The Unforgettable Guinevere St. Clair

The Unforgettable Guinevere St. Clair

Amy Makechnie

Atheneum Books for Young Readers

NEW YORK LONDON TORONTO SYDNEY NEW DELHI

ATHENEUM BOOKS FOR YOUNG READERS
An imprint of Simon & Schuster Children's Publishing Division
1230 Avenue of the Americas, New York, New York 10020

This book is a work of fiction. Any references to historical events, real people, or real places are used fictitiously. Other names, characters, places, and events are products of the author's imagination, and any resemblance to actual events or places or persons, living or dead, is entirely coincidental.

Text copyright © 2018 by Amy Makechnie
Jacket illustration copyright © 2018 by Abigail Dela Cruz

For information about special discounts for bulk purchases, please contact Simon & Schuster Special Sales at 1-866-506-1949 or business@simonandschuster.com.
The Simon & Schuster Speakers Bureau can bring authors to your live event. For more information or to book an event, contact the Simon & Schuster Speakers Bureau at 1-866-248-3049 or visit our website at www.simonspeakers.com.
Jacket design by Michael McCartney
Interior design by Hilary Zarycky
The text for this book was set in Bodoni.
Manufactured in the United States of America
0518 FFG
First Edition
2 4 6 8 10 9 7 5 3 1
Library of Congress Cataloging-in-Publication Data
Names: Makechnie, Amy, author.
Title: The unforgettable Guinevere St. Clair / Amy Makechnie.
Description: First edition. | New York : Atheneum Books for Young Readers, [2018]
| Summary: As ten-year-old Gwyn searches for a missing neighbor in her new town in Iowa, she learns much about her mother, who grew up there but has suffered from memory loss since Gwyn was four.
Identifiers: LCCN 2017053924 (print) | LCCN 2018000443 (eBook)
ISBN 9781534414488 (eBook) | ISBN 9781534414464 (hardcover)
Subjects: | CYAC: Missing persons—Fiction. | Memory—Fiction. | Mothers and daughters—Fiction. | Moving, Household—Fiction. | Farm life—Iowa—Fiction. | Iowa—Fiction. | Mystery and detective stories. | BISAC: JUVENILE FICTION / Family / Parents. | JUVENILE FICTION / Mysteries & Detective Stories. | JUVENILE FICTION / Social Issues / Friendship.
Classification: LCC PZ7.1.M34685 (eBook) | LCC PZ7.1.M34685 Unf 2018 (print) | DDC [Fic]—dc23
LC record available at https://lccn.loc.gov/2017053924

For the mothers:
Mary Cope, for saying "wonderful,"
and
Heather Hope,
for giving me the indomitable Gaysie

Children's games are hardly games.
Children are never more serious than when they play.
—MONTAIGNE

CHAPTER 1

I WAS TEN WHEN GAYSIE CUTTER tried to kill me. It was just like her too—always leaving a bad first impression. Her idea of a welcome wagon came in the middle of July, during my first Iowa heat wave, which was as hot as you know what. My little sister, Bitty, and I were minding our own beeswax, walking past one corn row after another to get a look at our new school and the playground's famed red rocket slide. I had my fingers crossed that it was totally wicked.

We stayed off the main road, walking along the bank of the Crow River, where it was cooler and somehow felt safer. I swear, it was so flat here that with one little tilt, we could fall right off the world.

"Hurry up, Bitty baby."

I could hear her behind me, dragging an old stick in the dirt, which was comforting, in a Hansel and Gretel kind of way—not that it was even possible to get lost here. We had a bet that by the time we got to the rocket slide, we'd *still* be able to see Nana on the front porch, wagging her finger at us.

Sludging forward, past identical green stalks, I decided to hate corn.

"Gwyn," Bitty moaned.

"Come on, honey," I called over my shoulder, using the word "honey" like any sweet, mothering sister would.

I peeked back to see Bitty's pitiful red face dripping sweat down the sides of her baby-round cheeks. I collapsed on the one rock that had shade, motioning for Bitty to sit next to me. In New York, the only river we had lived near was the Hudson, where these people called the Mafia put their rivals' dead bodies. I had a sudden and lonely affection for it.

Bitty collapsed next to me. "I want to go home. It's too hot here."

"It was hot in New York, too."

"I don't want to live here."

"We have to."

"Because of Vienna?"

Everything, really, was because of Vienna.

I splashed water on Bitty's face, jumped up, and said, "Come on, we're almost to the slide!"

Our objective cheered us enough to wade through yet another giant cornfield, to Lanark Lane, where the glorious rocket slide came into view. It was like a real rocket: solid, enormous, painted red with white wings, and a long slide coming down to earth. The top was a brilliant blue tip headed straight for the sky.

I didn't even have time to say, *Race ya!* before we were halfway there.

We would have made it too, if it weren't for the boy. His presence stopped us short.

He was facing away from us, awkwardly cutting a large,

green bush into nothing but sticks, using the largest pair of scissors I'd ever seen. Dressed in frayed, cutoff jean shorts and a black T-shirt, he balanced barefoot on a skateboard.

The backdrop to this butchery was an enormously grand farmhouse the color of a clementine. Crudely nailed to a porch slat was a warped piece of driftwood with CUTTER carved into it.

The boy made a large, impatient whacking gesture at the bush, chopping off the entire top.

"Ah heck," he spit. "She's not gonna like that."

"I've never seen anything like it," Bitty said solemnly. He turned quickly, surprised, but as soon as he saw us, his face became one wide, crooked grin. He tucked the scissors, which looked large enough to decapitate me in one quick whack, behind the bush. Cool as a cat, he flipped his skateboard up with a bare foot to walk toward us. The underside of his board was a cluster of black-and-white skulls.

"Pruning shears," he said, following my gaze. "Had to hide 'em." He lowered his voice and raised his eyebrows. "Don't want those to get . . . into the wrong hands." I couldn't tell—was he teasing or trying to scare me?

Despite my questions, I let Bitty pull me down the street. An interrogation would have to wait—we had a rocket slide to climb.

But the boy wasn't done with us.

"Watch this."

I heard the skateboard coming from behind before it passed, headed toward a homemade plywood ramp sitting in the middle of the road. He pushed off the ground with his bare foot. Crouching like a tiger on the approach, he attacked and flew. The wind carried him high into the air as he glided through space, his board flying with him, touching nothing but sky. He landed as neatly as he had begun, in the same crouched tiger position.

"Holy tamoly," Bitty whispered.

I briefly considered marrying him.

"Have you ever crashed?" I eyed his bruised knees and slightly swollen cheek.

He shrugged, flicking long, dark hair out of his eyes. "I was born lucky, Gaysie always says." He yawned, like it was nothing to be lucky.

"Gaysie?" It was a familiar name, one I'd heard my father use, but I couldn't remember why.

"Yep. I'm cutting a wreath for the funeral." He motioned back toward the clementine-orange house.

"She died?"

"No."

"Okay," I said, confused. "Well, I'm Gwyn. . . ."

"I know," he said, waving us off. "Everyone knows you were comin'."

"What's your name?"

"Jimmy. Want to see my tattoo?"

Bitty and I looked at each other. Iowa was supposed to be *Little House on the Prairie* and braids. There were not supposed to be tattoos in Iowa.

"Shoot," he said. "I'm just messin' with ya."

I nodded slowly, sizing him up. "Want to race?" I asked.

"I can run a six-minute flat mile. I was the fastest girl in New York."

He raised an eyebrow.

"It ain't braggin' if you can do it," I added, figuring "ain't" was a good Iowa word.

From behind us, a door slammed, letting him off the hook.

"That's Micah," Jimmy said. "You could say he lost his best friend today—well, except for me."

Jimmy skated toward the smaller boy sitting on the front steps. Bitty and I took a few steps forward.

At first glance, you could tell the farmhouse had once been impressive, with a large wraparound porch, storybook turns and curves, and a small tower I'd have liked to read a hundred books in. But the closer we got, the more foreboding it became.

The house was actually falling apart.

The rusted black mailbox was secured only with faded blue duct tape. The orange house paint was peeling, the front porch was bowed, and the gutters were broken or missing. Not to mention, distracting from any sort of charm were clashing fluorescent NO TRESPASSING and BEWARE OF DOG signs nailed to the massive maple trees out front. Who, I wondered, were they trying to keep out? Jimmy was the first human we'd seen in a mile.

"Rapunzel," Bitty whispered, looking upward at the small tower.

The boy Micah kept his head down as we approached. He was real skinny and his white hair was almost completely buzzed. His legs were pale, chicken-like, sticking out of bright pink shorts, and never before had I seen a boy wear sparkling silver, curly shoelaces. I instantly adored them.

"Hey, Micah," Jimmy called, ollieing over a small troll statue. "Look who I found."

Micah looked up, his teary eyes magnified behind thick brown eyeglasses. He stood and wiped his nose.

"Hi. You can come too. . . . She's waiting."

Jimmy followed Micah toward the backyard.

"Who's waiting? Where are we going?" I called out.

"To bury José," Jimmy said.

Far too curious to leave now, I pulled Bitty along. "Come on," I whispered. "There might be snacks."

Whoever lived in the clementine house was far more interested in flowers than paint and gutters. The backyard looked like a New York City art exhibit, with splashes of pink, purple, and yellow flowers everywhere. The sunflowers, not quite opened, nodded and beckoned us forward.

"Vienna would love these," I murmured with a slight pang, stopping to inhale a black-eyed Susan. I was so engulfed that I barely noticed a loud honking noise off in the distance.

"Beware," Micah said, looking around, "of the goose."

"Actually," Jimmy cackled, "Gaysie is who you need to watch out for."

"But who *is* Gaysie?"

This, actually, was the question I would forever be asking.

Jimmy smiled wickedly over his shoulder, then motioned to a long, wooden box that sat against the house. "Gaysie's coffin," he said. "Commissioned last month, 'cause she can't fit in a regular one."

I raised my eyebrows.

"Just in case. Things happen."

Honk! went the goose.

Jimmy motioned me forward.

Far out in the fields was a man moving slowly on a blue tractor. I wiped the sweat from my forehead. My watch read 8:42 a.m.

"It's so hot," I breathed.

"Heck-of-a-hot-spell," an enunciated voice said behind me. "Which is why morning burials are preferable to afternoon burials."

I jumped as Bitty clung to my backside. A giant woman had materialized from nowhere. She was enormously tall, as if she had dinosaur bones. Her muscles were large on top but sagged on the bottom, like there was too much person to fill. Following close behind her was a beautiful white goose. I stepped forward to pet it, but the goose let out a terrifying *Honk!*

"Stay!" the giant woman said, giving me a fierce look. Then she turned to the goose, revealing an ugly, purple scar from her hairline to her chin. "Shoo!" The goose obeyed, but not before aggressively flapping its large white wings at me.

"Tula, the Fighting Goose is all talk and no action today," the giant mocked.

She turned back toward me and raised her chin, sizing

me up. I recoiled. Hard, wrinkled lines ran down her face like dried-out riverbeds. Her hair was pulled back in a coarse gray braid and in her arms she held a big black garbage bag.

I swallowed hard. Was José in *there*?

"It's the people from New York," Jimmy said.

"I can see that," she said, nodding. "How marvelous to finally meet Guinevere St. Clair. You look like your father. I'm Gaysie Cutter."

My instincts told me to run. My father had said people would know us. He and Vienna had grown up in Crow, after all, and everyone knew everyone, but I didn't like how this Gaysie Cutter said my name, like she knew more about me than I did.

A large drop of sweat hung precariously from her upper lip, and I licked my own lips as it fell, hitting the bag with an audible *smack*.

Bitty decided to make her appearance by peeking out from behind me.

Gaysie startled and staggered sideways, the black garbage bag tilting toward me. I felt a great chill hit the center of my chest as a tiny sliver of black hair slipped out from under the plastic. Gaysie stared at Bitty, looking like she was seeing a ghost. "Well!" she whispered. "Aren't you the spitting image!"

It was true. I knew from pictures that Bitty was our mother, Vienna, many, many years ago.

I impatiently took Bitty's fingers out of her mouth, and she ducked behind me once more.

"Does she talk?" Gaysie said, delighted.

"Yes," I said indignantly.

"Wonderful! And so our adventure begins. Now, without further dilatoriness . . . shovels!"

I hesitated, holding my sister back. There were clearly no snacks. We should have never deviated from our rocket slide plan!

But Micah and Jimmy followed Gaysie toward the cornfields next to the river.

Georgia Piehl, New York prosecuting attorney and my father's dental patient, knew I wanted to be a lawyer more than anything. She had given me a gift when we left New York: *The Law: A to Z.* "Accessory" was letter *A: Somebody who aids somebody else to commit a crime or avoid arrest but does not participate in the crime itself.*

This woman was holding a dead body and walking off into a cornfield—and I was letting her. Could it be . . . a crime? The thought was both terrible and thrilling. I was only ten and about to become an Accessory. Was it possible to be disbarred before I even got into law school?

Alas, curiosity has always been my weakness, and ten seconds later we, too, were marching in the funeral procession mourning José. We stopped abruptly while Gaysie adjusted the weight in her arms.

"This is a solemn occasion for the Cutter family and Jimmy Quintel, who, for all intents and purposes, is a Cutter," she breathed heavily. "An important member of the family has passed on through the great veil that separates us from the heavenly beings." Micah kicked a rock. Gaysie fixed her eyes fiercely on him. "We've got to channel the Lord, boy. We've got to talk with Him, let the spirit move you!" She inhaled deeply and closed her eyes. I watched in fascination, having no experience with watching someone channel the Lord before.

Jimmy smirked, his eyes tightly shut except for a slit to watch me. I bowed my head and nudged Bitty to do the same. Slowly, and deliberately, Gaysie's voice became a low-pitched force.

"Lord, death comes to us all. It comes to us all, and we thank Thee for the life Thou gives us either big or small." Gaysie hefted the bag high in the air like an Amazon warrior.

"We offer Thy faithful servant unto Thee, commanding his spirit into *Your* keeping. We ask for Your great and magnanimous mercy as Thy servant did the best he could in the body he was given. And, Lord . . ." Her voice suddenly broke.

I peeked under my eyelids, grudgingly delighted by such a performance. Did she say "servant"? They were burying their servant in the backyard!

"Lord," she cried, "José was *well* loved! Yes he was, hallelujah."

Gaysie nodded, wiped her nose on her shoulder, and grunted like a pig. "Though hygiene and breath had *much* to be desired—Amen!" Opening her eyes, she looked around our small circle. "Final thoughts and tributes?"

"Dude," Jimmy said. "Remember that time he ate that nasty baby diaper?"

"*What?*" I interrupted. "Baby diapers?"

"Speculation on Jimmy's part," Gaysie said.

My palms were now noticeably damp, my feet stuck like concrete to the ground. Questions peppered my brain. Baby diapers, a servant, a secretive backyard burial. They didn't look like the kind of people who had servants. Why couldn't José be buried in a normal cemetery? Then again, I was new to town. Maybe this was an Iowa thing.

"Heavy," Gaysie groaned, lowering the bag. It thudded, dead weight on the ground. She clapped her large hands together and looked at us expectantly. "Six feet is ideal."

With only two shovels, we took turns and were immediately drenched with perspiration.

"How far is six feet?" I panted.

"About as tall as I am." My eyes went from Gaysie's knees to her bulging waistline to her broad shoulders, and finally up to her face. We'd be digging until next week. As if she could read my mind, she responded saltily by saying, "But three will suffice."

"Um," I said. "How did José die?"

"In his sleep," Gaysie said. "It was his time. He was suffering." Somewhat mollified, I dug my shovel into the hole, the long handle awkward in my skinny arms.

"Then again, he could've been poisoned," Gaysie said. "He was always eating something out of the trash."

"That diaper . . . ," Jimmy began.

"Enough," Gaysie said. She tapped the side of her head, close to her long scar. "José wasn't the sharpest knife in the drawer, but he was a faithful companion to this family." She took the shovel from Micah and launched a huge chunk of earth over her shoulder with such force that I startled and fell over.

"How is your mother, Ms. Guinevere St. Clair?"

"Fine," I said, struggling to get up.

"I'm going to bring her some flowers. She always loved my flowers."

"Yes," I said, frowning at my dirt-covered clothes. Nana was going to have a hissy fit. "Vienna loves flowers, but I'm sure she's . . . different than when you knew her."

"Well, we're all different than we were. Thank goodness for that."

Not, I thought, in Vienna's case.

Micah mumbled something, his face a mess of dirt rivulets that kept sliding his glasses down his nose while his dirty fingers kept pushing them back up.

"Enunciate so I can hear you," Gaysie said.

"I need a drink."

Gaysie bowed.

Micah and Jimmy walked back toward the house, leaving Bitty and me with the giant woman and a corpse.

"Micah's having a hard time," Gaysie said. "Very much like his father, sensitive, weak. I'm afraid for him. This world has a way of crushing the sweet and the soft." I glanced out into the fields at the man on the blue tractor.

"No, that's Wilbur, the old boy. You'll meet him and his mistress soon enough." *A mistress in Iowa!*

"Micah's father is dead. Cremated, ashes to ashes, dust to dust." Gaysie surveyed the field. "He's buried here too. But cremation is expensive, and as much as I loved

José . . . well, some men you have more of an affection for."

Bitty, who was too small to dig, took a tentative step toward a tree swing, looking at me for permission.

I nodded.

"I can see you take care of her," Gaysie said, heaving another large shovel of dirt over her shoulder. "You both lost your mother at too young an age."

"No," I corrected. "We didn't lose her."

"There's more than one way to lose somebody."

Gaysie sniffed, her T-shirt drenched with perspiration and clinging to her lumpy body. "That's probably deep enough. Why don't you get right in there and see?"

I pretended I hadn't heard, craning my neck for the wretched boys who had left me to bury their own servant. When there was no sign of them, my mood blackened.

"I'm too big," Gaysie added.

I glanced at Bitty, swinging happily. Next door was a small white house I hadn't noticed until now. The goose sat on the back porch, occasionally honking. A curtain fluttered before hanging still. A witness.

"Well . . . I guess."

I dropped my shovel in the hole and jumped down after it. It was cooler in the ground, an almost welcome relief from the humidity.

The hole wasn't six feet, but it was deeper than I expected, and when I put my hands on the ledge, the earth crumbled down my arms and onto my shoes. Immediately, a helpless feeling rose inside my chest, then all the way up to my hairline.

"Bitty?" I yelled.

"Are you frightened?" Gaysie asked. She sounded surprised. I tried to breathe in and out, to not lose control of my imagination as my father frequently suggested I did. I tried to hear him talking to me. *Use your brain and control your emotions, Guinevere.*

I jumped up to climb out, but my attempt only brought more dirt down. I could see nothing except for Gaysie's looming face. Her teeth suddenly looked like yellowed fangs. My hands began to shake. I opened my mouth but no words came out. My hands were clammy, almost numb.

And then Gaysie began to unwrap the bag. Did she mean . . . to put it in the grave *with me*? I'd be buried alive!

I pressed my eyes tight, my breathing becoming shorter. *Guinevere. Act!* I forced my face upward. Gaysie had stopped unwrapping and was looking down at me, a curious look on her face, almost as if she was amused by my last moments of life.

I could see the body poking out of the bag.

Black hair. Thick, unruly, snarled black hair. Matted and wet. The smell of fresh death. My voice came. I screamed, while Gaysie hovered above, ready to bury me alive and top me off with a dead servant. My screams gave me the adrenaline to lunge upward, clawing savagely with my fingernails as the cold dirt poured down my neck and under my clothes. I hung on the ledge as Gaysie got down on her hands and knees.

"Help," I whispered.

"Guinevere," she said. "You don't need my help."

I fell back in the grave.

Dirt fell on my cheeks and microscopic dust entered my eyes and nose, making me cough. The moments of my life flashed before me: Vienna teaching me how to play patty-cake, my father's smile, and—Bitty! I had to save my Bitty before Gaysie turned on her next.

With an unknown strength, I jumped and grabbed the grass above me. Using my feet and knees, I pulled myself up and away from the devil woman. If she had tried to touch me, I would have bitten her hand off. And blessed Bitty— she was running toward me, Micah and Jimmy close behind.

"What's the matter?" Micah asked, out of breath.

"Worthless!" I screamed.

They looked at one another, baffled by my outburst.

And then Gaysie did the oddest thing: She clapped, delighted.

Grabbing Bitty's hand, we ran the entire mile back home on the dirt road of Lanark Lane, not stopping until we were panting and crying on Nana's front yard behind the prim white picket fence.

"We will never ever go back there, Bitty . . . never!"

"We didn't see my school, or the rocket slide," she wailed.

"Bitty, hush now. I'll take you tomorrow."

We lay back, looking up at the light blue Iowa sky. "We'll never go back" was the phrase I uttered over and over: *We'll never go back.*

That wicked Gaysie Cutter was right about one thing.

I didn't need her help, nor would I ever ask for it, not as long as I lived and breathed. We lay on the grass until Nana called us in for lunch. By that time my mood had decidedly changed for the better for two reasons:

One, I had always longed for an archenemy, and two, I was certain I'd just beaten my New York six-minute-flat mile record.

CHAPTER 2

JIMMY AND MICAH CAME AROUND later that day and the next day after that, but I refused to speak with them. Maybe they were used to burying servants in their backyard, but I certainly wasn't. Besides, they hadn't seen Gaysie's face while she was burying *me* alive.

"Isn't Crow wonderful?" my father kept saying. I thought bitterly of Gaysie Cutter. Oh, if only he knew. No, not *all* of Crow was wonderful.

But my father didn't have time to think about that dreadful woman down the street, and I hadn't told him. He was a busy man. As much as I knew he loved me and Bitty, he had a singular focus for one person: Vienna. He had consulted every brain doctor on the East Coast, then the West Coast, and I guessed that now corn country was what he considered his Hail Mary pass, the key to unlocking Vienna's memories. He theorized that familiar settings and people could rewire her brain, that her brain was capable of healing itself. Since I believed in my father more than I believed in anything, I let him think that.

And truly, I didn't mind moving. I liked New York okay; it had been my home for as long as I could remember, but it was also associated with the heaviest sadness of my life.

Iowa was an exciting and fresh start, like the witness protection program.

Bitty and I had imagined we'd have fields to run through, silver lunch pails, and warm, home-cooked dinners that tasted nothing like the reheated hospital food we often ate. We would make friends with blue jays and field mice and keep cheeping bullfrogs in our pockets.

Sure, I would miss my old friends, including prosecuting attorney Georgia Piehl, whom I considered a true ally. But I was most sorry to leave behind Lolly, Moose, and Tomato. As one of Vienna's first nurses, at home and then at her care centers, Lolly was the closest thing we had to a mother. Moose and Tomato were her twin miniature schnauzers that went everywhere with her, so we were practically siblings.

"I wish you would come too," I had said more than once as we were getting ready to leave. Lolly shook her head.

"Honey, my heart hurts just thinking about you leaving me, but I've got a husband to feed and a grandbaby on the way. I guess I have to stay around here."

I tried not to resent the grandbaby part. Bitty and I were Lolly's babies. She had cradled, comforted, and read to us, and she'd taken more grief from Vienna than anyone deserved. Through it all, Lolly loved my mother fiercely.

If I were to tell a secret, I'd whisper that I'd have rather moved to Iowa with Lolly than Vienna.

Since there were no subway systems in Iowa, we bought our first car for the trip. It was a scarlet red, of course, because red was Vienna's favorite color.

"Most people in Iowa own a car," my father said, stuffing more bags into the trunk.

"Next you'll be riding a tractor," Lolly said. "And some cows."

I became instantly fixated on the cow.

"I need a cow of my very own," I declared, imagining myself arriving on the first day of school riding one, Queen Guinevere atop her royal bovine.

"I hate cows," Vienna said, watching us pack.

"You can't hate cows. You're from Iowa. You were probably a farmer and went to cow shows," I said.

"I hate cows."

"Do not!"

"Do too!"

"I cannot abide this conversation," my father said, pinching the bridge of his nose. "Guinevere, your mother truly does not like cows. They scared her as a child. Could you, perhaps, not be an agitator?"

I frowned.

Five minutes later Vienna had forgotten our conversation entirely until I mooed.

"I hate cows," she said.

My father gave me the look of death, so I bowed my head and mooed silently out of principle.

And so it was, in the middle of a sweltering July, that we left our school friends but also our best friends—the doctors, therapists, and brain specialists we saw every day—for the big Midwest sky, somewhere in the middle of America.

We bravely said good-bye to Lolly, but I'll admit to tears when I looked back and saw her growing smaller and smaller.

"I'll come visit," she had promised. "See if your mama still remembers me."

Yeah. Good luck with that.

We drove through New York, Pennsylvania, Ohio, Indiana, Illinois, and finally—Iowa. The trip put twelve hundred miles on the odometer, and my father got a speeding ticket on Interstate 74, but the closer we got to corn, the more relaxed he became.

"Where are we going?" Vienna asked.

"Neverland, of course," I said, looking out the window.

Usually my father did not allow us to lie to Vienna, but even he had a soft spot for Peter, Wendy, and the Lost Boys.

"And Nana will be there." Bitty clapped her hand over her mouth and giggled at the great luck of having a grandmother named after a character in our favorite story, even if it was the dog.

Vienna grabbed my father's arm and said in her soft-spoken voice, "I love Neverland! Can we go right now?" He smoothed her blond curls and smiled.

Vienna clapped her hands like a small child because this was who she was now—a child whose memory no longer included me or Bitty; we were the lost children in her Neverland.

When we passed a sign that said, WELCOME TO CROW, POPULATION 4,261, I began to sniff.

"What's that . . . *smell?*"

My father laughed. "Who likes cows now?"

"I hate cows," Vienna said.

I kicked the back of her seat.

Eventually, we drove into Crow, a small town that followed the lazy, meandering Crow River. At first glance the river ran slow and deliberate, but underneath I could see the swirling of an undercurrent. This gave me a secret thrill.

We pulled up in front of a large white farmhouse as Nana came down her tidy flower path. With an obvious effort to remain calm, she gingerly embraced her daughter.

"Where's Dad?" Vienna asked immediately. Nana smiled and redirected, "I'm so glad you've come home, darling."

When we entered the living room, my father took in the wallpaper, the old-fashioned giant pink, red, and yellow roses on all four walls.

"I wanted to change it several times," Nana said quickly. "But I thought . . . I shouldn't."

My father smiled. "Thank you, Nancy. Familiarity is just what she needs."

I could see his pleasure when Vienna smiled at the old photographs on the walls and the hand-sewn doilies on every surface. When she ran her fingers over the piano, Nana was at her side.

"I just had it tuned—so you could play."

Vienna sat and played a song from memory, something that always struck me as all wrong: the way her brain could remember music but not people. Her fingers were uncoordinated and spastic, moving more like webbed duck feet, and yet she could remember the notes and finger position-ing. Often, her clumsiness caused frustration and tears, but not this time. She sat and played a disjointed Chopin while Nana stood, clasping both hands to her chest as if to protect her heart.

Instead of listening, Bitty and I went upstairs to see our new room. We would be sharing Vienna's old bedroom and the same lovely white furniture hand-picked by Nana for her five daughters, all of whom had shared the room at one time or another. It even had the same old-fashioned pink-and-white-flowered bedspread Vienna had once slept under.

I would have preferred stripes.

So many people came over to welcome my parents back to Crow that first day that *Those poor, poor children* echoed in the halls nonstop. To prove otherwise, I skipped through the house and laughed extra loud until Nana said I sounded more demented than happy.

That first night, our father stayed with us until we were almost asleep, before heading out to check on Vienna. No surprise, she was having trouble adjusting to her new residence, a small care center in town. Perhaps one day soon, my father postulated, Vienna might be ready to try some overnight visits again. All of us together again, like a normal family. Poor Jed St. Clair. How could he forget the disastrous results of those New York experiments? Like the time Vienna forgot she was banned from using the gas stove and singed her eyebrows off.

He tucked us into a double bed, turned out the light,

nnie

it's just easier that way," my father

s if we observe first, we can tell what to call
'Mom' doesn't always work out so well."
it?" Nana said with a strained voice. "Eat up."
bite, unable to swallow. If I had a real mother,
would have added "darling" or "honey" after
to eat lumpy, mushy gruel.
ot dawdle, Gwyn," Nana added, her back still

thinkers are often mistaken for dawdlers."
my father smile behind his journal.
l, think and eat at the same time. Land sakes!"
d, then disappeared into the pantry. A sound sus-
y like that of a can opening echoed through the

hat is *that*?" I asked, swallowing abruptly. *"Beer?"*
uinevere," my father said. "Really."
new what was really in that can. It was a well-known
hat Nana was perfect, but I had recently discovered
ne vice: Diet Coke. I kept the idea of bribery in my
pocket should the need ever arise.
But I was also dismayed at the thought that Bitty and I
essitated Diet Coke with breakfast in order for Nana to
through the day. Our father had asked us to try very hard
be good girls. Nana, he said, had become accustomed to
ving alone. She liked things just so and was trying to cook
ealthy meals so we wouldn't die under her care. Mothers,
e said, bore many burdens. For example, I once overheard

then paused to sit. Little Bitty put her arms around my neck, and I started my usual story.

"Peter came to the window," I whispered, "because it was Wendy's last night in the nursery. Nana was tied outside." Bitty giggled again. ". . . and when they flew to Neverland, Wendy with the yellow hair found the Lost Boys."

"Wendy with the yellow hair," Bitty whispered.

"Yes," I said. "All night Wendy told stories to the Lost Boys. She sang and rocked them to sleep until they remembered their mothers again. Then all the boys wanted to go home too and not be lost anymore."

Bitty sucked her thumb and fell into sleep beside me. Soon I was in my own Neverland slumber too, hovering between the real world and my imaginary one, where our father never sat all alone on the edge of my bed.

CHAPTER 3

I DREAMED OF THAT BIG LADY," Bitty announced at breakfast a few days after José's burial. "She was scary!"

I gave her a small kick under the table along with
a murderous look.

"What? I didn't tell!" she said.

"Tell what?" Nana asked, turning from the stove.

I put on my best wide-eyed, innocent face, which was
the wrong tactic, because Nana narrowed her eyes like I
had just robbed her jewelry box. As far as my father and
Nana knew, we had only wandered into the Cutters' backyard and gotten distracted by Jimmy and Micah on the way
to the rocket slide.

Instinctively, I had not told on Gaysie and her little let's-
bury-Gwyn party. I was still thinking of the words "accessory" and "crime scene." After all, my fingerprints were on
the shovel, so I had scared Bitty into keeping her trap shut.
Sometimes, I told her, criminals come back for retaliation.
The image of Gaysie Cutter coming after us sealed her lips
as tight as superglue.

"Was there an interaction with Ms. Gaysie?" my father
asked, lowering the science journal he was reading. On
the cover was a big and colorful picture of the brain, his

most favorite
trade, but he w
"hippocampus"
ory worked. Bec
anatomy of the br

"Gaysie Cutter
entangled with on y

"Yes," I said, u
"Did you know she co
she's not even dead yet

My father chuckled.

"Cuckoo," I added.

"Sometimes, Guinever
ing, "we do not recognize
should, just because they're

"Daddy. This is nothing li

I swear I saw Nana bite he
agree on one thing: our obvious

My father just chuckled a
brains, something I found most
allowed to read at the table. I looke
healthy breakfast: thick Oliver Twist

"Did Vienna like gruel as a kid?
pathetic voice. "Now she eats pancake
day."

"It's cracked wheat," Nana said.
you're Oliver Twist now?"

My father gave me a look.

"Do you always call your mother Vienna

26 • Amy Makec

"Sometime
answered.

"Lolly say
her," I said.

"Doesn't
I took a
I'm sure sh
ordering m

"Let's
to me.

"Grea
I saw
"Wel
Nana sa
picious
kitcher
"W
"C
I
fact
her
bac

ne
ge
to
li
h

my father say that Vienna's condition was the great tragedy of Nana's life. But from where I sat, Nana should be happiest of all of us; she had at least had the best of Vienna.

I grudgingly slid a small spoonful of mush into my mouth and looked up as Nana tidied the kitchen. She was wearing an ironed shirt and jeans, a spotless kitchen apron, and clean and practical indoor house slippers. Nana reminded me of a perfectly tied bow. Even in New York when she had visited, even without company, she was proper and polite, a woman who always buttoned her top button.

"Well, we'd better get going to see Vienna," my father said, folding his journal under his armpit. "Thank you for breakfast, Nancy. What do you say, girls?"

"Thank you, Nana."

"Carry over your own dishes," he said. "Your Nana is not to wait on you hand and foot."

I carried over my bowl. Impulsively, I turned and gave Nana a hug.

"Oh!" she said, fluttering like a pigeon. "Thank you, Gwyn. You . . . are so much like your mother sometimes."

Startled, I skedaddled out to the front porch, away from the comparison, and almost keeled over from an overpowering foul smell.

Bitty buried her face in my shirt.

"I thought they didn't have pollution in Iowa," I gasped.

My father stepped onto the porch, inhaling deeply. "Pollution," he scoffed. "That, my dears, is the smell of home. Fresh morning manure. As natural as anything else on the earth." He straightened the rolled-up sleeves of his white dress shirt and tucked his hands in his khakis, a man content.

I gave a dying breath for Bitty's benefit.

"Drama, Guinevere," he said. "Too much drama."

Instead of turning right and walking down Lanark Lane toward Gaysie's house, we thankfully went straight ahead to Main Street. We walked half a mile on a dirt road, green fields on either side. Corn was yet again the sightseeing highlight until I spotted a cow.

"Look, Dad," I said pointing. "Hint, hint."

"That's a Holstein. I think you're more of a prize-winning Jersey."

My father reached down and took our hands. He was happy this morning. Maybe because he loved Crow, Iowa, and maybe because this was the beginning of another great experiment with Vienna's mind. I was more resigned to our fate, but if my father was happy, I was happy. That's all I needed from Crow, really, even if nothing changed with Vienna.

We reached Main Street, which looked like something out of an old TV show, and passed Arnie's Supermarket, where a man in a white apron was sweeping the sidewalk.

"It's so quiet," I whispered. "Where is everyone?"

"You're not in New York anymore," my father laughed. "Hello, Arnie!" he called out. The man raised his hand in a wave. The little town was new to me, but we were greeted as old friends, and it surprised me how *friendly* my father was. We walked past a church, all white and sparkling in the early-morning sunshine, complete with a ringing bell.

"Crow," my father said, "has everything we need and most things we want—pizza, a post office, Petey's Diner, the deli, a bank!"

"Movie theater?" I challenged.

"Better," he said. "A library, which is next door to your mother—and I happen to know Ms. Priscilla already has a stack of books waiting for you."

I jumped up and down and pulled my father down the street toward the library, until he stopped abruptly in front of a tiny gray house. It was vacant, with wide steps and a blank sign hanging over the stoop.

"This is where I'm going to work. It was your grandfather's dream that I come back to practice dentistry with him here. Shame that he never got to see this day."

Crow was small, but it had room for my father. Old Dr. Frank happily retired as young Dr. Jed, who had almost become an oral surgeon, became Crow's new dentist. A regular old dentist. It was a difficult fact to reconcile. My father was not a quitter. But he *had*—right in the middle of his oral surgery residency, after all that studying and test taking. Because of Vienna, he'd never become the great surgeon he could have been.

"You could practice next door," he said, winking at me.

I imagined myself in a law office like Georgia Piehl. Sometimes Bitty and I had helped out in the back at my father's practice in New York, emptied trash, watered plants, and cleaned dental instruments. Whenever she came in she told me all her best law stories. Once, she said, a man had cut off his own hand while trying to escape through a courtroom window.

When we left New York, she told me to write anytime, scribbling her address down for me. I kept her note tucked in my jewelry box with my best treasures.

"Well, I'm going to open a Yum-Yum Shop," Bitty said. "And make candy and doughnuts all day."

"Doughnuts next to my dental practice?" My father laughed. "At least it will keep me in business. But the best part of this location is your mother is just down the street in a terrific facility. We can have lunch together every day, visit familiar settings, get some exercise, associate with old friends. Neurons will form, rewire even. . . ."

He turned and began to whistle, hands in his pockets as he walked down the street. I watched him a moment before moving.

Maybe he was right. Many of the things we tried didn't work, but I knew my father. He was not a quitter; he was a man who fixed things.

"Officer Lytle!" My father called out.

Bitty and I gaped as Officer Lytle, a real-life *police officer*, actually *punched* our father good-naturedly *in the shoulder* and enveloped him in a great bear hug. "So great to have you back, Jed. Let me get a look at your girls." He squatted down. "None of this 'Officer Lytle' stuff. You can call me Uncle Jake." He held out his hand to Bitty, who smiled. "Ah, aren't you just like your mama?"

"I'd like to call you *Officer* Jake," I said, holding out my hand and admiring his neat uniform and golden badge.

"I'm very pleased to meet an officer of the law."

After a solemn salute, he clapped my father on the back again. "Girls, I could tell you some stories about my buddy here."

"And I would like to hear them!" I said, leaning forward eagerly.

Officer Jake laughed. "Now, listen, you all need to come and see Suzy, my wife. Number four is in the oven, about to pop any minute, and did I tell ya? It's another boy! Suzy's been cryin' for months she wants a girl so bad. You've got to come by. She'd sure love to spoil some cute girls."

"Congratulations!" my father said. "I'm happy for you."

"How's Vienna?" Officer Jake asked. "I hear she's . . . settling in?" An almost imperceptible look of discomfort passed across his face. This was how it always went. Everyone was curious about Vienna, but few were comfortable talking about her.

"She's doing well. That's where we're headed. Why don't you come along?"

"Can't right now. Duty calls. But I'll be by. . . . Tell her hello?"

We waved enthusiastically.

My Iowa days were looking up. A police officer was someone every future lawyer needed to have on her side.

We walked past the library, to Vienna's new home. The care center was a modern building with pretty green gardens and a rock-lined walkway. It was lovely until *that woman* ruined it.

Bitty saw her first and let out a tiny scream. Following

the direction she pointed, I saw a familiar bunch of flowers being carried by a ginormous body with large man feet.

Trailing behind were those two boys, Micah on foot and Jimmy riding his skateboard.

I pulled my father back inside before he could notice, hoping with all my might that those flowers weren't coming into Vienna's room.

Vienna now lived in cheerful Room 12, painted a banana yellow. A nurse was making the bed, pulling up a handmade, patterned quilt my mother was rumored to have rocked me in when I was a baby. I knew this because my father frequently repeated this piece of information to Vienna, who had yet to remember rocking any babies. The nurse turned.

"Whoa," I said.

She was the prettiest and youngest nurse we'd ever had, with long, dark hair and shiny pink lips, matching her hot pink scrubs.

"Hi there!" she said. "I bet I know who you are!" When my father appeared behind us, she brightened further. I felt his hands on my shoulders.

"Annabelle, these are my daughters, Gwyn and Bitty." He motioned toward her. "Girls, Annabelle is one of your mother's nurses. She's also new in town."

"No offense," I said, "but what are your credentials?"

Annabelle laughed like I was joking, showing very straight and very white teeth. My father liked healthy teeth, a sure sign of good character.

"Annabelle's worked with patients who have suffered a

brain injury like your mother," my father said before turning to Annabelle. "For better or worse, the girls are practically experts on the subject of brain trauma."

"Is that right?" Annabelle said.

I gave her a solid wink.

"She was born with a slightly abnormal heart rhythm," I said with authority. "But no one knew until it just *stopped* in the produce aisle." I sighed dramatically. "Her brain went without oxygen for a *perilously* long time. Bitty and I are practically orphans."

"Guinevere."

"Yes, Daddy?"

"Oh my," Annabelle said, producing the clucking sounds I was going for. "This was long QT syndrome, correct?"

"Correct," my father said.

"Usually there are early episodes that indicate a potential problem."

I waved her textbook explanation away. "A few fainting spells," I said airily. "But no one knew they were warning signs. Of course Nana blames herself for that *fateful* day."

Annabelle put her hand on her chest and leaned toward me. I met her gaze with woefully tragic eyes. "Actually, in most cases," I whispered, "there are no signs—only death."

"There will be plenty more time to talk," my father interjected, breaking my spell.

Annabelle quickly resumed a professional demeanor.

"She's been asking for you all morning," Annabelle said, turning to my father.

"She's always very excited to see Daddy," I said, rolling my eyes. "He's like her Justin Bieber." We'd seen the Biebs walk through Central Park once. Girls were screaming, tears coming down their faces while they jumped up and down. Vienna was kind of like that with Jed St. Clair.

"She wanted to call you this morning," Annabelle said.

On cue, I put my backpack on the floor and pulled out the bright red card stock with my father's cell phone number, printed in big, bold numbers. Vienna knew how to dial a phone number, but she couldn't remember the digits unless they were taped on the phone. Calling my father multiple times a day was one of her favorite activities. She fixated on the same four things:

1) I'm hungry. What's for breakfast?
2) I'm tired.
3) I've got to go to the bathroom.
4) Where's Jed?

Where's Jed? was the most important item on the list, probably because he could take care of the rest of the list.

"Your mommy is down the hall in physical therapy."

"Vienna," I interjected. "We call her Vienna."

"Oh! I'll get . . . *Vienna* before her breakfast gets too cold." Annabelle tapped a tray of French toast sticks and slipped out of the room. My mouth watered as I realized I was suffering from severe processed-food withdrawal. My father had done his best, but before Nana's extreme health initiative, we'd eaten our share of Goldfish crackers and frozen dinners.

At that moment the bouquet of flowers burst into the

room. Bitty and I grabbed each other. But instead of the giant, out came Nana's blue seersucker button-up. Bitty and I exhaled, releasing our grip on each other.

Nana faced me with her hands on her hips.

"You'll never guess who I just ran into—Gaysie Cutter!"

"How unfortunate."

"She brought these beautiful flowers for your mother." Nana raised her eyebrows. "*And* she apologized for scaring you! Of course, I had no idea what she was talking about. Apologizing isn't something Gaysie Cutter does often."

I chewed on my lip. Gaysie was admitting guilt. This could definitely work in my favor.

"Gwyn?" Nana asked. "What happened?"

"I'm glad she's sorry."

"Sorry for what?" My father turned the pages of *Brain Today* magazine.

"Attempted murder." There was a pause between page turns.

"She buried my sister," Bitty offered. I stifled my scowl, realizing that sympathy was my best defense.

"Excuse me?" Nana said, puffing up her chest. "Gwyn, what in the world?"

"Well," I said, "I guess I should have told you before, but I believe I have been manipulated."

My father put the magazine all the way down and squinted at me. "Manipulated?"

"Exactly. She made me do it!"

"Explain."

"Dig a grave for José the servant."

Nana gave out a small cry.

"José," my father repeated.

"I'm not even sure what he died of—maybe a baby diaper, I don't know. She said for sure he was dead, so I helped her because cremation is so expensive and because she kind of made me do it.

"But then," I pushed on, "she made me get *in* the grave so she could bury me with José and wouldn't help me get out! Luckily, I escaped and saved Bitty."

"Wait. José?" Nana paused her hand-wringing. "Is that the . . . ?"

"Servant," I said.

"José," my father said, "is the dog."

I let this sink in for a minute before jumping out of my chair.

"The dog!" I yelled. "José is not the dog!"

"He is, indeed, the dog."

"Well, why didn't she just say so?" I kicked my chair, and my father caught it before it fell over.

"A prosecutor," he said carefully, "asks the right questions and gets the facts before presenting them to the jury." At this personal insult, I burst into tears.

"Gaysie Cutter told me to climb into the grave that was really, really deep!" I blubbered. "And I swear she was going to put that 'dead dog' on top of me and bury me with it! I couldn't get out and she wouldn't help me. She wanted me to die and I hate her!"

"Gwyn!" Nana said. "Language!"

"'Hate' is a very strong word," my father said.

"That's why I used it!"

"Guinevere."

"Sorry," I said, wiping my nose. "Vienna says it."

"That is an utterly ridiculous argument and you know it."

"Gwyn is obviously traumatized," Nana said, her face all pinched up. "It's like history is repeating itself—trouble involving Gaysie Cutter! You all haven't even been here a week, and *look what I've let happen.*" She didn't actually say that last part, but by the look on her face I could see her brain thinking it. And I suddenly loathed her, too, the way she thought everything was her fault. Not for the first time, I wished practical Nana would just cry or smash a plate.

"Come here," my father said, pulling me down to his lap. I leaned against his chest and inhaled the smell of his aftershave and starched shirt.

"She *was* scary, Daddy," Bitty said.

He nodded. "I admit Gaysie Cutter is an odd woman, one of the most unusual characters you will ever meet in your life. She's not, shall we say, easy to color with one crayon."

Across from us was Vienna's bed, where her pink Love-a-Lot Care Bear sat. The two intertwined hearts on Love-a-Lot's chest stood for the closeness and loyalty of true love. Vienna often pretended Love-a-Lot was Jed. Like cupid's arrow, Love-a-Lot could "create a crush in no time!" and "Love will find a way, and if it doesn't, I will!"

Love-a-Lot was totally embarrassing.

I frowned and folded my arms.

"You know what the brain is capable of, Gwyn," my

father continued. "It sees what it wants to see. Perhaps your imagination got the better of you."

I shook my head.

"Believe me," he said, following my gaze to Vienna's bed, "there will come a day when you will be glad to know her." I tucked my head under his chin, wondering if we were really still talking about Gaysie.

"Jed!" a voice screamed from down the hall.

"I keep waiting for my arrival to be old news," my father chuckled. I resentfully slid off his lap as he stood, stretched out his long limbs, and stepped out into the hall to wait for Vienna.

Formerly known as my mother.

CHAPTER 4

J ED!"

He waited in the doorway, coaching her down the hall until she shuffled into the room.

"Jed, Jed, Jed," she said.

Vienna. Still beautiful, blond, and dark-eyed, yet the lively, warm fire everyone talked about had dulled like once-hot embers. Supposedly, we were lucky. Vienna spoke. She didn't drool. She walked. She wasn't a vegetable fed through a tube. Just looking at her, you might not know anything was wrong at all.

Only in the eyes. There was trouble behind the eyes. And then, of course, if she opened her mouth. Vienna looked at Nana and gasped like she was seeing her for the first time. "When did you get so fat?"

You had to admire Nana's impenetrable shell now. Her expression hardly changed.

Vienna pointed at me and whispered to my father, "Why is that girl looking at me like that?"

"You know who that is. Gwyn doesn't like you to be rude, remember?"

Vienna stuck out her lower lip in a pout. She sat slowly, glancing at me as I continued to glower. Lolly would have told me to stop, but sometimes I just liked messing with her. But since she was so highly distractible, Vienna abruptly lost her focus on me. She giggled, still holding on to my father's arm. "We are going out."

"You've had a busy morning," my father said. "How was physical therapy?"

Vienna looked blank.

"Did you eat breakfast?"

"Yep!"

"What did you eat?"

"Sausage, pancakes, and orange juice," she said automatically. My father glanced at the French toast sticks, dismayed.

"Vienna," he said, motioning to Annabelle. "Who is this?"

"The nurse."

You see, although Vienna had a major brain injury, she was smart. Sometimes she was able to answer the way she thought she was supposed to, even though she couldn't remember.

Since The Episode in the grocery store when I was four, Vienna could not remember a single thing after the age of thirteen. But she often didn't act even that old. Her behavior was young and unpredictable, like a bratty baby. Even Bitty was more mature.

"What are the names of your children?" my father pressed.

"Guinevere, Elizabeth, and Gus," she recited, not actually remembering.

"Gus was your cat," I said.

Annabelle stepped forward.

"Woo-wee, you have big bosoms," Vienna said, clapping her hand over her own mouth.

I sighed loudly.

"Annabelle is your nurse," my father said smoothly.

"Lolly is my nurse. She's my best friend, like totally best friends forever," Vienna said.

"But now Annabelle is your nurse."

"Where's Lolly?"

"She's not here. You live back home in Crow now, remember? You had a brain injury and you live at this care center now."

Vienna looked up at him carefully. "Baloney." Except she didn't say "baloney." She said a bad word, and Nana tried to cover Bitty's and my ears, but ended up just knocking our heads together.

"Look at these beautiful flowers, Vienna," Nana said, changing the subject.

"Gaysie!" Vienna said, clapping. "Where's Gaysie?"

"She's not here," Nana said.

"Oh . . . Gaysie," Vienna said slowly. Her hands fluttered, her speech slurred into panic, and she began to sob. "It was an accident. Bad. Bad. I didn't mean . . . Where's Myron?"

"It's okay, honey," my father said, wiping her tears with his hand. "What are you remembering?"

"This is not the right time to ask, Jed," Nana said briskly. "You know it's an upsetting subject."

Vienna's outburst and Nana's reaction snapped me to

attention. A *bad, bad* accident? An upsetting subject? My favorite! I leaned forward and touched Vienna's hands. "What do you mean?"

She snatched her hands away and threw a cold French toast stick at my face. It bounced off my nose and fell on the floor. I picked it up without changing my expression.

"Thanks," I said, taking a bite.

Vienna swiped her entire plate of food onto the floor.

"I think it's time to go," my father said.

Nana gathered us quickly and herded us to the door as Annabelle whispered, "Don't take it personally, honey."

"Easy for her to say," I said as Nana walked us quickly down the hallway.

I knew better than to get upset by Vienna, but I could still feel my face burning.

"Nana, what did Vienna mean?" I asked. "An accident? Who's Myron? Why would Gaysie bring Vienna flowers? How does she even know Vienna?" I took another bite of the cold French toast before Nana could confiscate it.

"Old friends," Nana said darkly. "And your *mother* doesn't know what she's talking about half of the time." She plucked the French toast stick out of my hand and deposited it in a garbage can.

The sound of Nana's small heels click-clicking echoed down the hospital corridor as I hurried to keep up with her.

"Why's it an upsetting subject?"

"For heaven's sake, Gwyn! She's rambling about a past that is best left there."

"Oh no, Nana! Don't you remember? We're here to

uncover her deep, dark secrets." I meant it as a joke, but Nana's face turned pale, sending my curiosity into over-drive. "Was there a lot of blood?"

Nana stopped in her tracks. "No, there was not a lot of blood! Banish those"—she made a swirling motion over my head with her hands—"those *thoughts* right out of your head!"

My nana obviously did not know me very well.

Nana grabbed Bitty's hand and marched us back down Main Street and onto the dirt road toward home. We had walked everywhere in New York, but never on dirt roads with tractors. The one passing us had a man on top who looked older than dirt.

"Hello, Wilbur!" Nana called after him, back to her composed and well-postured self.

The man turned to look at us, a shy smile on his face.

"Howdy," he called. He wore a real cowboy hat and raised his hand to wave. I realized he was the same man from Gaysie Cutter's fields. "Real nice day we're having."

"Kinda hot!" I yelled after him.

"Guinevere, be polite," Nana said. "You'll find that the Midwest is a friendly place. We try to be kind to one another."

"Gaysie wasn't nice to *me*."

I was expecting a scolding for back-talking, but Nana seemed to actually consider my statement and pursed her lips together.

We followed behind the tractor until Wilbur passed Nana's house and headed down Lanark Lane. I stared after it, knowing that I had vowed to never go back to that horrid woman's house. Except now there was upsetting information, an accident, and somehow Gaysie and Vienna were involved—and Nana wouldn't talk!

"Gwyn!"

I skipped inside, giving one last look down the dirt road that led to an orange house. Life in Crow was looking up.

CHAPTER 5

DESPITE MY CURIOSITY, WE DIDN'T see Micah or Jimmy for days, not until Bitty and I discovered the river. In New York we never swam, only played in water shooting out from hydrants on hot concrete during the summer months. But now we played in the stretch of river right behind Nana's house, where the water was warm and slow and shallow. I tried not to be frightened of all the small fish and slugs and bugs floating up from the squishy mud bottom. One afternoon our father read *Huckleberry Finn* to us on the banks of the Crow.

"The Crow River leads all the way to Tom and Huck's Mississippi." He looked down the graceful river that snaked endlessly between cornfields.

My face must have lit up a little too much.

"It's five hundred miles," he said, eyeing me. "That's a *long* way."

This only led me to the conclusion that Bitty and I needed our own Tom and Huck.

We knew two boys.

I avoided face-to-face contact with Gaysie Cutter by writing a letter of invitation. When the boys wrote back the very next day, I just knew, from Micah's typewritten note on turquoise paper, that we were destined to be the best of friends. And that is what happened. They were forgiven for their early offense and Micah and Jimmy accepted us into their friendship like we'd always been a part of it.

As July slipped into August, our lives took on a sort of structure and routine, every morning starting at the breakfast table, where Nana warned of the river and *those boys* and *that woman.*

"The water barely covers our ankles, Nana! And I watch Bitty every second." Which was kind of true.

"The river is fine," my father said, looking up at me from the brain journal he was reading. "As long as you stay right behind the house, where it's shallow. You only get into trouble farther up, when it gets deep and the current picks up." I nodded encouragingly at Nana, who sputtered like a tea kettle at my father's rare contradiction.

"Today, I'm going to bring Willowdale with us," I said.

"To see your mother?" Nana asked.

"No! To pick up Micah and Jimmy."

"Vienna hates cows," Bitty added.

Just days earlier, my father had surprised me with my very own registered cow.

Most cows are mutts, named something like Sadie, Bessy, or Freckles, but my cow came with an ancestral pedigree, recorded physical assets, and fat statistics. Instantly smitten with my golden-haired pet and her large chocolate-drippy eyes, I named her Willowdale Princess Deon Dawn. Never in my life had I given anything the name of "Princess," but that's what my cow was.

"First you won't go near the Cutter house and now you spend all your time there." I could hear the disapproval in Nana's voice, especially as she had introduced me to several perfectly nice but perfectly boring girls the week before. When I mentioned Micah and Jimmy to them, I got the sense that nobody, and I mean nobody, was calling up Gaysie Cutter to arrange a playdate.

"I don't talk to Gaysie," I said.

"How are you going to get Willowdale there?"

"I'm going to ride her." I smiled, pleased with myself.

"Well, I have heard it all now!" Nana dropped her cleaning rag right onto the floor. "Jed, do you hear this? Cows are not horses."

My father raised an eyebrow.

"It's really not funny, Jed. You're encouraging her."

"Guinevere, I'm afraid, is the type of child who will have to learn many hard lessons from personal experience. Who does *that* remind you of?"

Nana shook her head and began to intently scrub the floor.

"Who?" I said.

"Your mother had a penchant for mischief," Nana said. "Thankfully, she grew out of it and became a lady."

I went outside, mulling over this new information, trying to picture Vienna running wild around Crow. Sniffing the air, I also wondered when manure would start to smell appealing.

Despite Nana's strong words against it, Bitty and I awkwardly rode on golden-haired Willowdale Princess down

Lanark Lane, to Micah's house. I would never admit it in a thousand years, but Nana's disapproval was well-founded. It was terrifying and terribly slow riding atop a large moving animal. Willowdale Princess Deon Dawn had a very large mouth and giant teeth that were always dripping with saliva as she meandered here and there, chewed on grass for long stretches, and stared at nothing for even longer stretches. Just when I'd get comfortable, she'd lurch forward, nearly making me topple right off.

I finally ended up pulling her by the rope tied around her neck while enduring a thoroughly slow and scenic tour down Lanark Lane. By the time we arrived at Micah's, I was drenched with sweat, and fuming.

I tied Willowdale's rope to an orange porch slat.

"Be good," I instructed before Bitty and I ran through the plowed corn path, hearing the honking of the goose, and arriving just in time to see Jimmy swing across the river on a rope swing and drop himself in.

"Hey!" Micah called to us. He stood on a rock, wearing green swim trunks and a glorious homemade purple cape.

"What took so long?" Jimmy yelled, coming up from the water and flicking his black hair out of his eyes.

"I brought a surprise!" I yelled.

Though I wasn't an expert swimmer, I stripped down to my bathing suit and jumped in. It was a deliciously cold and wonderful feeling, unlike anything I'd ever experienced in New York. The current was slow, and I shut my eyes, letting myself get carried down a moment, the sweat and grime washing off my body. I resurfaced and walked against the current, thigh deep, back to Bitty, who tentatively put her feet in the water as it slowly swirled around her legs like a curl of hair.

While Bitty played, I climbed onto a large, warm rock where Micah sat.

"Where's the surprise?" Micah asked.

"At your house—but let's swim first."

Micah looked down at the water.

"Come on, scaredy cat," Jimmy said, wading toward us.

"Jimmy, stop." Micah frowned, pulling his bony knees to his chest.

"Ah, come on," Jimmy said, climbing up next to us in sopping-wet cutoff blue jeans, and lying down on the warm rock. "It's like two feet deep."

"Maybe if I had an inner tube to float on," Micah said doubtfully.

I lay on my stomach, watching the dark water swirl in currents.

The water was shrouded by trees and forest, but every so often scattered light escaped through, shooting out yellow and white shades all over the leaves, rocks, and speckled water.

"If we had an inner tube we could sail down the river to the Mississippi," I said.

"We're not allowed," Micah said. "It gets real deep. Ma's predicting a real wet spring and it's gonna rise even higher."

"She says that every year," Jimmy said.

"And if it floods, all the corn will die," Micah said.

"Once the river flooded the whole town, and everyone had to evacuate and all the corn was drowned—that's a true story." He shivered and exchanged a look with Jimmy.

"What?" I asked.

Jimmy shrugged. "He don't like the word 'drowned.'"

"You mean he *doesn't*?"

"Whatever. There was a bad sledding accident a long time ago right on this river. Gaysie crashed right through the ice."

I perked up.

"That's why Gaysie's all messed up," Jimmy continued, tracing an imaginary scar down his face. "And no one likes her, and it's why Micah is scared to have fun."

"Am not!"

"But why doesn't Micah like the word 'drowned'?" Bitty asked fearfully.

"'Cause of Myron," Jimmy said.

"Myron," I whispered. Vienna had said his name. "Who's Myron?"

Jimmy and Micah glanced at each other.

"Tell me!"

"He's the one who didn't make it," Micah said sorrowfully.

The hair on my arms stood straight up as I was brought back to my near-burial, with Gaysie hovering over me.

I had a million questions, but seeing the terrified look on Bitty's face, I swallowed them and lightened my voice. "Jimmy is right, Micah. Look how shallow the water is here. No one's going to drown."

I knelt down to touch the water. I wanted to see the soul

of a boy named Myron, but instead I saw my reflection wobbling all over the place, brown hair that never lay flat and my father's deep, dark, thinking eyes that blended right into the river rocks. Bitty's hair was curly and wild too, but blond like Vienna's. It gave her a cute, impish style, whereas mine looked only like I forgot to brush.

"Well, I'd still ride to the Mississippi," Jimmy said, throwing a rock at my reflection, scattering it farther in the water. "I'm not afraid. And when I get to wherever I'm going, I'm gonna be a barber and have a tattoo and never come back."

"I've never known anyone who wanted to be a barber," I said.

"He's going to call his shop Lucky's and give me free haircuts," Micah said, rubbing his head.

"You'll come back. You'd miss your family."

"Nope," Jimmy interrupted me. "No, I would not."

I could see why he wouldn't miss Gaysie, though I didn't know if he had any other family, considering he seemed to always be at Micah's house. "Well, you'd miss Micah, then."

Jimmy considered this. I wanted him to say he'd miss Bitty and me, but he didn't.

"My father came back to Crow," I said, swatting at a mosquito.

"He even likes the smell of cow poop," Bitty added.

We were interrupted by a black blur flashing through the trees on the other side of the river.

I leaped up, and the blur disappeared with a thrashing noise through the trees.

"What was that?"

"Maybe a giraffe?" Bitty asked.

"Ah, it's just the Creepers," Jimmy said, standing. "Let's go get a Popsicle." He made his way down the bank and began to walk across the river.

"Who are the Creepers?"

"Why do you ask so many questions?"

"She's practicing to be a lawyer," Bitty answered for me. I scrutinized the woods. All was quiet again, like nothing had been there at all. I shivered. Sometimes quiet Iowa was way scarier than crazy, loud New York ever was.

"I wish it had been a giraffe," Bitty said.

"Race ya!" Jimmy yelled, taking off ahead of me.

"Cheater!"

The creek was only a couple hundred feet from Gaysie's house, and I was fast, but Jimmy gave me fierce competition, making it out of the cornfield just ahead of me. I was gaining when he stopped so abruptly we both crashed to the ground.

Before I could yell at Jimmy, I froze in horror.

Gaysie's yard was a disaster. The goose was flapping its wings, honking in distress. Flowers of every color were strewn about, stems broken off, begonias trampled. And there was Willowdale, satisfied with the meal she had inhaled, right on top of the baby pool, now squashed flat. Her golden tail swished back and forth as she stared at me. Around her neck was the rope and a broken orange slat pulled from Gaysie's wraparound porch.

I heard the sound of Gaysie's raised voice before seeing

her emerge from the side of the house, stomping, hands flailing wildly about her. I wanted to sink into the earth and never come out again. Following behind Gaysie was a very confused-looking Wilbur.

"There!" Gaysie boomed, her eyes blazing hot with anger as she pointed at the mess. "There!"

I trembled, a squeak coming out of my throat. Micah looked at me, distressed.

"Was that your surprise?" Jimmy asked.

Gaysie continued to rail.

"Well, now, Gaysie," we could barely hear Wilbur stammer. "I don't know what . . ."

"You don't know—of course you don't, because you're an imbecile!"

Honk!

"Shut up!" Gaysie roared at the goose. It waddled away toward the little white house next door and honked, but from a safer distance.

"I just . . . ," Wilbur began, taking off his cowboy hat to fan himself.

"What kind of man brings a brainless blockheaded animal of the bovine variety into *this* backyard *knowing*," Gaysie said, her voice rising as she gestured in big, wide circles, "the bestial behavior cattle are prone to. It's ruined! Look around you—it's ruined. It. Is. All. Ruined. And it's not just my work—it's all of your work too!"

"She was going to enter the Crow flower bazaar," Micah said. "And win first place over Dottie and Lavinia."

"They don't like Gaysie," Jimmy added. "Say she's

crazy and prone to flying off the handle. Can't imagine why."

"I'm so dead," I whispered, beginning to chew my nails.

"Yep," Jimmy said cheerfully. Gosh, sometimes I just wanted to hit him.

Gaysie wiped her hand across her nose.

"The mess you have made is just beyond me. The stupidity of your actions! Days—months—years of work! I honestly cannot believe a grown man with even half a brain would fail to foresee the consequences of his actions. I'm not speaking to you ever again. Go away and sit in your little house out of my sight," Gaysie cried, gesturing to the small cottage that sat away from the main house, where I had recently learned Wilbur lived. Though why he'd want to live near such an awful woman was beyond me. She turned and cried out again, "My sunflowers!"

Watching Wilbur not saying anything, not even trying to defend himself, was too hard to bear. I took a small step forward, gripping the back of my small neck with my hands. The curtain moved from inside the house next door. The goose honked. Gaysie's voice grew louder and louder.

I walked to my death slowly, across the lawn and past Willowdale, who continued to lazily chew on Gaysie's grass.

"Naughty!" I hissed at her, then turned to Gaysie. "Mrs. Cutter?"

She turned to snarl at me. "Micah said you're an up-and-coming lawyer, but don't even think of defending this stupid man who cares more about being out with his blue mistress than paying attention to good sense."

The mistress again!

"Uh, you see . . . ," I rushed on. "Willowdale Princess Deon Dawn is *my* cow, and I'm a very bad cow owner! I'm training her to act like a horse instead of a cow, but, uh, I've failed. She was very wicked to ruin your porch and your flowers. . . ."

"Wait," Gaysie said, holding out her hands to stop the universe. "You're telling me that this *thing* in my yard"—indicating Willowdale—"is *your* cow?"

"Yes."

She took two aggressive steps toward Wilbur. There was a collective flinch.

"Unbelievable!" she spit out. "You stand there and say absolutely nothing to defend yourself!" Gaysie turned and marched into the house.

Bitty reached up and took my hand, which was now wet and clammy.

"I'm so sorry, Wilbur," I said, dragging my feet over to him. Seeing Wilbur up close was an education on sun damage. I had never seen so many sunspots or such wrinkled leather on anyone's face before. He turned to me, his eyes gentle. "I didn't know she'd do that," I said.

"Yep, cows can be beasts, all right," Wilbur said.

"And Gaysie, too," I said.

He looked at me and laughed a short bark. "Huh! That woman is like a hurricane meeting a tornado. Sometimes," he said conspiratorially, "I'm actually afraid of what she'll do. I wish you all the luck." He gave me a wink before shuffling to Gaysie's, his old shoulders stooped. He knocked on the door.

"Come in!" Gaysie yelled. "And you too, girls!"

I squeezed Bitty's hand tightly before stepping inside the monster's lair. The boys followed. The walls were a surprisingly happy sunflower yellow but decorated with small pieces of stuff Nana would call "clutter."

Wilbur patted both boys on the back, poured himself and Gaysie a cup of coffee, placed the cup in front of her, and settled down into a chair.

"Best part of the day," he said. "Coffee break with Gaysie Cutter." I made a face. How could that be anyone's *best part of the day*?

"Don't you try to butter me up," Gaysie said to Wilbur. "I'm still angry." She was sunk down into a chair, eyes closed, fanning herself. She was doing some sort of breathing exercise—breathe in and hold . . . hold . . . hold . . . and exhale slowly, like one of those birthing shows I watched in the hospital lounges. Jimmy and Micah were already into the Popsicles as if my impending death was no big whoop. Bitty and I stood in the doorway until Gaysie finally opened her eyes.

"Sit," she commanded. We sat.

"Oh, my temper. My terrible, terrible temper." She gave herself three mighty whacks across her own cheeks. "Wilbur Truesdale, I apologize!"

"I'm very sorry," I said again. "It was irresponsible of me to tie her to the porch."

"Well, we can certainly agree on that."

Wilbur, now safe from wrath, closed his eyes, pulled down his hat, and seemed to fall asleep instantly, sitting upright, despite the steaming mug of caffeine in front of him.

"Willowdale what?" Gaysie asked me.

"Princess Deon Dawn."

Micah stood and stretched, walked to the middle of the kitchen, and began to lower himself into a gymnast's split position.

"Hurts just looking at you," Jimmy said. "Please, just stop."

Gaysie looked at Micah. "Son, what are you doing?"

"Showing you my split, so you won't be mad at Gwyn anymore. She's already scared of you."

"I am not!"

Gaysie turned to me and raised an eyebrow. I felt my face go hot.

"Training a cow to act like a horse?"

I nodded.

"Well, I believe you just might be the girl to do such a thing."

"You have to practice every day," Micah said, holding his hands elegantly out to the side.

"*Your* cow!" Gaysie said loudly, pounding down hard on the table. She began to laugh so hard, tears rolled down her face.

"Stop it, Mom. You're going to make me pee," Micah said, balancing precariously. Gaysie took one look at him trying to lower into the splits in his green swim shorts and purple cape and burst out laughing again.

"You only have yourself to blame," Gaysie heaved, her large chest moving up and down. "Contorting yourself into such a position. Oh dear, my bladder is not what it used to be . . . oh dear."

Bitty and I stared wide-eyed as Gaysie shook with laughter before easing herself off the wooden kitchen chair and waddling out of the kitchen, a big wet spot dripping from the back of her pants.

"That," I whispered to Bitty, "is a very strange woman."

Wilbur sat up from his nap, put his hat back in place, and finished his cup of coffee. He stood and shook my hand and then Bitty's. "Never a dull moment around here. Now that she's speaking to me again, it's back to work."

As much as I was relieved not to be dead, I pondered his earlier words. What had Wilbur meant, *afraid of what she'll do* . . . ?

CHAPTER 6

SCHOOL STARTED ON WEDNESDAY, THE last week in August. It was a day we'd never forget, because that was the last time we saw Wilbur Truesdale.

The morning began with the color pink. Nana had plainly refused to answer any of my renewed questions about the accident and Gaysie, even using the insulting word "pestering." She busied herself with packing something called hummus in our new, matching pink lunch boxes, and those in our new, matching pink backpacks. I slipped in three books, including my newly beloved *Huckleberry Finn*. Our father hugged Bitty and me good-bye and told us to have fun. Nana imparted advice: "Use a Kleenex, not your sleeve" and "Mind your p's and q's" (whatever those were) as if we'd never been to school before.

My last farewell was to Willowdale Princess, who was faithfully waiting for me by the backyard fence. I petted her nose and bravely let her eat out of my hand, which was still terrifying, what with her big, slobbery tongue and gigantic teeth.

"I wish I could bring you to school," I said, giving her the last of my apple. "I'd tie you to the bike rack, but after what happened at Gaysie's . . ." Such a shame. I had so wanted to make my grand entrance riding a royal cow.

For the first time in our lives, Bitty and I ran to school instead of riding the subway, calming my nerves for the first day. We ran down Lanark Lane until we came upon Jimmy, riding his skateboard in front of Micah's house. He was attempting a new trick and was actually wearing all his clothes and a pair of shoes.

Also, he had a brand new hairstyle: a Mohawk.

"Whoa, Jimmy," I said. "What happened to your hair?"

"Did it myself," he said proudly, running his hand across the top.

"Micah!" I hollered excitedly at the house. "Hurry up!"

I heard nothing from Micah, but the door of the little house next door opened a crack, and a head of reddish-orange hair peeked out. A crabby voice yelled, "Hush up!"

It was Ms. Myrtle, the old witch who had made it her mission to ruin our summer by yelling at us from inside her house every day we passed by before noon. Usually we just ignored her, but sometimes I couldn't help sticking my tongue out.

A door slammed. Bitty and I turned to see Micah running down the front stairs, nearly tripping over his sparkling shoelaces. His hair was neatly parted, weighed down by comb marks and smelling strongly of hair product. He was wearing his brown-rimmed glasses, a Boy Scout shirt, and clashing green-and-yellow-striped shorts.

I was pretty sure he was going to get beat up on the very first day.

"I *really* like your sparkly silver shoelaces," Bitty said encouragingly.

Micah beamed, puffing out his small rib cage under-neath his Scout shirt.

"I didn't know you were a Boy Scout," I said.

"He got kicked out," Jimmy said, skating past us. "For wanting to make pies instead of campfires. But he makes a real good pie."

"I like pie," Bitty said.

"Ma says that girls like a man in uniform," Micah said, smiling his endearing, toothless smile. I vowed that no one would be beating him up today.

We were almost past Ms. Myrtle's house when we heard Gaysie's voice. Turning, we saw her out on the porch in dirty work clothes.

"Farewell, young scholars!" she bellowed just as Wilbur came hobbling around the house.

"Yoo hoo, Wilbur . . . my *exquisite, absolutely resplendent* flowers are still scattered all over the lawn! I hope it's cleaned up before you disappear with that mistress of yours!" Gaysie hollered.

"Wilbur's picking up all the flowers that weren't ruined by your cow and putting them in the house," Jimmy said. "The whole place stinks, thanks to you. Almost makes me want to move out."

"I said I was sorry. Where do you really live, anyway?" I asked.

"Why do you ask so many questions?" he asked back.

"She's practicing to be . . . ," Bitty began.

"I know!" Jimmy yelled.

"She sure doesn't like that mistress," I said.

"You do know the Blue Mistress is the tractor, don't you?" Jimmy asked.

I stopped walking. "A *tractor*?" This news was altogether much less exciting than an actual mistress.

"Wilbur spends so much time with his that Gaysie calls it his Mistress," Micah said. "And it's blue."

"You thought Wilbur had a real blue mistress!" Jimmy cackled. "Who'd ya think that was? A Smurf?"

I furrowed my brow, picking up a fallen crab apple to throw at him.

"Hush up!" came the crotchety Ms. Myrtle again.

Bitty suddenly yanked on my hand, making me drop the apple. "Goose!" The white fluff came waddling, just as we passed Ms. Myrtle's front walk. Bitty and I ran, but Micah stood still, holding out his hand as the goose came closer and closer to him.

"Micah!" I screamed. But the goose didn't eat him. Instead, it stopped and let Micah gently pet its head.

"How does he do that?" Bitty asked.

"He's a goose whisperer," I said reverently.

"Get off my property, you nasty child!" Ms. Myrtle railed from inside. She sounded like she was on her last breath, but still couldn't resist a nasty comment. Unrattled, Micah kissed the goose right on the beak and skipped toward us.

"Ha!" I yelled, sticking my tongue out at Ms. Myrtle's house. "I bet she let that goose out on purpose so it would eat us."

"I saw that, you bratty little girl!"

I could hear the old woman yelling, Gaysie hollering, and the goose honking as we ran to our first day of school, toward that red rocket slide shooting right to the moon.

It was already the most exhilarating first day of school I'd ever had.

"Put my kiss in your pocket, honey," I told Bitty, outside her classroom. "To remember me." I instinctively felt my own pocket, a small, fragile memory surfacing of Vienna. Bitty looked up at me mournfully, her eyes wide and already tear filled.

"Gwynnie, I want to go with you."

"Be brave like Wendy."

She turned, greeted by a smiling first-grade teacher while I felt my heart go walking right out of my body.

Micah slung his arm around my shoulders just as a big boy with greasy, disheveled hair walked by, knocking his elbow into the back of Micah's head.

"Sorry!" he laughed over his shoulder, big, dirty buck-teeth sticking out of his mouth, eyes trained on me.

Jimmy's eyes narrowed.

"Travis Maynard," Micah said, rubbing his head. "Eighth grader, head Creeper. Archenemy Number One."

My eyes followed Travis and the other Creepers down the hall. Gaysie had become my archenemy when she tried to bury me alive, but Travis didn't look like a harmless marshmallow either.

"Let's go to the library and check out a wrestling book," I said.

"You don't check out a library book to fight Travis Maynard," Jimmy said.

"And he would know," Micah whispered. "They're cousins. But Travis hates Jimmy because of me."

"Ohhhh. Why because of you?"

Micah shrugged a bewildered shrug. I concurred. How could anyone hate Micah?

"Well, listen. You can find anything at the library!" I began. "Kung fu, snakebites, poisonous elixirs . . ." Jimmy ignored me and led us down the hall. There were two classrooms per grade at Crow Elementary, but the three of us entered Mrs. Law's sixth-grade classroom together. My nerves were all jumpy again as I wondered about my new class, suddenly missing Public School 57 in NYC, where Brian Peppernick had surely found someone else to annoy.

"Mr. Quintel," a firm-looking woman greeted us. Jimmy sighed and handed over his skateboard.

She turned to me. "I'm guessing you are Guinevere St. Clair. We are *so* excited to have you join us."

"Yes," I said. "I just took my sister to first grade. She can read because I taught her, and her name is Bitty."

Mrs. Law nodded seriously, her perfectly straight gray hair brushing her jawline.

"You have the perfect name for a teacher," I said sincerely.

She smiled and gestured her arm for me to enter the classroom. Fifteen students curiously eyed me.

Mrs. Law had me sit next to Penny Jankowski in the back row, a pretty girl with light freckles and blue eyes. I'd met her a few times that summer, thanks to Nana's match-making. Penny was nice and all, but not nearly as exciting as Micah and Jimmy.

"Hi, Gwyn. Are you for-real friends with them or something?" Penny tilted her head at Micah and Jimmy, making a face.

"We're best friends. Like the three musketeers. Plus my sister, Bitty."

"Welcome to sixth grade!" Mrs. Law said from the front of the room.

"Did you know Jimmy was held back in kindergarten?" Penny whispered. "He's really, like, twelve."

"So what? I skipped first grade, so I'm really supposed to be in fifth," I said.

"Have you met Micah's mom?" Penny whispered, making a crazy sign around her ear.

I was no fan of Gaysie, but I couldn't help thinking, *You should meet* my *mom.*

"We have a new student this year," Mrs. Law said. "Guinevere?" I scooted my chair back and stood up straight. All eyes came to rest on me. Jimmy flipped me the bird under the desk.

"Guinevere just moved to Crow to live with her grandmother, Nancy Eyre—who made the most delicious soufflé for the playground raffle last year—and her mother and father, and her little sister who has just started first grade." Mrs. Law winked and walked toward me. "Over the summer we made something for you and your mother, who we know is going to get better!"

She handed me a homemade booklet with drawings, well wishes, and signatures.

"Thanks. You can call me Gwyn," I said to Mrs. Law.

"All right. Gwyn it is," Mrs. Law said. "Gwyn, can you tell us where you moved from?"

"New York City."

"That sounds very exciting!"

I nodded, thinking of Vienna's temper tantrums, which were usually the most exciting event of the day.

"And what are your aspirations in life?"

"Oh, I'm going to be a lawyer," I said. "Like the prosecuting attorney Georgia Piehl. I know all about her cases. Once she had to try a man who sold his twin baby girls so he could buy a moped. My father is Georgia Piehl's dentist, and she has very nice teeth . . . and thank you for the book."

"Well. You are very welcome," Mrs. Law said, looking slightly scandalized and partly amused. "You tell your mom to feel better."

I heard the word "mom" somewhere in the room, and a few kids glanced toward me.

"Let's get started!" Mrs. Law said from the front of the classroom.

Mother. Mom. Not Vienna. I held the handmade book tightly, suddenly feeling a great wave of homesickness for a person I hardly knew.

I shook it off, turning my face to the tall windows to let the morning light lay on my face, seeking out my father's words. . . . *Serotonin is a neurotransmitter, a chemical that induces a happy feeling when the body encounters light. Let me tell you about the day you were born, on a perfect, sunny day.*

It didn't work. All day long I felt the stares of classmates. Maybe they were only curious about the new girl, but I had a feeling it was more than that. It was like they already knew everything about me and my family, that we had been discussed around the dinner table while eating meat loaf and corn. After school I took my grumpiness out on Micah, who was adjusting his Scout necktie as we walked home.

"Why are you wearing that shirt?"

"I thought you liked it."

"You're not even a Boy Scout."

Micah deflated like a dead balloon.

"Ah, shove off, Ms. Know-It-All," Jimmy said, skating a slow circle around Micah.

Bitty looked at me, wounded. I had broken an unspoken code. We weren't mean to other people. Ever. Our father said that was one of the great benefits of having Vienna as our mother; we knew and accepted different. I threw my backpack on the ground.

The goose hissed, honking as it ran toward us. *Honk, honk.*

"Now you've done it!" Jimmy said, steering his skateboard so perfectly that he ollied right over the goose. "Wahoo!" he yelled, his fists in the air. "See that? I. Am. Awesome!"

"See that?" I yelled. "YOU. ARE. NOT!"

Bitty and I ran to Micah's front porch, but not Micah. Again, he petted the goose, whispered, and worked his goose magic.

"How do you do that?" Bitty asked when he came to sit down next to us.

"The goose thinks Micah's its mother," Jimmy said.

"I was the first thing she saw as a gosling," Micah said. "She remembers me." Micah turned to me. "She remembers you, too."

"The mean goose?"

"No, your mom."

I looked at him, startled.

"I visit her with my mom."

"You visit Vienna?"

"We bring flowers, and she really likes them, and she talks about you—and Gus."

I rolled my eyes. "Gus was her cat. She doesn't really remember me." But I folded my arms across my body, wondering. "I'm sorry about what I said—about your Boy Scout shirt. I didn't mean it. It's a great shirt."

"Nah," he said. "It's okay, girls never like me. They always like Jimmy."

"Oh no!" I said. "I'm sure all the girls loved it."

"Come on, let's get a Popsicle," Jimmy said. "It's freakin' hot." We followed him into the kitchen and stopped. It was deathly quiet except for the small squeak of a rocking chair coming from the other room. Moving closer to the living room, we could see someone was sitting in it, wrapped tightly in a brown blanket.

"Ma?" Micah whispered. There was dirt all over the floor, traced back to muddy boots sitting in the middle of the kitchen. As my eyes adjusted to the shadowed room, I noticed the dirt in Gaysie's hair, and smudged on her face. On the floor lay dirty old jeans and a men's shirt smeared with red, like when I'd had a bad bloody nose last winter and it dripped all over my pants.

"Ma?"

When she didn't answer, Micah tiptoed closer. Gaysie made no sound, just continued to rock, her face turned away from us. Micah put his hand on her shoulder.

"Ice," she whispered. Micah went to the freezer, grabbed a bag of frozen peas, and brought it to her. She began speaking in a low voice, and Micah leaned down to hear. His eyes went wide. His face turned white.

"Should I get Wilbur?" Micah asked. Gaysie made a low noise that sounded like Willowdale crying.

Micah turned. "Go, go, go," he yelled. We followed him outside as he jumped down the front stairs, fell, and got back up before running toward the backyard.

"What are you doing?" Jimmy yelled.

Micah kept running, his bony legs wobbling like a calf until we were all the way down by Wilbur's tractor.

"What are we doing?" Jimmy repeated.

"Uh, uh, looking for . . . ," Micah stuttered and trailed off, getting down on his hands and knees.

We knelt down and began combing the grass and dark dirt, but with no idea what for.

"She's sometimes a little crazy, you know that, Micah,"

Jimmy said. "Is she seeing dead people again?" He looked at me, a wicked, goading smile on his face.

"What do you mean, *dead people*?"

"Be quiet, Jimmy. Keep looking!" Micah yelled.

"Well, tell us what we're looking for!" I yelled back.

Micah shoveled frantically in the dirt. "Um, um, um." The ground looked soft and oddly lumpy underneath the tractor, so I crawled closer.

I was all the way under the tractor digging when I lifted my hands up.

"Is this . . . blood?" I whispered. My hands were covered with chunks of brown dirt, but there was also something else, something red. I looked up, seeing smears of red and brown all over Bitty's shirt, Jimmy's face, and Micah's clothes. Then my eye caught sight of something underneath the tractor wheel.

"I know what we're looking for," I said, pointing. There, lying on the dirt, gray and fat like an overcooked sausage, was Gaysie Cutter's finger.

She said she'd have our heads if we called an ambulance, so Bitty and I ran all the way home, after Jimmy had picked up the finger and put it in the freezer like I told him to— right next to the Popsicle box.

"Gaysie cut off her finger!" I yelled, bursting through our front door.

We watched our father speed off faster than a NASCAR driver before Bitty and I were hustled to the bath. Afterward we sat down for a silent dinner, one I could barely swallow. We were in bed before my father was home, but late that night, he came into our room, his face troubled. He had taken off his shoes, but his clothes were dirty and rumpled.

"What happened?" I whispered.

"An accident lifting the back of the tractor."

"Can they reattach it?"

He shook his head.

"Gaysie sure gets in a lot of accidents."

"What do you mean?"

"Well, Vienna said there was an accident, and Jimmy and Micah told me about a boy named Myron—"

"Yes, yes," my father interrupted quietly. "It was a very sad day. One I don't like to think about." He shook his head. "We all used to be such good friends."

"Did you say *friends*?"

"Yes, me and Gaysie. Vienna, too."

I sat back, aghast.

"Your friendship with Micah and Jimmy feels so familiar to me." He laughed at my expression. "Is that so hard to believe?"

"It's just that you're so . . . different from each other."

"Maybe now, but back then we were just good pals."

Good pals. I made a face. "Daddy, Jimmy said something about Gaysie seeing dead people." I thought he was going to laugh it off. Instead, he became very serious.

"Well, she had an . . . experience that day she likely talked too much about. People didn't understand or didn't want to. Plus, she was the oldest of us. In a small town, it was hard for her to ever get out from underneath what happened. You know, I like to think Crow is a little bit better every day, but it's hard for people to forgive and forget, to move on and let go."

He rubbed his eyes. "Ironic, isn't it, given why we're here. I'm sure some people think we're crazy with what we're trying to do for Vienna. But Gaysie? She deserves better than she got."

I bit my tongue instead of saying something wicked like I wanted to.

"Now, Guinevere, get some sleep." He kissed me on the forehead and walked to the door.

"Dad . . ."

He held up his hands. "No more questions. Sleep."

"Okay, but was Wilbur at the hospital?" I called after him. "If he wasn't, she's gonna be even more mad at him for what happened, because it was his tractor—I mean, Mistress!"

My father turned, his face lit by the hall light. "No, he wasn't there. But Wilbur can handle himself with Gaysie. Now shhh . . . good night."

But it was too quiet to sleep. I tossed and turned, longing for the sounds of city driving to lull me into a sound slumber. Instead, I dreamed of fingers and dripping red blood. I dreamed of Gaysie Cutter sledding and hitting thin ice. I dreamed of Wilbur and the Blue Mistress, waking with a dread I couldn't shake.

We went to Micah's before school on Thursday and Friday, and all the next week, but never saw Gaysie or Wilbur. Not once. The Blue Mistress remained strangely quiet and still, and even the reclusive Ms. Myrtle was unnaturally mute, not once yelling hateful comments out the front door, even when I purposely walked on her lawn.

CHAPTER 7

ON SATURDAY, THE LAST DAY of August, it was blazing hot. After we took Vienna on a short walk to the library and back, where she recognized Ms. Priscilla but asked her why her hair looked like a skunk tail, the only place for me and Bitty was the river.

That morning I introduced my comrades to the legend of King Arthur and his queen. Naturally, I was Queen Guinevere. Nana let us use some old sheets (that didn't look at all old) for capes.

Jimmy came forward, shirtless from swimming, in his wet jeans, carrying a sword he had made out of a long stick and duct tape. He knelt before Micah, Bitty, and me.

"Noble servant," I said, motioning for Bitty to come forward while I put a wreath of sticks on his head.

"Ow!" Jimmy yelled, twisting away.

"Quiet, fool!" I commanded. "For your faithful and honorable service you shall be knighted Sir Lancelot. May you be ever valiant in your quests." I held out my hands, and he gave me his homemade wooden sword.

I brought it down on his left shoulder and then his right.

"You are hereby knighted Sir Lancelot, Knight of the Round Table. You shall serve me, Queen Guinevere, and King

Arthur, and my maid, Elizabeth, all the days of your life."

Micah stepped forward. "I am Arthur Pendragon! It is better to die with honor than live as a coward!" He bowed toward Lancelot.

"You may arise," I said, holding my hand out.

Jimmy stood and bowed.

"Death before dishonor," I said.

"Death before dishonor," my court repeated.

Jimmy nodded, tore off his cape, dropped his weapon, and yelled, "Cowabunga!" before bombing into the river.

"That kind of ruins the moment!" I yelled, wiping my forehead. But it was so hot that Bitty and I plunged in after him.

Micah still didn't swim. He sat on the rocks watching us splash, laugh, and float on the water. We took turns having sovereign power until we got tired.

"How is Gaysie?" I asked. "Is her finger back on?"

Micah shook his head and shuddered. "They couldn't attach it. She's been in a real bad mood."

"How'd it happen, exactly?"

"Working," Micah answered. "And she's always telling *me* to keep *my* hands off the Mistress."

"I need a Popsicle," Jimmy stated. I sometimes wondered if he ate anything else.

"The ones next to her finger? No thanks!" I said. "Let's go to my house."

"Too far," Jimmy said, climbing onto the bank. I reluctantly followed.

We walked through the field and past Wilbur's small cottage.

"Where's Wilbur been?" I asked.

"Don't ask us," Jimmy said.

We walked back to the cottage door. Micah knocked three times. No answer.

The four of us peeked in the window. It was tiny, with one room and a small bathroom with the door wide open. But no Wilbur.

"Come on," Micah said hopefully. "Maybe he's at the house."

My heart thudded, as usual, when I walked into Gaysie Cutter's kitchen. Jimmy quickly looked around.

"Not here."

Micah opened the freezer and pulled out the Popsicle box, tipping it upside down. Empty.

We heard footsteps across the ceiling and then a slow lumber down the stairs. My heart went from thud to pound. I backed up closer to the door, Bitty tucked behind me. Gaysie entered the kitchen with a large load of laundry in her arms, not acknowledging us. Her face was red, sweaty from the heat, but flat and expressionless.

She walked into the small laundry room adjacent to the kitchen. Her right arm was raised slightly, still wrapped in gauze, the edges tinged with dark, dried blood.

"It's too hot for you to be taking up space in my kitchen. Go swim," Gaysie yelled.

Micah looked at Jimmy. They exchanged unspoken words. Jimmy raised his eyebrows. Micah gulped and stood still.

"Any . . . more Popsicles?"

"Look with your eyes not your mouth, boy!" Her rage reminded me of what Wilbur had said: When Gaysie was mad she was a tornado meeting a hurricane.

Jimmy narrowed his eyes and folded his arms like a sheriff overseeing a duel. Bitty and I inched even closer to the back door. Micah stood still and small in the kitchen.

Gaysie kicked the dryer and walked out, heaping a wet load of bedding into Micah's arms, before stomping back to the laundry room. "If you're not going to swim, go hang the laundry and stay outside."

"You could ask Wilbur to fix the dryer," Micah squeaked.

"No. I can*not* ask Wilbur."

Micah stood in the kitchen, holding the wet laundry, drooping under its weight.

"Where's he been, Ma?"

The question triggered a load of other ones. Why had Gaysie been lifting the tractor without him in the first place? Why hadn't Micah and Jimmy seen him? Where *was* Wilbur?

Gaysie ignored Micah's question, but came out of the laundry room and slammed an inner tube onto the counter. It was in the shape of a clown and its head bobbed maniacally back and forth.

"Hang the laundry. Go float," she snapped. "I'm too tired and upset for you to be here. My hand is aching something fierce."

Despite all my questions, I silently begged Micah not to say another word, as anyone with half a brain could see this volcano was about to explode.

Micah stood still, his arms full of wet clothes.

"Micah," I whispered.

"Hush up," Jimmy hissed at me.

Micah glanced at Jimmy, who stood with his chin raised proudly.

Gaysie turned slowly to face Micah. "Go."

Time stopped. We stared at Micah. He gulped and raised the load of laundry slightly higher to cover his face.

"But, Ma," Micah said behind the wet clothes. "It's . . . it's . . . a baby floatie. I'd sink."

"Do something!" I hissed at Jimmy.

Jimmy focused his eyes on Micah but stayed silent.

"Jimmy!" I said. "What kind of friend are you?"

Keeping his black, intense eyes focused on Micah, Jimmy's voice was low and dangerous.

"I'm his *best* friend."

Gaysie picked up the giant bobbing clown and handed it to Micah.

Very slowly, Micah reached his hand out from under the mound of wet clothes in his arms. I saw Jimmy's shoulders droop with disappointment. As much as I feared for him, I also felt my spirits drop. Micah should stand up to the beast.

But then Micah dropped the floatie on the floor.

Mother and son stood looking at each other. Micah did not bend to pick up the clown. Bitty grasped my arm with both hands and buried her face into me.

When Micah didn't move, Gaysie swung down and grabbed the floatie off the floor, slamming it on the counter.

Using her undamaged left hand, she grabbed a steak knife from the counter and raised it in the air. Our mouths dropped open in silent screams. And then she brought the knife down and stabbed the clown. It squeaked gasping breaths as the blade came down again and again until the clown deflated into a small, rainbow-colored, plastic heap on the counter. Gaysie lowered the knife so that it hung parallel to her side, the tip sharp and shiny.

"There you go," Gaysie said. "Now you won't sink— you'll have to swim!"

I grabbed Bitty and pushed her out the back door. Seconds later Micah followed, dropping the load of laundry in front of the clothesline without a word.

Jimmy came out last, his face drawn.

Micah shook out a wet, pale blue pillowcase and reached up on his tiptoes to hang it awkwardly with a clothespin. I grabbed some laundry, stealing glances at Micah as I tried hanging pants to dry, a chore I had never done before. Jimmy grabbed a wet shirt that looked like Wilbur's and slung it sloppily over the line.

We finished hanging clothes as Micah silently cried the entire time, his tears hitting his glasses, then diverting like a slow and silent river down his face.

"Brother . . . ," Jimmy began, "you did good."

Micah blinked slowly and shook his head.

My fists curled into tight balls as I glared at the clementine house. Did it make her feel good to make a sweet boy feel so bad? It wasn't any wonder Wilbur was staying away. Who would be friends with a wretched woman like

Gaysie Cutter? I picked up a rock, wanting to throw it at her window and watch it smash into a million smithereens.

Instead, I spit on her hanging pants.

I didn't care what Nana said about the word, I hated her so much.

CHAPTER 8

THE NEXT DAY, MY FATHER stepped back from the dental sign he was painting. "How's that?"

We were in the backyard with an easel set up, overlooking the fields of green, the sunset turning a golden yellow, the color of Vienna's hair. My father was not using pink paint as Bitty had suggested, but a soft white, gray, and blue.

"I wish I could paint like you." I reached over the wooden fence to pet Willowdale. She tossed her head and came closer.

"Practice," he said. "Painting well is ninety-five percent practice. The great Merzenich would say that practicing a new skill under the right conditions can change millions of connections between the nerve cells in the brain. Isn't it fascinating," he continued, "that we can change the very structure of our brain and our capacity to learn? There's very little such thing as natural talent." My father repeated this information so often that both Bitty and I could quote long passages of neuroscience as easily as *The Little Red Hen*.

Though I believed my father, I doubted I'd ever be able to paint anything anyone considered a masterpiece.

He, however, used his hands as an extension of his mind, a gift he could have used as a surgeon, but now used to extract teeth and paint pictures for Vienna, small snatches of beauty on white canvas. Her favorite was the one of a mother holding her baby. Sometimes, when she was gazing at it, I secretly pretended she knew who that baby was.

My father looked up at the sunset about to hit the horizon. Because the Midwest was so flat, the sun hit the corn crops from very far away, drawing closer until it peaked and backed off into twilight. At its peak it appeared to take up the entire earth like fire; reds, yellows, and bright streaks of orange all the way to space. There was no fog, smog, exhaust, or hard, blinking lights to dilute the effect. And when night came, the stars came too, dotting the sky like brilliant diamond flashes. The only competition was the moon, sometimes as big and fat as the round fiery sun; it was a bold beauty you never ever saw in the city.

"The end of the summer harvest," my father said as a tractor—not blue—rolled through the back fields, pulling a giant swisher through tall, overgrown grass. "It will be cut, left to dry, fluffed, then gathered into hay bales."

"Did you know Gaysie calls Wilbur's tractor 'the Blue Mistress'?" I said.

"Scandalous!" he replied, making a small touch-up. "Wilbur sure loves that tractor. He's shy. Until Gaysie and Micah, all he had was Blue. He's been a real good friend and neighbor, like a grandfather to those boys."

"I don't know why Wilbur likes Gaysie at all," I said.

"It's not like she's nice to him, always swatting at him and changing her mind about 'do this, do that.' She killed Micah's floatie yesterday—stabbed it to death on the kitchen counter."

"That is most unfortunate."

"Floatie murderer," I said darkly, remembering Micah's tears. "Just plain old mean. I don't blame Wilbur a bit if he never comes back." But even as I said it, I wondered. Where would a farmer as old as Wilbur go?

My father turned to look at me. "What do you mean, if Wilbur *never comes back?*"

"Well, Daddy, he's always around and suddenly he isn't! We haven't seen him for days."

Just then Nana pulled into the drive, interrupting us. Bitty waved at me from the backseat, as my father and I walked to the car.

"Next summer," Nana said, loading my arms up with groceries, "Gwyn and I are going to be gardening buddies, and we won't have to buy all this produce from the store." I followed her in, wondering how she could consistently forget that I hated vegetables—especially corn.

Bitty held up a cantaloupe. "Nana let me pick the best one!" A strange and familiar swoosh of terror went through me.

My father came in and washed his hands, the gray paint swirling down the drain.

Nana turned, hands on her hips.

"I just spoke with Dottie at the grocery store. Wilbur didn't show at the barn raising this past weekend, which is odd, don't you think? And he didn't come this morning to till my garden like he promised."

"Gwyn just said he hasn't been around for a few days. Maybe he's sick or out of town," my father said.

Nana shook her head impatiently. "Why wouldn't he call?"

"Send Gwyn and Bitty over to Gaysie's to ask, if you're worried," my father said. "I'll start supper."

"I don't think Wilbur's at Gaysie's," I said. "I already told you, he doesn't come by anymore. I think they had a fight—maybe a *lover's quarrel*."

"Guinevere!" Nana clucked. "Wilbur is old enough to be Gaysie's father! Do as your father says and go—no dawdling." I went to grab my jacket as Nana continued to talk.

"Dottie went to visit Ms. Myrtle, and *she* said that Wilbur's tractor hasn't moved for days—and if anyone knows anything, it's Ms. Myrtle. She keeps tabs on the entire neighborhood."

"Maybe he's fishing. Always did like a good fish fry."

"I don't think so!" I yelled.

"That man!" Nana said, exasperated. "Ride your bikes. You'll go faster."

"Come on, Bitty," I said.

"And put a helmet on," Nana added.

Bitty nodded and lifted the heavy cantaloupe over her head. My heart began to hurt at the sight.

"And make sure you stay on the right side of the road," Nana said.

My eyes were fixated on Bitty as she stood up onto her

tiptoes and very carefully placed the cantaloupe on the edge of the counter. Slowly, she took her hands away. The fruit balanced precariously before settling. I slowly exhaled.

Bitty walked toward me, but I continued to watch. The cantaloupe wobbled slightly forward.

"It's gonna fall," I whispered.

"Gwyn?" my father asked.

Watching that cantaloupe, I found myself thrust back to the grocery store when I lost my mother, standing by a yellow SALE! sign.

I could hear her light, happy voice. She walked easily then, without shuffling. She was Mama, not Vienna.

I was four years old and riding on the outside of the grocery cart, holding on with both hands. She leaned over the bin of cantaloupes, knocking on them to get a good one. I breathed in the smell, right at nose level; earthy and slightly sweet. Bitty was nine months old and strapped in her car seat, starting to fuss. Mama undid the buckle, picked Bitty up—*Sweet pea,* she said to me. *Could you please hand me a pacifier for our baby girl?* Sweet pea. I was always her sweet pea.

Had she known it was coming?

She suddenly stopped and became still. Her eyes locked into mine.

Sweet pea.

I remember her eyes, her dark blue eyes staring at me, the cantaloupe falling from her hand.

Sweet pea.

"Gwyn?" my father asked again, shutting off the sink

and shaking me out of my memory. But my heart was pounding so hard I could feel the beat in my bones. Instinctively, I reached out both hands. I lunged forward, trying to catch the melon, but it fell, hitting the floor with a loud thud, cracking open.

Too late.

I covered my ears and screamed.

We made it to Micah's on our bikes ten minutes later, after I'd almost given Nana a stroke. She apologized about a hundred times in the space of three minutes, mentioned seeing a psychologist, and promised never to buy cantaloupe again. My father had closed his eyes like he was steadying his insides, and reached for me. I tore off with Bitty before there were tears from either one of us.

When we reached the Cutters' ratty driftwood sign, the opera music was so loud it rattled the windowpanes we peered through. Jimmy, Micah, and Gaysie were eating spaghetti. There was one extra plate at the dinner table. It was empty. A small, uneasy knot began to lodge in my stomach.

"Bitty," I whispered, inching away. "Don't . . ."

But she was already knocking.

"Enter!" Gaysie yelled. We jumped at the sound of her voice.

"Sorry," Bitty squeaked.

Bitty held my hand tight as we entered the kitchen and walked to the table.

"Nana's looking for Wilbur . . . ," I began.

Gaysie held up her bandaged hand a moment, closed her eyes, and hummed the final notes of the opera, which sang from a small portable CD player on the kitchen counter. I grimaced at the dirty gauze on her hand, at the place where a finger was supposed to sit. Didn't she know anything about clean dressings and infection control?

"Ah," she said, tears rolling down her face. "That voice, that voice!" She shook off her emotion and blew her nose on her shirt. "Wilbur's favorite. Now. You are looking for him," she said in a brisk voice. "As you can see, he's not here."

I eyed the extra dinner plate.

She fixed her eyes on me.

"I've been having the same dream for days now," she said, changing the subject. "It involves you, Guinevere, and the river. Water is not something to be trifled with, do you hear me?"

"Yes."

She turned to Bitty, who was hiding behind me again. "What's the matter with you, Elizabeth? Honestly, I don't know how anyone can say the name 'Bitty' with any sort of dignity."

And just like that I hated her again. It was no wonder Wilbur was gone, that no one in town liked her or wanted to be her friend.

"Come here," Gaysie said. "Let me see what you're made of."

Bitty showed us exactly what she was made of by bravely walking forward until she looked like a tiny, shadowed Jonah about to be swallowed up by a giant whale.

Gaysie squeezed Bitty's shoulders and arms and looked her right in the eyes.

"There's a lot of smart in that pretty head of yours. You make sure to use it!" Bitty smiled and, shockingly, sat down at the table. I wanted to jump up and shout, *I object!*

Gaysie leaned back in her chair and patted her large stomach. "Mmm, full as a tick." She looked at me. "Hungry?"

"Um," I said, thinking of Nana cooking.

"Sit!" Gaysie ordered.

Micah patted my back as I sat, his smiling, big brown eyes magnified behind his thick glasses. Jimmy nodded his head across the table and opened his full mouth of chewed-up spaghetti.

"You're disgusting," I said.

Gaysie came back to the table with two plates piled high. "We've already said grace. And that sauce is made from our very own garden, isn't it, boys?"

"Yep," Micah said.

"Garlic, onion, tomatoes, of course, eggplant, squash, spinach, and zucchini!" Gaysie said.

I snapped my fingers, remembering why I was here. "Nana sent me because Wilbur was supposed to help her dig a garden."

A shadow crossed Gaysie's face. I suddenly noticed how ragged it looked, how red her eyes were, like she'd rubbed them raw. Even the scar down the side of her face looked more purple and pronounced.

She leaned forward, changing the subject again. "What I want to know is why Elizabeth never talks."

"She . . ."

"Shh!" Gaysie said, glaring at me. "Elizabeth needs to find her voice. You're quite the number to try to follow, you know, mother and older sister rolled into one." She turned back to Bitty. "What do you have to say, Elizabeth?"

Micah burped and Jimmy asked for seconds. Gaysie kept her eyes on Bitty, waiting.

"I dropped the cantaloupe and made Gwyn scream."

My face colored at Bitty's betrayal.

"You see?" Gaysie said. "Now we're getting somewhere!" She turned to Micah and Jimmy. "Stop eating like pigs. I didn't raise you to behave like barnyard animals!"

I looked at Jimmy, wondering again why he never went home and instead spent his time with *her*.

"Now, why did you scream over a cantaloupe, Guinevere?"

I looked down at my shoes. *None of your business, that's why.*

When I didn't speak, Gaysie said, "I saw your mother this morning."

I looked up.

"I get such great pleasure bringing her flowers," Gaysie said, animated. "Her whole face lights up. There's no guile, no pretense—and we both know she'd tell me if she didn't like them."

True. That sounded like Vienna.

"I know something of head injuries," Gaysie said, her finger absently stroking the long scar on her face. "Jimmy and Micah told you about me, didn't they?"

I glanced at them.

"Oh, it's not a secret," Gaysie said. "Though we all have a couple of those in our back pocket. If I were a more perfect woman, I would be more like your father, who's never kept anything from you."

I nodded, but slowly. My father didn't lie to me, but the longer we were in Crow, the more I wondered about what he'd chosen not to tell me.

"You don't know the details of the accident, Guinevere, but you want to, don't you?"

I kept my eyes on her, wishing I didn't want to know anything about Gaysie.

"I don't know why Vienna has to live the way she does when I escaped with little more than a scratch." I looked at Gaysie's face. Her long scar was more than a scratch. "Life isn't always equitable, is it?"

Bitty shook her head.

"I didn't have it easy as a child. My parents were . . . not kind people. I was smart and loved learning, but life was difficult. I was never pretty like Vienna," she said. "Not even mercifully plain. Not athletic. Very clumsy with big feet. The closest compliment I can remember is 'sturdy.' And every day I went to school smelling of pig slop."

"Pig slop?" Bitty said.

"It's true. I smelled like pig slop because my step-father raised pigs, and oh!" Gaysie banged the table with her fists. "Those swine smelled so bad! You can imagine how terrible it is for a young girl to show up at school smelling like slop. I endured the insults, the foul smells, the too-small hand-me-downs. But there was that one thing . . . one thing I desperately longed for!"

"A shower?" Jimmy asked.

"More than a shower!" Gaysie said. "What I *desperately* wanted was for someone to need me." She looked longingly at Bitty and then to me. "Guinevere and Bitty, you are so remarkably lucky."

Bitty needed me, that was true. And I needed her. But I thought of that feeling I got deep down sometimes, a restless longing sort of feeling. An image of Vienna came to mind, screaming my father's name every time he appeared. The way she asked for him every five minutes. She never screamed for me. If need was love, then Vienna didn't love me. Vienna needed only one person, and that was my father. I sometimes thought that this *need* is what kept him tethered to her, even when she was awful.

"I didn't have a family like yours," Gaysie said, as if mine was the epitome of bliss. "But I did eventually find true friends, your parents and Myron, and oh, what a grand thing it was." She blinked rapidly, as if pushing forward a memory. "I would have done anything for them.

"But our last real adventure was something we shouldn't have done, and that's how the accident happened. Vienna, Jed, Myron, and I put my sled on the biggest hill in town."

I felt myself going into shock, and my mouth dropped open.

"Didn't you know?" Gaysie asked.

I sat, frozen solid to my chair. *They were there!* Why had my father never told me this story?

"We had been forbidden to even try it."

"Try it?" I managed.

"To sled down that spectacular hill! You know the one, right on the town line as you enter Crow, next to Dingle." Gaysie laughed, far away in her recollection. "We were attempting the biggest dare in Crow—sledding down the hill and right across the frozen water to the other side of the river. We had made it too, several times that winter. What a ride! But that last time, well, it was nearly spring. The ice was melting. We crashed right through."

"Her head split in two," Jimmy said.

"She died," Micah added.

"I'm quite certain my death was instantaneous," Gaysie said. "And I wasn't altogether sad. In fact, I felt relief. No more pig slop, unbearable home life." Gaysie's eyes became distant, seeing something beyond us. "The light came. It was so warm, so beautiful. All my pain was gone, every bad feeling, all the horrible things done to me—gone!" Gaysie snapped her fingers. "Heaven," she said, "is a place you never want to leave."

Gaysie swallowed carefully, and I had a sharp and uncomfortable pang of conscience. Had I misjudged her? Was I being cruel like the other kids had been? I thought of Nana and my father, and even Vienna. An unusual family, yes, but what did I know of pig slop and a harsh family? Gaysie's eyes became heavy with tears that pooled under her red eyelids.

"If you were dead, then how did you come back?"

Gaysie tilted her head at me. "Because I realized that there *were* people who needed me."

Either Gaysie was a masterful liar or she believed this story without a doubt. But I wanted to know: How exactly does one die and come back to life? How long was she underwater? How cold was the water? How long was her body deprived of oxygen? I knew the statistics and they were grim. What was the extent of her head injuries? How had everyone gotten out of the water but Myron? And who exactly needed her to come back? Did she mean her friends? *My parents . . .* or someone else?

I opened my mouth.

"That's all for tonight," she said with a decisive nod, and walked to the kitchen window.

The sun was setting over the cornfields, day heading into night. I sat, stewing. How could she leave me hanging like that?

"Is Wilbur coming to dinner tonight?" Micah asked, his voice like an eager puppy's.

"No. Wilbur is not coming to dinner." The way she said it, with such finality, made me sure that Gaysie knew the where and the how and the why. For all her talk of no secrets, Gaysie was keeping a few. She turned slowly and looked longingly at the empty dinner plate. "But I had to set a place anyway. Just in case."

After we ate, we got on our bikes, the sun completely gone to sleep. Micah and Jimmy, told to accompany us home, turned on their headlamps. Gaysie came out onto the porch.

"Don't you dare talk to anyone," she yelled. "You're just the sort of children the circus would love to borrow!"

"Can you yell any louder?" Jimmy yelled back at Gaysie.

"Oh, you bet your bootstraps I can yell louder than that!" she hollered, her voice echoing all the way down the street.

Jimmy shook his head and led the way down Lanark Lane. It was spooky, with the sun almost down, the air cooling and becoming so dark I couldn't see the road ahead. Bitty whimpered beside me. I imagined this was the sort of night the Headless Horseman of Sleepy Hollow would appear.

"Come on, Bitty!" We pedaled faster, but it only brought the panic closer. *Control your imagination*, my father would say. I suddenly thought of the Creepers. Were they allowed outside after dark? The only lights were from Micah's headlamp and the few that dimly shone out the occasional farmhouse window. I shivered though it wasn't cold, with a feeling that someone was watching us. Corn, now tall enough to hide grown men, monsters, and ghosts, rustled on either side of the road. I wouldn't have been able explain how or who, but I just knew: We didn't bike home alone that night.

I didn't have time to think more about it though, because when we arrived home it was to Nana who was annoyed we had stayed so long, annoyed we'd intruded on Gaysie's dinner, and annoyed we hadn't found out anything about Wilbur's absence. My father left for the care center before I could ask him anything about sledding and Gaysie's version of events. It was after visiting hours, and I wished they wouldn't let him in. I wished they'd see the tired shadows under his eyes and tell him to go home and sleep. And part of me wished he'd just stay with us, instead of always running to her.

We climbed into bed, and Bitty hugged me around the waist as I began our Peter Pan story. I was barely to the Lost Boys when she whispered, "Is Jimmy a Lost Boy?"

"He has Gaysie, I guess."

"Then Gaysie is like Peter Pan, right?"

"More like Captain Hook," I scoffed. We lay quiet in the darkness of our bedroom, looking out into the vast sky that was just outside our window. The stars were bright, the night cold. I think we both fell asleep thinking of a girl named Gaysie: a lost, ugly little girl nobody loved, nobody wanted. Never feeling needed. I could not imagine her ever being small or having a mother or a father. But I guess she had been a little girl once, had run around Crow—had played with my parents! She had even died, like Vienna. Wasn't it extraordinary that they had both come back to life, but with scars of different sorts?

CHAPTER 9

A T LUNCHTIME THE NEXT DAY I sat in a noisy cafeteria, surrounded by my classmates, pondering everything Gaysie had told us. There was laughing, trays clanging, sneakers squeaking on the linoleum, but it all drifted far away, even my questions, when I opened my lunchbox.

I took a bite of cantaloupe I had purposely cut and packed myself that morning. My father said the only way to face your fears was to face them head-on. So there they were, cut up into nice, even squares in a Tupperware dish. The squish in my mouth though, the sweetness on my tongue, brought the memory surfacing.

She began to fall.

Holding Bitty with one hand, her other arm swung wildly into the stacked cantaloupe. The fruit rolled forward, slowly at first, then faster as one by one, each cantaloupe took a suicide plunge all the way to the hard grocery store floor. At that moment, something disastrous was happening inside my mama. I yelled and stuck my arms out to stop the falling fruit, but her eyes found mine once again. Bitty was falling too. *Our baby girl.* She was going to hit the ground, her little, round head the shape of a small, round cantaloupe. There were no words. I just held out my arms. She dropped Bitty into my arms, like she was saying, *This is your baby now, sweet pea.*

My mama's eyes closed and she continued to fall, hitting her head on the cold, white-tiled floor with a sickening thwack and thud. That fall wasn't what wrecked her though. Her heart had stopped. She wasn't breathing. No oxygen was circulating to her brain. Bitty wailed as I squeezed her, the cantaloupes still falling all over and landing, one after another, on top of my mama's legs, back, head, and hands.

A woman stopped, snatched Bitty from me, and began screaming for help. Alarmed, I knelt down, tears and hysteria coming over me. "Mama, get up! Someone has the baby, and cantaloupes are all over the floor and we're going to have to pick them all up!" And then I was screaming it. "Get up, get up!"

She didn't answer me.

My father explained the brain like it was a tree. All the branches making up the tree are the brain's millions of neurons that need oxygen. The longer your brain is deprived of oxygen, the worse the damage will be.

Strangers put their hands on her chest and pumped while counting in quick, deliberate rhythm.

How long can a person go without oxygen? I've experimented. My longest time ever is one minute and twenty-three seconds, which is pretty long, but I almost fainted, and my face turned a scary purple color. At five minutes brain cells begin to die. The tree branches shrivel.

Extraordinary efforts were taken to save Mama's life

that day, I found out later. But it wasn't enough. She was taken by ambulance, my father beside her. Paddles were applied to her chest, an electric shock was delivered. She was given numerous IVs. Still, the heart did not pump. Six minutes without oxygen turned into eight. Nine. Ten.

She was twenty-four years old and declared dead at 10:23 a.m.

It was then my scientist of a father tried a new hypothesis. He dropped to his knees and pleaded for a miracle.

That's exactly what he got.

Vienna's heart began to beat on its own again.

It was a miracle. She came back to life. If you could call it that.

I spit the cantaloupe into my hand.

CHAPTER 10

A S THE WEATHER TURNED COOLER, my questions about both the sledding accident and Wilbur's whereabouts remained unanswered. I saw Officer Jake peering through the windows of Wilbur's cottage one afternoon after school, and Micah said Gaysie was avoiding him because he was a pompous nincompoop, but I thought that awfully odd. If Gaysie's only real friend was missing, why would she be avoiding the best person to help her find him? Through my superior eavesdropping skills, I heard rumors that Gaysie Cutter had finally driven Wilbur away, and that he was in hiding. It was followed by a laugh and a chilling silence.

Others, including my father, said Wilbur was an independent sort, not the kind of man who checked in. But my suspicions grew, especially when one morning before school I saw Officer Jake talking with Gaysie in the backyard, close to Wilbur's tractor. They gestured with their hands, animated. The field was overgrown and recently blanketed with cold, wet dew.

"I'd give my pinkie toe to know what they're talking about," I said to Micah. Today he was wearing a handmade-looking yellow-and-orange poncho, the hood pulled up around his face. "In fact," I said, "you go on ahead." I skulked around the trees, trying to get closer.

"The longer he's gone, the worse it looks," Officer Jake was saying. I'd only just settled in when Gaysie loudly said, "Curiosity killed the cat, Guinevere."

I skipped away. Wasn't it too bad for her that I was Guinevere St. Clair—and not a cat?

"Hurry up," Jimmy said, skating ahead. "Mrs. Law is on the warpath." This was unfortunately true after we'd arrived half an hour late last week due to Bitty's recent show-and-tell: a perfectly intact squirrel who had recently met its demise in the middle of the road. Since moving to Crow, I had observed that squirrels, next to Jimmy, were God's most reckless creatures. The squirrel we found was so perfectly alive-looking, we weren't even sure it was dead until we poked it and it didn't move. Jimmy plopped the coolest show-and-tell ever right into Bitty's backpack.

But it made us late to school, and it wasn't even worth it, since Bitty's teacher, Mrs. LaRue, shrieked and threw the backpack across the room, scaring all the first graders to tears. Of course, Bitty didn't get into trouble, because she was a sweet, motherless child, but I sure got it later when Nana got called to the office.

Still, I'd been feeling restless for days, with so many questions about the past no one would answer.

"I dare you, Jimmy Quintel," I said, moving past Ms. Myrtle's house, "to knock and run."

"*Booooring,*" he said.

"You're just chicken!" This, of course, was a very ridiculous thing to say, since Jimmy Quintel was many things, but chicken was not one of them.

Jimmy careened so close, I thought his skateboard was going to hit me.

"Come on, guys," Micah said, pulling me along.

"Can I knock?" Bitty asked.

"You want that goose to eat you?" I said.

"Oh, so it's okay for the goose to eat *me*?" Jimmy said. "It's too easy to knock and run. She can't even chase you. I dare *you* to spit in her mailbox."

"Jimmy," Micah said.

"She won't do it. She's too scared," Jimmy said lazily, rolling ahead on his skateboard.

"I am not."

"*Baawwwwwk!*" Jimmy said.

I observed Ms. Myrtle's mailbox, which was affixed to the house, right next to the front door.

"Why isn't the mailbox on the road like everyone else's?"

"Probably because witches can't be seen in daylight," Jimmy said.

I had never actually seen Ms. Myrtle except for a flash of red hair or one wrinkly hand sliding out the front door to take her mail out of the box.

Stalwart, I marched across the grass with Bitty following me. Jimmy and Micah made it to the maple tree and covered their eyes. I could hear Jimmy cackling.

I opened the mailbox and hesitated.

Jimmy bawked like a chicken.

I closed my eyes and spit.

"Get off my porch, you nasty girl! I'm going to tell your grandmother on you!"

Bitty screamed, while Micah and Jimmy yelled for us to run. Mortified, I jumped off the porch and ran breathless to the maple tree, looking back to make sure Ms. Myrtle wasn't flying on her broom after me.

It was Bitty I saw. She had not run. She stood frozen, locked in a staring contest with the goose who had waddled around to the front. It honked, and Bitty startled. The sight was so horrifying that I screamed out for her.

Micah and I began running toward her. The goose, however, had a distinct advantage with a much smaller distance to cover. It was not afraid of us, either. On the contrary, it was outwardly defiant, posturing at Bitty, angry and hissing.

"Bitty!" I screamed. "Move!" But she didn't move. Her face was white, her mouth open. I knew that terrified feeling. It was like being in Gaysie's open grave with a dead dog hanging over you.

The goose came up to her face—they were about the same height—and honked. When she didn't move, it made a pecking motion toward her. "Stop it, you stupid, stupid bird!" I screamed.

But the goose went in hard and nipped Bitty's cheek.

"Bitty—run!" My voice became a panicked cry.

The bite woke Bitty from her frozen stupor, and she finally stepped back, but fell on the sidewalk. The goose toddled around her once, then went after her again, honking loudly. Ms. Myrtle's front door opened, and an old and wrinkled arm reached out, grasping at the air. Bitty was crying, trying to shield her small face.

It was Jimmy who reached her first. He flew down the

road on his skateboard, ollied over the curb, and picked Bitty up like Superman, shielding her from another lunge from the goose. When I reached the goose, it nipped me hard on the shoulder. I gave a great kick, but missed the mark and fell. Bold and defiant, it made another lunge toward me. I screamed a bloody-murder scream.

Micah, with wild eyes, hesitated just one second.

Then he grabbed the goose by the neck, and sweet, gentle Micah wrung its neck with both hands. He wrenched it hard before dropping it on the ground, his mouth open in horror. The world went silent. We stared down at the lifeless animal, its beautiful white feathers fluttering with a slight breeze. I half knelt and grazed them with my fingers.

I took Bitty from Jimmy, cried at the blood on her cheeks, and carried her on my back all the way to school.

The searing image that stayed with me though, was when I looked over my shoulder, just to make sure the goose hadn't revived and come after us for revenge. No, it lay still and dead. It was Ms. Myrtle I remember, the one and only time I ever saw her leave her house. She sat on the grass sobbing, holding the dead goose in her arms.

Bitty was immediately sent to the nurse. I sat with her as her face was bandaged and Nana was called. Yes, the nurse said, we were fine, just a run-in with a local goose.

Jimmy halfheartedly punched me in the shoulder on the way to class, his way of showing affection, I supposed.

"Ow," I said. "Where's Micah?"

"Sobbing his eyes out in the bathroom."

The news made me want to sob my eyes out too.

"Every once in a while," Jimmy said, holding out his hands like he'd hold a twig, "Gaysie just SNAPS! You never know when it's coming. I guess that's what happened with Micah." Jimmy lifted his eyebrows in admiration. "You've got to admit. It's about the bravest thing he's ever done." Jimmy entered the classroom, but I stood still a moment longer.

"Gwyn?" Mrs. Law popped her head out of the classroom.

SNAP. And yet I owed Bitty's life to Micah! He wasn't a goose murderer, only protecting us.

Blindly, I hung up my jacket, walked to my seat, and sank down, trying not to think about the dead bird. It had all happened so fast. Jimmy was wrong. Micah wasn't like Gaysie. And sure Gaysie snapped at Wilbur, but . . . was it like Jimmy said? Had Gaysie really *snapped*?

When had we last seen Wilbur? I mulled it over, realizing it was the day Gaysie cut off her finger. She had sat in her living room, rocking, bleeding. There had been blood under the Blue Mistress, too. I had gotten it on my clothes and hands that day. And poof—we had never seen Wilbur again. We had assumed all of the blood was from Gaysie's finger, but was it? Or was it connected to Wilbur as well? I almost groaned out loud. What kind of lawyer was I? Days and days had gone by, and now all that fresh evidence was gone!

A hard, cold thought came. Something had happened to Wilbur that day, and Gaysie Cutter was in the middle of it. How was I going to prove it?

CHAPTER 11

WE ARRIVED HOME FROM SCHOOL to find my
father sitting at the kitchen table.

"Sit," he said, patting the seat beside his.
Bitty came in behind me, a large bandage on her cheek. He
inhaled sharply as she climbed up into his lap.

"I'm sorry, Daddy," I said quietly.

"You killed Ms. Myrtle's goose?" my father asked.

"Jed, for heaven's sake," Nana said, touching Bitty's
side. "Look at your baby's face."

"I didn't kill the goose," I said quietly, but I lowered my
eyes. I might as well have.

My father rubbed his forehead and closed his eyes. "We
need to go see Ms. Myrtle."

We walked up the road to where Gaysie was waiting outside her orange farmhouse, Jimmy and Micah beside her.
Jimmy was tapping his foot impatiently, arms folded, tossing his hair out of his eyes every few seconds. Micah stood
still, eyes red with guilt and grief. His purple-and-yellow,
paisley-swirled shirt was untucked and rumpled. Gaysie's
lips were pursed tightly, her hands folded in front of her as
her body rocked back and forth. She said nothing until my
father began to walk us over to the dreaded Ms. Myrtle's.

"Jed."

He turned.

"Let the children do this."

He looked at me, then nodded.

"Daddy!" I whispered. "You can't leave me!"

He gently turned me to face the lion's den. "I'll be right here."

"But not Elizabeth," Gaysie said firmly. "She's been through enough today."

"But . . . ," I protested. Bitty's face was our best supporting evidence!

"Go," my father said.

I climbed the front stairs, averting my gaze from the mailbox. Micah, too shell-shocked for words, was dragged up by Jimmy, who knocked on the old aluminum door. We paused to listen. The curtains were drawn, not a sliver of light shone through.

"Maybe she's not home," I said.

Jimmy knocked harder.

"What!" a voice demanded.

Jimmy looked at me.

"Uh, it's Guinevere St. Clair. We wanted to say—we're sorry," I said diplomatically, knowing a hostile witness usually looks like a guilty witness.

Jimmy impatiently pushed the front door open and entered.

"Jimmy!" I whispered. "You can't just . . ."

But he did, and we followed him into a dimly lit living room. Micah let out a cry when he saw a worn yellow baby blanket in the middle of the living room floor, the dead goose atop it. Limp and peaceful, it looked like it could just be sleeping. I stared at it until Micah's sniffles required assistance. I reached out and held his hand tight. We sat awkwardly on a dusty, rose-colored couch that smelled like Vienna's care center. My eyes flicked around the room, at anything besides the dead bird.

The room was bare except for one couch, one chair, a piano, and a large, empty cage. Inside was a bowl and fresh newspaper.

There were no pictures on the wall, no television, no books.

My eyes adjusted to the dim light as I finally saw Ms. Myrtle. She was as old and wrinkly as an ancient potato, and her expression looked like she was sucking on a very sour dill pickle. How strange it was, seeing the whole of her, sitting in a chair.

Ms. Myrtle cleared her throat.

She held her hands tightly together to control her shaking, and it looked like it took great effort to keep her very long neck upright. She reminded me of a turtle. At any other time, "Myrtle the Turtle" would have sent me into hysterics.

"I'm sorry for what I did," I began again, glancing out the window at Bitty. "We didn't mean . . ." The look on her face cut me off. She was frozen, staring out the window.

"Vienna . . . ," Ms. Myrtle's crabby voice whispered. "Vienna is the mother of that child."

"Yes," I said. "Of both of us."

"Vienna was my piano student," she said, motioning to the instrument in the living room, her expression suddenly less sour. The complete deviation of conversation caught me off guard. One of my earliest memories was sitting on Vienna's lap while she played the piano, her voice sounding like what I imagined angels to sound like. Sometimes I could still hear that voice in my head.

"She was very talented," Ms. Myrtle said. My heart beat more quickly. So many people mentioned Vienna, saying how beautiful or spirited she was, but I didn't know much else. Ms. Myrtle had really *known* Vienna.

"She still plays," I said thickly. "It's one of the only things she remembers how to do."

I had not intended to say anything personal to the witch, but I couldn't help it.

Ms. Myrtle sniffed, her orange hair moving slightly, the tip of her nose red, gnarled hands curled and twisted together. "She was so nice to my boy."

"Your *boy*?" I asked.

Ms. Myrtle gave Micah such a ferocious look that I was even more confused.

Jimmy elbowed me hard. "Get on with it," he whispered.

I shook off the spell that had come over me and put my lawyer skills to work. After all, we needed adequate representation.

"We wanted to say we are sorry about your goose," I began again. "Micah loved the goose, and he'd never ever in a million years hurt another living thing and definitely not the goose who thought he was its mother!" Ms. Myrtle's eyes narrowed as I continued. "Micah is sweet and good, and Bitty was being attacked—he had to save her!" As the neighborhood spy, I was expecting compassion; Ms. Myrtle knew the true and gentle Micah who wore silver, curly shoelaces. Micah sniffed back a ragged sob.

She did not offer compassion. She looked disgusted and angry.

Ms. Myrtle raised her eyes as she lifted a wrinkled, gnarled finger and pointed at me. "And you are a very bad girl! I saw what you did to my mailbox. You shame your mother's name." I shrunk an inch, stricken.

"I'm truly sorry for . . . that. Sometimes, you see, my father says I get a wee bit carried away, especially when it comes to double dares." Jimmy sighed. I hurried on, "Please forgive me for my complete lack of manners and neighborly kindness!" I batted my eyes for extra innocence.

If she refused to forgive me, I briefly considered negotiation. But Rule 14 from *The Law: A to Z* was: *N: Never Negotiate with Terrorists.*

We waited for Ms. Myrtle's reply. We sat in silence except for the tick-tick-ticking of a hidden clock, as if she kept Captain Hook's pet crocodile in her basement. *Ticktock, ticktock.*

I jumped a mile upon hearing a knock at the front door. My father's figure appeared outside the front window. Relieved, I hopped up and pulled Micah along. We skirted the dead goose in the middle of the floor before Micah turned at the front door.

"Um, Ms. Myrtle?" Micah asked. "What are you going

to do with . . . ?" All eyes turned to the beautiful, lifeless goose.

She shook her head pitifully. "What do you think? Gaysie Cutter knows how to bury the dead."

Jimmy pulled open the front door. My father nodded at Ms. Myrtle.

"Ma'am. We're very sorry."

"Jedidiah," she said stiffly.

As we walked down the stairs Ms. Myrtle called out. "Micah!"

He turned, his eyes begging for a crumb of forgiveness.

"I *hate* that shirt you're wearing."

He stumbled down the stairs after me, then ran to the back of the house and hurled. My feelings exactly.

Gaysie waited for us on the lawn as I stomped over, glaring at her superior, smug smile. I clenched my fists, thought of how I had been so afraid of her, of how she had killed Micah's floatie and made him cry even after we'd found her fat sausage finger, how she'd called him weak.

"Micah is the bravest and nicest and best boy I know," I said. "He loved that mean goose but he loved Bitty even more. He's sweet and—it's his superpower! Don't *ever* tell me he's weak again. Not *ever*!"

She drew herself up tall, her eyes boring down on me. She was pretty good at staring contests, but today I was better. I glared right back at her, my backbone made of steel. Never would Gaysie Cutter have power over me. I would never be afraid of her again. I would find out what she did to Wilbur and prosecute to the full extent of the law.

CHAPTER 12

THAT NIGHT, AFTER OUR HUMILIATING Ms. Myrtle experience, I lay in bed thinking about Vienna playing the piano, a little girl Ms. Myrtle loved. A girl who was nice to her boy. I admit, I wanted to love Vienna too. I wanted to be nicer to her, to help my dad try to make her better, more like that girl she had been—so why couldn't I? I had avoided the care center like the bubonic plague pretty much since we had gotten here. My father said that some people were harder to love, but it bothered me, how excruciatingly hard it was.

My mind wandered back and forth from a younger Vienna to a younger Gaysie. Gaysie was hard for me to even *like*, but Vienna apparently had. What were they like at my age, when they had all gone down that hill? If Gaysie had really died, why had she been allowed to live again and not Myron? And why had Gaysie come back with all of her memories—and Vienna hadn't? There were so many variables that could change how things turned out. For instance, who and what had caused the sledding accident? Was someone at fault? What if someone had refused to go sledding that day? Would Myron be alive? What if someone had gotten Vienna's heart started earlier? Would we still have her?

When Vienna came out of the coma, it was nothing like the movies make it look. In the movies, when a mom opens her eyes, she instantly smiles and holds out her arms to her beloved children. There's a happily ever after.

My father said the brain could actually change and rewrite history the way we wanted, that photographs could trigger memories that never actually happened, that the many books I read planted narratives in my head that weren't even true.

But never once did he question the accuracy of my memory on the day Vienna awoke. We were both there, and, believe me, that's a memory I have tried to forget.

After her heart started, her brain did not. She slept for four long months.

My father was first and foremost a man of science, but in the hospital he began speaking of miracles. We spent many evenings in the hospital chapel. He would open the Holy Bible as he sat in the pew and stare at the book without turning pages.

"Guinevere," he said, "faith is an experiment. It must be demonstrated before being rewarded."

"It's a miracle she survived at all," the doctors said.

"It's a miracle her heart is still beating."

And then: "It's a miracle she's awake."

Miracles could not be explained by my father's science, by the doctors, world-class brain specialists, or nurses. This is how Vienna's case changed my father. Before, all things could be explained from a scientific point of view. But then suddenly they couldn't.

On the day Mama woke up, my father carried me into the room. I was wearing a yellow dress that was now too tight around my armpits and shoulders, but it was her favorite.

She lay in the hospital bed covered with a sheet, hands curled up close to her chest, body rigid and tight.

"Vienna," my father said. "It's Gwyn. Guinevere. Your special girl." I leaned over the cold hospital bed rail to hug her, tentative at first, then fiercely. She made no movement except to bring her hands and arms in closer and tighter to her body. When I breathed into her neck and said, "Mama," she turned her head to the other side and made a fearful noise in her throat instead of pulling me close and wrapping me tight.

The only person she reacted to besides my father was Nana. We didn't know it at the time, but they were the only people she recognized—though somehow—much, much older, and she didn't know why.

Days passed, weeks became months. When she finally spoke, she was Vienna Eyre, age thirteen. And never a day older.

Not once did she say my name or ask for her sweet pea.

Back then I called her Mama.

But after that day, she was never my mama again.

My father began talking. He talked and talked and talked, tried to hit upon something she could grab on to. He told his wife that she was twenty-four. She didn't live in Crow, Iowa, anymore. She was married, had two children, and was living in New York City while her husband studied to be an oral surgeon.

That's when she began swearing.

She may have loved Jed St. Clair as a child, but she didn't know him as a man. She did not remember getting married. She didn't know her own father was dead. She remembered her sisters who came to see her, but was confused that everyone looked ten years older.

She didn't remember holding me just after I was born, stroking my head and saying I was the most beautiful baby ever. She didn't know that she had watched me learn how to roll over, crawl, and walk.

She didn't know that she had loved me.

After she came out of her coma, I was sure that if I touched her enough, looked into her eyes long enough—she would remember.

But that moment never came. She never remembered me.

Why? I wanted answers so badly, I ached for them. But no matter how hard I looked I could never find them.

Guinevere St. Clair did not exist.

I believe that was my father's first true heartbreak.

I know because it was mine, too.

CHAPTER 13

THE GOOSE KILLING IS HOW piano lessons with Ms. Myrtle began. Understanding a mean, old, sour pickle, my father said, would help rid the hate in my heart. He didn't actually say "mean, old, sour pickle" but I'm sure that's what he meant.

"But, Daddy, my heart is perfect," I said, riding Willowdale around the backyard. "The doctors tested it a million times, and, anyways, Ms. Myrtle will probably eat Bitty when she comes with me."

"Bitty will not be attending," he said. "It will be good for her to be more independent, and music lessons will be good for you. Music makes extraordinary demands on the brain. Liszt's Sixth Paganini Étude requires a staggering eighteen hundred notes per minute. Musicians have several areas, including the motor cortex and cerebellum, that are far superior . . ."

I gave him a deadpan look.

"You'll also be able to play music with your mother, who I hope you'll be visiting more often," he added.

My mood darkened.

"Why is it always about her?" I burst out. "Ms. Myrtle actually liked Vienna. She hates me! You're sending me to my doom. I heard a ticktock in the house, and I bet . . ."

"Guinevere." My father paused. "This *is* about you. It's about your development as a well-rounded individual."

"I'd rather die than go into that house," I sniffed. "I hate . . ."

"Ah!" he said, backing up toward the house. "Don't say it." He turned to go inside.

"Then I'll think it!" I yelled after him.

"You can think it," he said over his shoulder. "But you can't say it. I'd rather you not even think it. Remember . . ."

"I know, know." All my mean thoughts were going to get stuck in my brain, and I'd never be able to rewire myself and be a nice girl.

"You start next Thursday," he said. "I'm counting on you."

I leaned down over my cow's neck. "Oh, Willowdale Princess Deon Dawn. I have an unusually cruel father." My sweet cow tossed her head in agreement.

On the bright side, maybe Ms. Myrtle would have dirt on Gaysie.

September had brought the scattered and random brilliance of red, orange, and yellow leaves, flushing out the humidity and brightening the little town of Crow, making it easier to let go of summer.

We crunched in fallen leaves to and from school, made leaf tunnels, and breathed in the comforting smell of bonfires. During those days I often thought of Wilbur, becoming more and more certain something terrible had happened to him when he didn't show up. One afternoon, after constant questioning, my father let me accompany him to Wilbur's cottage.

Gaysie wasn't home, so we just walked across the backyard. My father tried the cottage door.

"Windows are locked too."

"How did you know?" he asked, giving me a look.

"Well, I was worried about our old boy," I said innocently.

"Hmm. A bit strange."

"What is?"

"No one locks their doors around here." He furrowed his brows. "Certainly not Wilbur."

"Maybe you should break it down with your foot. Give it a big hi-yah karate chop!"

Instead, he peered in the window. I stood next to him on a big rock, lifted onto my tiptoes, and peered in alongside him. It looked the same except maybe more empty.

On the mantel was a picture of Gaysie, Micah, and Jimmy standing by the Blue Mistress, all smiles. I stared at it. They were like a family. No wonder Micah and Jimmy were blind to Gaysie's shadiness. And my father . . . his loyalty to women was his greatest blind spot.

He looked toward Gaysie's house.

"What are you thinking?" I asked eagerly.

"Nothing." But I didn't believe him. He was always thinking.

My father sighed, put his hands in his pockets, and walked back across the grass. I thought for a moment before scrambling to catch up to him.

When I did, he was speaking to Gaysie, who had just pulled into the driveway. And he was actually *smiling*! As if they really were *friends*.

"Hello, Guinevere," she said.

I nodded sullenly and walked past her, feeling a burning inside for answers and an anger at my father's stubborn refusal to see what I did. Was it truly a blind spot . . . or was it worse? Did his friendship with Gaysie also extend to covering up . . . a crime? I felt ill.

We didn't speak all the way home. He was lost in his thoughts, and I could not find a way to voice mine.

Unfortunately, Thursday piano lessons were not forgotten. The next Thursday we walked home from school as Micah, who was mostly recovered from the goose killing, told us about a story he'd written on his typewriter. My name, Guinevere, had inspired him, and he had decided to write an Arthur Pendragon story with an ending the way it should have been written. This time Guinevere would redeem herself instead of betraying the once and future king. He used a typewriter because Gaysie didn't allow computers in the house (that was how the terrorists watched you). Living next to Ms. Myrtle, I guessed her paranoia was understandable.

We stopped in front of Ms. Myrtle's house. "I'd rather be tortured and eat rats," I whispered, "than go into that house again."

"Have fun," Jimmy said, skating away, his Mohawk blowing in the breeze.

Out of the corner of my eye I saw Gaysie, far out in the

green fields, way past the late-summer crops. The blue tractor remained still, a thin plastic tarp now pulled over the top.

"Micah, where exactly could Wilbur be?" I asked, purposely casual.

"I just can't figure it out," Micah sighed, genuinely puzzled. I closed my eyes so he wouldn't see me rolling them. "He's never been gone this long."

"How long has it been?"

Micah surprised me by being very specific. "Twenty-one days," he said. "Gwyn?" He turned to face me. "Do you believe everything happens for a reason?"

I looked him in the eye and was about to say *no*. No way was I supposed to have a mother like Vienna. There couldn't be a reason for that.

"'Cause I think," Micah said, "that you moved here so we could find him."

"Find Wilbur?" I asked, surprised.

He nodded.

I was so touched by his faith in my super-sleuthing skills that I leaned over and kissed his cheek. He blushed a shade as red as his overalls.

I was up to the challenge, of course I was. But as I looked out into the fields, my eyes caught on Gaysie again. I thought of that first day when she had tried to bury me, how she had a tendency to "fly off the handle," how she *snapped*. No one just disappeared for three weeks. If Wilbur had been gone for twenty-one days without saying goodbye to Jimmy or Micah at least, the most likely explanation was . . .

I gulped. Poor, sweet Micah. How could anyone be prepared for his own mother to be the only plausible murder suspect?

I knocked and pressed my face into the front window of Ms. Myrtle's dark house.

"Get your greasy face off my window!" her voice screeched. I fell backward and landed hard on a green prickle bush.

I glanced down the road, contemplating a runaway. Surely my father did not expect me to endure such personal degradation.

"Come in and get off my bush!"

Unhappily, I pushed the door open. I wondered if Gaysie really had buried the goose and what or who else she'd put in the ground. *Gaysie Cutter knows how to bury the dead*, Ms. Myrtle had said.

Ms. Myrtle sat in the same chair as before, holding a cat that looked suspiciously like Mr. Thompson's recently reported missing feline.

Despite my misery, my father would have been pleased at the brief pang of empathy I experienced. The old woman was clearly sick, her face a gray, unhealthy pallor, and she shook with each breath of air. Maybe I would hold off on reporting her for cat burglary.

After I washed out her mailbox she made me wash my hands at the kitchen sink. I obeyed, looking down the dully lit hallway. Dull, dull, dull. The whole place was devoid of excitement; no wonder she looked out the window. It pleased me, for the first time, to think that she spied on me for entertainment.

I sat on the piano bench, facing a small spinet that looked out a large side window with a view of the Cutters' backyard. This and the wide front window gave Ms. Myrtle a remarkable panoramic view of Lanark Lane. I imagined her sitting for years watching Micah and Jimmy grow up, seeing Bitty and me walk by with Willowdale. Had her own boy walked down this street with his friends? Did he ever come home to visit her now? Did she miss him? Is that why she was so ornery? Or had her orneriness driven her boy away? I avoided looking too hard at the front yard, where the goose incident had gone so wrong.

"You're old to begin piano. . . ." Her mouth gaped open like an oxygen-deprived fish trying to remember my name.

"I'd be happy to leave," I said sweetly. "My father is making me come so I can play Paganini Étude and improve my motor cortex and cerebellum."

"Paganini Étude?"

"It's really so I can play with Vienna."

"Vienna," Ms. Myrtle whispered. Her whole face softened like microwaved butter. "Dearest Vienna."

She resumed petting the cat.

"I love cats," I said, holding my knees, "even though I'm allergic."

"Don't touch him," she said. "You might decide to kill him, too."

"That cat looks just like Mr. Thompson's," I answered back.

Hunched over and frail-looking, she walked toward me, struggling to clasp the poor meowing cat with her gnarled hands. She sat shakily down on the bench, close to me, smelling like mildewed carpet.

"Vienna began playing with this book. She was my favorite student," Ms. Myrtle said.

My fingers touched the pages as I imagined Vienna Eyre as a little girl, opening the book and playing "A Playful Pony."

"Why?" I asked. "Why was she your favorite?"

"She was very talented and learned things quickly," Ms. Myrtle said. "She was a sweet and smart little thing and kind to my boy. She would come visit with her cat, bring little presents, and talk and talk."

I suppressed a smile. I was always being told I talked and talked.

The cat jumped out of Ms. Myrtle's lap with a yowl. Large tufts of cat hair floated toward me. I sneezed, but tried not to touch my eyes.

"Gus?" I asked.

Ms. Myrtle smiled for the first time. "Gus," she said. "Yes, my boy loved Gus."

"Does he still like cats? He should go visit Vienna. My dad would sure like that. The more she can remember, the better."

Ms. Myrtle stared at me, her smile fading.

"Play."

Silenced, I began to play random notes on the terribly out-of-tune piano. She seemed to have forgotten that she hadn't actually taught me anything yet.

"Ah," she said. At first I thought she must be appreciating my natural musical ability, but she was gazing out the window that overlooked the Cutters'. I followed her eyes out toward the cornfield. Kneeling by the Blue Mistress was Gaysie. She looked like she was praying, wearing her ratty old men's shirt, a faded pair of jeans, and a bandanna tied around her head.

"Did you know Wilbur is gone?" I asked. "He was here one day, and the next . . ."

Ever so slowly, Ms. Myrtle's head began to shake back and forth.

"Wilbur doesn't leave Gaysie," she said. "I'm old and sick, but I've been sitting here for years. Watching. I've seen it all. People say Wilbur wanders off, but he never has for this long."

"Seen it all?" I pounced. My eyes caught Micah and Jimmy coming down the street, back from bringing Bitty home. Jimmy was trying a new skate trick and holding on to the tail of his board.

"Death attracts certain people, hovers like a rain cloud," Ms. Myrtle said. "I've seen a lot, living next door to that woman. I could tell you many stories. And you like stories, don't you? I've heard you tell lots of stories with your loud voice."

Gaysie was stomping around her backyard, her face hard to see but looking contorted with tears and frustration.

"She knows where the man is," Ms. Myrtle said ominously.

"You mean Wilbur?"

"Child," she said, "don't be a dope."

"I am most certainly not a dope."

"I saw you in the grave that first day," Ms. Myrtle said.

"My father says that she probably wasn't trying to bury me," I offered, shocking myself even as I said it. "It was the dog's funeral."

"The whole yard is a cemetery," Ms. Myrtle said. "I wouldn't doubt if George Cutter, her deceased husband, ended up out there." She looked at me and narrowed her eyes. "Did you know it's against the law to bury what she's buried?" Ms. Myrtle shuddered. "Gaysie knows it too. She's been fined, even threatened with jail time! Yet she keeps on doing whatever she pleases. And what about me? Imagine having to live on a burial plot."

"We should tell Officer Jake," I said excitedly.

Ms. Myrtle breathed uneasily in and out, her eyes boring holes in me. Why didn't she tell if she knew so much? Was she afraid of Gaysie too? Is that why she was telling *me*? Was this the final call to battle?

My brain catalogued the multiplying charges against Gaysie just as I heard the sound of the dump truck braking, far down the road. It triggered a most serendipitous thought—today was dump day! Rule 20 from *The Law: A to Z: T: Trash as Evidence. Oh, Guinevere*, I scolded. I should have found a way to confiscate Gaysie Cutter's trash immediately after I suspected her of a crime.

But maybe it wasn't too late! Maybe she had held on to evidence!

I listened as the dump truck came closer and closer, stopping at each house down the road with the sound of its heavy brakes, followed by trash being emptied, the truck crushing its weight. I hurriedly plunked out a few notes for Ms. Myrtle's benefit. By the look on her face, I was certainly not my talented mother's daughter. Little did she know I was also performing a complex sting operation in my head.

After an incongruous rendition of "My Playful Pony," she finally made her way to her chair and sat down, gasping for air. Her eyes closed, and her head rolled back and forth several times. Seizing the opportunity, I grabbed the music, shoved it in my backpack, and bolted. As I opened the front door, the cat scrammed past me, danced across the yard, and leaped atop one of the trash can lids. I followed. Just as I reached the trash cans, I heard my archenemy's voice—Gaysie! Panicking, I made my own flying leap behind the barrels. The cat meowed loudly at me.

"Here, kitty, kitty!" I whispered.

Gaysie grew louder and louder, swearing like Vienna on a bad day. I peeked out, saw Gaysie stomping toward me. The cat's tail curled around my nose, and I stifled a sneeze in my shirt as Gaysie stopped to kick the side of the house, tear past-prime lilies out of the ground, and throw them aside. In her left hand she held a glass coffeepot. I knew that pot. It was the one I'd seen Wilbur pour numerous cups from.

I stopped breathing as Gaysie continued to walk toward my hiding spot. *Oh please, oh please, oh please make her stop.* She did, five feet away from the trash. The cat meowed.

"Scram!" Gaysie roared. The cat jumped over my head and ran across the street. Oh, how I wished to be a flea on him.

My only hope was speed. I knew I could outrun Gaysie any day of the week. I readied myself in a sprinter position, not even daring to peek, all the while despising my fear. I knew if Ms. Myrtle had awoken she was watching, but she would do nothing to protect me. The rumble of garbage trucks echoed down the street, an easy place for Gaysie to throw my body.

Something hard hit the garbage in a splintering crash. Glass shattered and showered down behind my head. The black coffeepot handle ricocheted off the ground and hit my hand, making a small cut.

"Take it!" Gaysie screamed. "Take it . . . just take it—you've taken everything else!" At first I thought she was talking to me, but when her voice faltered, I quickly peeked out to see her fist to the sky. She went into the house, banging the side door behind her. I crouched like the cat, shook small shards of glass out of my hair, and peered over the garbage cans. *Hurry!*

I reached down quickly, feeling the bags. Paper crunched, my hand felt something warm and squishy, and my nose wrinkled at the smell of decaying food. I glanced at Ms. Myrtle's house, hardly believing I was practically in cahoots with the old bat.

I grabbed the top of the plastic bag. The metal can tipped over as I pulled it out, making a loud clanging noise. I ran, the heavy white plastic hitting the back of my legs with each kickback of my foot. The farther and faster I ran, the heavier the bag became, but when I lowered it slightly, the plastic caught on the road. I continued to run, half carrying, half dragging the spilling garbage to Nana's barn. Willowdale looked at me with interest as I approached, a long trail of trash behind me. Dropping the trash bag, I ran back to pick up a soup can, a shaver, a piece of soap, a newspaper, wrappers, and an old toothbrush. I left the hairballs, and kicked the coffee grounds to scatter just as the dump truck stopped and snorted down the road. It was making its way to Nana's.

Behind the barn, I heaved at the wet, rotten stench of garbage on my clothes, hands, and legs. Tearing open the bag I discovered last night's lasagna dinner oozing like slime. There was oatmeal and school papers and hair clippings. I examined them. Micah must have had a haircut from Jimmy again, and Jimmy was going to fail English with those quiz grades. There was a milk jug smeared with peanut butter and jelly. But there was nothing close to remarkable. No bloody knife, no secret diary, no smoking gun—nothing!

However, as I was putting things back in, I did notice something at the very bottom. There were two unopened gourmet coffee packages. I knew how much Wilbur loved his afternoon coffee with Gaysie. Why was she throwing it away?

Once again I heard the sound of the dump truck braking.

Shoving the trash back into the ripped bag, I rolled it up as best I could and darted to the curb. The blue-and-white dump truck stopped.

"Nick of time, huh?" Mike, the trash collector, said. I

nodded, plugging my nose, darted back behind the barn again, and collapsed. I leaned my head against the outer wall, breathing in and out, relieved to have the trash away from me. I regretted listening to the witch Myrtle. In addition, I smelled like a skunk.

Still, a nagging tickled my brain. It was the coffee. Why would Gaysie throw away gourmet coffee and the coffeepot unless she knew for certain Wilbur wouldn't be coming back to drink it?

I sat by the barn for a long time. Clouds moved overhead, the sun began to dip. I touched my backpack that held Vienna's old music, then rose, brushed off my clothes, and walked into the house. I hung my backpack up and left my shoes by the side door.

"I'm home," I called to Nana and Bitty before walking directly to the bathroom.

I stripped off my clothes and got into a scalding shower. I washed my hair, scrubbed my hands with soap, washing between my fingers and under my short, bitten fingernails. I scrubbed all the way up my arms until they were lobster red. I dried thoroughly, using a pretty rose towel Nana had embroidered.

When I entered the kitchen, Bitty was coloring at the kitchen table while Nana stood at the counter, chopping up squash for dinner.

"Guinevere, did you just take a shower?" Nana asked, surprised.

"I've taken a shower before."

"Not voluntarily. How was your first piano lesson?"

"She gave me Vienna's music."

"Vienna's!" Nana exclaimed. "Oh, show me. Show Vienna when she comes for dinner." She smiled and began to hum.

"Vienna's coming to dinner?"

Nana smiled. "Your father thinks she's making progress."

That was news to me.

Nana paused and sniffed the air. "What's that smell? Smells like . . . garbage!" She sniffed again.

"*P U!*" Bitty exclaimed.

I said nothing.

"Are you all right, Gwyn?" Nana asked, stealing a look at me.

"Ms. Myrtle got a cat." I rubbed my nose and sneezed.

CHAPTER 14

ON FRIDAY MY FATHER MADE plans to take Vienna to the movies in a neighboring town. They were going with their oldest friends as a way to "help Vienna." He hypothesized that the more Vienna became familiar with the people from her past, the more connections her mind might make with the present. I was skeptical of my father's enthusiasm, secretly hypothesizing to Bitty he just wanted to go to the movies and eat Milk Duds without us.

Vienna sat on the couch next to me, her eyes shiny with excitement as she hugged her Love-a-Lot Care Bear.

"I'm going to the movies," she said to me. "With a boy!"

"I know."

I waited. Ten seconds passed. She looked at me, confused. "What's happening?"

"You're going to the movies," I said. "With a boy!"

"I am?" She clapped her hands. "I love the movies!"

When Officer Jake walked through the door, she shrieked and clapped her hands again—until she saw his very pregnant wife, Suzy. Vienna screamed and pointed at her stomach.

"Suzy? What happened?!"

Officer Jake and Suzy froze for one mortifying moment. I helped them out by doubling over with laughter, falling off the couch, and slapping my knee.

"Oh, Vienna!" I said. "Suzy is old now—no offense—and she's married to Officer Jake. They're having a baby."

"Officer Jake," she echoed, confused.

I turned to him and Suzy. "You're going to have to say that a million more times tonight. She doesn't remember anything after she was thirteen, so the baby will confuse her. . . ." Suzy stared at me.

"This is Jake and Suzy," my father began. "Remember . . ."

"I know!" Vienna said. "We go to school with them, duh."

He smiled. "Honey, Suzy and Jake have three kids and are about to have another one!"

"Shut-*up*!" She couldn't stop staring at Suzy's stomach.

Suzy stepped forward, red-faced, and said, "Vienna. It's . . . so good to see you." *Liar.*

"Are we going to a movie?" Vienna asked. "I love movies, it's like my favorite thing *ever*. Suze, can I borrow some lip gloss? I get to choose the treat. Oh my gosh, I'm so excited!" My father helped her out the door as Officer Jake and Suzy stood in the doorway a moment longer.

"I don't think I can do this," Suzy whispered.

"You'll get used to it," I butted in. "She just remembers you from before, not now. If you spend enough time with her, she'll start recognizing you." Of course, from personal experience, this could take a very long time. Vienna now knew my face and name, but never connected me to before.

Suzy put her hand to her chest as if I was the most pathetic thing she'd ever come across.

"Have fun!" I called. Officer Jake nodded, but before closing the door, I slid a note into his jacket pocket.

"What's this?"

"Information I have come across," I whispered. "You can put me in jail and torture me all you want. I'll never reveal my source." I'd gotten that straight out of *Morgana Cross, A Sherlock Holmes Protégé.*

"Okay, then," he said with a wink. "You all have a lovely evening."

Nana sighed when they left. "Poor Jake and Suzy."

"Yep," I muttered, slamming the front door shut. "The psych ward takes some getting used to."

"Guinevere."

"Yes?"

"Go play. Be home in half an hour."

We found Jimmy and Micah sitting out on the porch. "What are you guys doing?" I asked. Micah, who was wearing his glorious purple cape, pointed to the living room. Squinting, I saw Gaysie behind the front window. Rocking in the dark.

"What's going on?" Bitty whispered.

"There's a search party going out for Wilbur tomorrow," Micah said. "I think it made her sad."

"A search party," I breathed. My eyes narrowed at the shadow of a rocking Gaysie. "This is perfect," I said. "'Cause, guess what I brought?" Jimmy eyed the law book that I pulled from my backpack. "So, who's in charge of the investigation?"

"Lytle," Jimmy said.

"We've got to be in on that search party."

"Can't," Micah said, sitting down on the front porch, his long, dark purple robe splayed out dramatically.

"Can't," I said, "is a four-letter-word."

"Yeah, Micah," Jimmy said, throwing the rubber band ball at him. Micah swatted at it.

"At least try and catch it!" Jimmy said, exasperated.

"She already said we can't go," Micah said. "Adults only. Besides, what if we found . . . something we didn't want to find?"

"Like a dead body?" I asked, excitedly chewing my nails. Micah frowned.

"A dead body?" Bitty squeaked.

Micah's face turned pale at the thought. Even Jimmy looked rattled.

From inside the house Gaysie released a long, mournful noise.

"Come on, Gwyn, let's go," Bitty whispered.

"You guys want to come?" I asked.

As we began to ride, Micah's long purple cape flew behind him in the breeze.

"Did you finish your story?" Bitty asked Micah.

"Well," Micah began. "I'm sorry to tell you, but Queen Guinevere is going to be beheaded."

"Beheaded!" I yelled. "What for?"

"For betraying Arthur Pendragon."

"Micah! I would never . . ." But suddenly the note came to mind, the one I had handed to Officer Jake.

"Guinevere *did* betray King Arthur in real life," Micah said.

"But, Micah, you're the author," I said. "You get to rewrite it!"

Micah focused on the road. As the least athletic child I had ever known, he had at least finally learned to ride a bike.

I pondered my renewed beheading. Did Micah suspect I was a traitor? I felt a stab of regret at my disloyal actions: my secret thoughts, stealing the trash, the note in Officer Jake's pocket outlining all Gaysie Cutter's suspicious behavior. Perhaps I *was* a traitor. Just like Queen Guinevere. But wasn't it for all the right reasons? Wouldn't I be vindicated in the end?

Up ahead I saw something that made me forget my betrayal. The Creepers and their little Creepers-in-Training. They grudgingly nodded at Jimmy, who skated ahead of us. Their bikes were low, their knees hiked up to their chests as they rode in slow, lazy circles. I recognized the bucktoothed Travis Maynard from school. We hadn't had a run-in with them since the first day, but now I regretted never checking out that wrestling book.

"Go, Bitty baby," I whispered. "Go fast." Bitty bent her head and pedaled straight ahead. They let her by, grazing her up and down with their eyes, laughing at her concentrated gaze. My face felt hot with anger, but I kept going, head up and pedaling after her. Travis Maynard's black, greasy hair hung in his face as he watched me ride.

I heard Travis say in a high voice, "Hi, I'm Micah. I'm a girl."

"Nice cape," Eddie the Creeper said and smirked. I slowed and glanced behind me.

The Creepers had put their bike wheels together, blocking Micah's path. He looked so small, his pale face anxious. I turned my bike around, fear stalling me. There were too many of them. They talked loudly and laughed. One of them tossed a rock at Micah's tires, and a piece broke off, hitting his face. He blinked quickly, trying to look brave as he attempted to ride around. Gaysie's face suddenly came to mind, proud and stubborn. I shook her right out of me. Gaysie Cutter was most certainly *not* an inspiration.

I took a deep breath and booked it back to Micah anyway.

"Look who it is," a big kid with yellow hair said. "The girlfriend."

"Nah," another said. "She's too ugly to be a girlfriend." I unwillingly saw my wild, unkempt hair and felt utterly wounded.

"Hey, babe." Slurping loudly, Travis Maynard took a drink of Sunkist soda, belched, and blew it in my face.

"Hey, yourself, stink breath!"

"Her mom's the nutjob," the yellow-headed Creeper said, slinging an arm over my shoulder. The air went out of me.

Travis laughed before abruptly yelling a holy wet terror. I turned to see Micah, his face white but focused, pouring the Sunkist soda over Travis's head.

"What the . . . ," Travis yelled, orange soda dripping

down from his hair and onto his face and clothes.

Micah, realizing what he had done, abandoned the bike and began to run, the empty soda can clattering in the road.

A look of pure rage overtook the Creepers' faces, and they set off.

"Run, Micah!" I screamed. His purple cape splayed out behind him, the wind carrying it upward, revealing skinny legs and those silver, curly shoelaces sparkling in the last bit of daylight. *Please . . . please, let that boy fly.* A miracle, my father said, was a divine, extraordinary, and unexplainable event. As I clenched my handlebars, I suddenly understood that desperation, to believe in something that seemed absolutely impossible.

Micah wasn't going to fly without some help.

I found my legs and began to pedal. I could see the Creepers gaining on him. Travis reached out to yank Micah's cape. He pulled hard, and Micah tumbled backward onto the road.

"No!" I yelled.

And then our miracle came. Jimmy. He was riding fast on his skull-marked skateboard. He deftly brushed strands of hair off his forehead, the look on his face juxtaposed between intensity and ease. Pure confidence. He leaned back into the ride, coasting freely before pushing off again, like he'd been born with a skateboard glued to his feet. He jumped into their path, doing a trick.

And this was what gave Micah his escape. He crawled forward, lifted himself off the pavement, and began to run again. I heard Eddie ask, "Why you with them, Jimmy?"

followed by Travis's horrible laugh. Distracting them, Jimmy did a flip trick.

I rode fast while Micah ran to the safety of Nana's porch, not looking to see what Jimmy did next. We huddled, me patting Micah's back, thanking him for defending my honor with a Sunkist soda. All the while I could hear Travis saying, "I'm gonna kill that kid."

It seemed to take forever as we waited for Jimmy to appear again. Finally, he came, coasting down the road alone. He sighed when he saw us, Micah sniffling as we sat on Nana's front porch.

Instead of being grateful for my assistance, Jimmy lit into me.

"You know what's worse than Micah not being able to defend himself?"

"What?"

"*You* trying to defend him."

"Jimmy—"

"You're a *girl*."

"So?" I asked, rising.

"So it just makes everything worse for him!"

I pushed him off the steps just as Nana came out of the house.

"Guinevere St. Clair," she scolded. "Shame on you! You let Bitty come home alone, and now you're fighting like a wild tomcat. It's rude and impolite!"

"Bitty wasn't alone," I began. "Jimmy brought her home."

"And this is the way you thank your friend? Thank you,

Jimmy," she said stiffly before turning back to me. "Gwyn, say good-bye and come in the house!"

"Come on, Micah," Jimmy said.

Micah offered a wave and walked down the street after Jimmy. I watched after them, feelings raw as I looked down the darkened street, seeing the faint swoosh of a purple cape and hearing the rolling sound of a skateboard on a gravel road.

Later, I lay awake listening for my father to come home from the double date.

When he did, he handed me the note I'd put in Jake Lytle's pocket. The white paper glowed in the moonlight.

I scowled, insulted at the lack of discretion and seriousness with which my evidence had been handled.

"I didn't read it," he said. "But Jake said it's about Gaysie."

I crumpled it up and stuck it under my pillow. Officer Jake was as traitorous as Queen Guinevere.

"Gaysie is a good person," he said. "She's . . . had a really hard life, and I'd like you to show the same compassion to her as you've shown to your mother."

I covered my face with my pillow to hide my shame. Who was this girl he spoke of? Compassion toward my mother had always been in short supply.

He gently lifted the pillow off my face. I sat up straight and folded my arms.

"Daddy, she knows something about Wilbur. I know she does."

He looked at me awhile.

"I think we need . . . to hope for the best outcome," my father said slowly. "Who knows, maybe he'll come walking home tomorrow and we'll laugh that our worry was for nothing." But even as he said it, I heard the doubt creep into his voice again.

Suddenly exhausted, I scooted down into bed.

"Daddy, remember I told you about the Creepers? They were so mean to Micah tonight when we were coming home. And Jimmy says I only make things worse by trying to help Micah, because I'm a girl. It's not fair."

"Ah," he said. "But you already know that."

I frowned. "Poor Micah."

"Why *poor Micah*?"

"His father is dead, Wilbur hasn't come back, his mother is guilty, and those Creepers are really out to get him now—and I think it's mostly because he likes sparkly shoelaces! His life pretty much stinks."

"If you put it that way—but guess what? Life changes. It gets better. Nothing is permanent. And, Gwyn, no matter what Jimmy or anyone else says, you keep looking out for him. That quality is what I love most about you. Everyone is looking for a hero, someone to believe in. You can bet that even Travis Maynard is looking for one too."

I looked into his deep, dark eyes.

"Now," he said, tucking the covers under my chin, "go to sleep, my brave Guinevere."

"Daddy? Can I say . . . ?"

"What?"

"Sometimes, even when I try real hard, I can't remember what Mama's face was like. I remember things we did, but—I can't remember *her*." Something in my father's body shifted. There was a hardening in his grip, and he was quiet for so long I almost drifted off to sleep.

But on the edge of my dreams I thought I heard him say, "Don't be too hard on those boys. On Gaysie. On yourself. Not everyone gets the life they want."

CHAPTER 15

MY FATHER WAS OBSESSED WITH the creatures upstairs, the creatures being the hundreds of neurons in our brains. He said they were busiest at night and even when we slept, the creatures upstairs kept right on problem solving. Often, when my father went to bed puzzled, the answer would be right there in the morning, like an unwrapped present. The brain was so alive to him that he spoke about it as if it were a real person.

I was sitting at the kitchen table on Saturday morning when the creatures delivered the goods.

"Ah!" I shrieked, standing up quickly, clattering the breakfast dishes. Startled, Nana turned.

"I just remembered I had a dream about Gaysie!"

"Your imagination is something I'm starting to worry about." She said, "I keep telling your father you're spending too much time down the street."

I clanged my fork down on the table, and Nana jumped again.

"The search party is today!" I said. "That's why I dreamed about her!"

"For heaven's sake, Gwyn!" Nana said, holding her heart like any great actress would. "You're so dramatic!

And you're not going, so don't even think about it."

"Oh yes, I am!"

"Oh no, you're not!"

"You're going, right, Daddy?"

"I am indeed going, after I see Vienna."

"See? We're going."

"I said *I'm* going."

"You're not going anywhere near that search party," Nana said. "Of course, it's up to your father. . . ." Nana looked at him expectantly.

"Gwyn will not be at the search party," my father said.

"I made Vienna a picture," Bitty said.

"*Your mother* a picture," Nana corrected. "Bitty, you stay with me this morning. Your sister can bring it for you. Jed, please take Gwyn with you. She needs to burn off some energy."

I skipped along the road, happy to have my father all to myself for a few minutes. The air had turned sharper, the leaves bright with color. It was almost easy to forget that in a few hours we'd be finding Wilbur. Despite my suspicions, I truly didn't want to think about Wilbur as anything but alive, so I skipped over the dead-or-alive detail part. This was a case of a lifetime! Maybe they would even let me prosecute Gaysie!

I breathed in the cold air, coughed as it hit my lungs, and skipped more quickly to keep up with my father. He was a very brisk and purposeful walker. The walks to and from home were the only personal time he ever had. He did not play golf or sports like other dads. He didn't jog or have any hobbies besides painting, occasionally, and even that was always for Vienna. He had his children, a disabled wife, work, and a large collection of brain research that was always a mile high and never finished.

"So," I said, "do you think they'll find him?"

He looked sideways at me, and I tried to temper my excitement. "You're still not going."

"Daddy!"

"He'll come home. I'm sure it's just a misunderstanding. He could be shopping for tractor parts, for all we know."

"Daddy," I said. "It's been *weeks*."

He looked at me and blinked. "No. Really?"

"Yes! Ask Gaysie. The last time I saw him he was at *her* house."

"Meaning?"

"Isn't it obvious!" I said, trying not to raise my voice. "She *SNAPS*. Just the other day—and I didn't tell you this because I'm still gathering evidence—she threw a coffee-pot so hard at me, I was nearly decapitated!"

He looked at me. "*At* you?"

"Well, at the garbage can, but I was right behind it."

"Is this the evidence you gave to Jake? Circumstantial? Speculative? That she has a bad temper?"

I mulled that over. Circumstantial. Speculative. What I needed was a direct link.

And I was going to get one.

We walked past my father's office, admired his newly hung dental sign, but didn't stop until we were in front of the care center. Instead of going in right away, my father sat on a bench next to a yellow-flowered bush, just past its prime. This was fine by me. I was never in a rush to see Vienna.

"Gaysie planted this bush and did all the landscaping." He nudged me. "You know, Gaysie does many nice things you don't even know about."

"You never told me you were friends," I said darkly. "She did! She even told me about the sledding accident."

He looked at me, surprised.

"And you're offended by it?"

"You never told me."

"I apologize. It happened a long time ago. And it's a painful subject."

"How could you ever be friends—I'm surprised she didn't try to drown you!" My tone came out as an accusation.

"Gwyn," he admonished quietly. "That is a terrible thing to say."

I looked at my shoes.

"The fact is, Gaysie Cutter saved my life and your mother's life that day."

"What!"

I frowned at this new and heroic portrayal of Gaysie. It was an incongruous twist to my investigation. "How could you even be friends with her?" I burst out. I meant now, but my father looked backward.

"When you're kids, you don't care so much about what people think or wear or look like—adults condition you to that. Gaysie was funny and whip-smart and had a wicked imagination. She made up the best games. But afterward, Gaysie was in the hospital for a long time. During that time there was a . . . shift in the way the town saw the whole event."

"What do you mean?"

He shook his head. "Don't we all try to find someone to blame? A reason for everything? And, Guinevere, I'm not sure there always is a reason. For a man like me who has spent his whole life relying on facts and concrete answers, that's a hard truth to reconcile."

I was about to protest when he kept going.

"Myron." He swallowed, like it was hard to say the name. "He was a well-liked child. Gaysie . . . was just different, and it was her sled. No matter what we said, people went for the easiest scapegoat. After the accident it was just never the same for her."

"Because Myron died?"

My father's eyes looked sad. "Yes. We grew up that day."

He sighed. "This Wilbur business. It's no good for Gaysie."

"Why?"

"Wilbur's the closest thing she has to a friend since Vienna and I left." He took a sideways glance at me. "Missing for weeks, you said?"

I nodded. "That's why you should let me come to the search party—we're bound to find something!"

My father closed his eyes. "I pray that's not how we find him."

I raised my eyebrows.

"Think about this," he said, looking at me. "Who has the most to lose by Wilbur being gone?"

"Gaysie," I conceded.

"So why would she be involved in his disappearance?" He fingered the yellow bush again. "It's a shame there was a frost last night."

I felt an abrupt chill, thinking of old Wilbur, badly hurt or lost somewhere, shivering through a cold, dark frost. My father kept referring to the sledding incident as an "accident." But I wondered. A dead friend. A missing friend. A coincidence . . . or a pattern?

There were so many things I wanted to say and ask about Gaysie Cutter, but I silenced myself when my father leaned back on the bench and closed his eyes again, the sun bright and shining on his face.

His cell phone rang.

"One minute, Vienna, I'll be right there," he murmured before turning it off. I pretended there was a tied knot on my lips that wouldn't open unless carefully untied. I sat as quiet as a caterpillar. I did not understand Gaysie Cutter, but I did know my father. He needed this minute.

CHAPTER 16

T HIS IS BORING," JIMMY SAID, legs hanging out of Micah's second-floor bedroom window while dangling a yo-yo. "If Wilbur was out there all this time we would have found him five times by now."

"The entire town is here," I said, holding up my binoculars.

Ms. Myrtle, of course, was spying from her own window, while Mr. Thompson was loudly asking about his missing cat.

I saw Penny's father and older brothers, a pack of police officers, including Officer Jake. Pastor Weare and his sweet-as-pie wife, Luanne, were herding people into groups. There was Petey, the diner owner; our gym teacher, Mr. Zabriski; and Mrs. Law, wearing blue jeans and a baseball cap. I spied the Creepers hanging out on the perimeter on their bikes. From the way they were ducked down, I could tell they weren't supposed to be there either.

Technically, Nana could not be mad at me, since I was not actually *at* the search party. I was just playing at Micah's, merely a passive observer who happened to be perched in a second-story window at the same time as the search party. It was an excellent loophole.

I held my law book and binoculars while dictating notes

to Micah, who typed out my brilliant observations on his typewriter. Jimmy was supposedly handling surveillance. Attached to the house was a zip line that could carry Jimmy a hundred feet across the yard if needed. I looked down and felt faint.

"Hey," Jimmy suddenly said. "Where's Gaysie's coffin?"

Bitty and I looked. Sure enough, the commissioned coffin was gone. What was left was a worn patch of dead grass.

Micah shrugged.

"Seriously, Micah?" I said. "A missing man and a missing coffin? A coincidence? I think not!"

"It's not a big deal," Jimmy said. "The only reason she had it made was because she had wood from an old closet she didn't want to go to waste."

"And yet," I said testily, "it's *gone*."

Jimmy climbed out the window to get a better look, but his foot slipped. Bitty and I made a grab for him.

"If you fall out, it'll ruin the search party," I yelled. "At least wait until it's over to kill yourself!"

Jimmy, happy to make me so angry, laughed and climbed back onto the windowsill.

Micah came to join us at the window. Instead of looking down, he looked out into the fields. Most of them were finished for the season, but without Wilbur, Gaysie's hay hadn't been cut or baled. A small patch of depressed-looking corn stood abandoned too.

"There's Daddy!" Bitty said.

"Quick!" I said, pulling her down. After a few minutes we peeked back out and saw Gaysie appear, her large backside facing us. I looked through the binoculars.

"Holy heck," I said, my eyes opening wide. "She's holding a shotgun!" Micah groaned and typed. I could feel excitement fizzing inside me like Pop Rocks. The gun was pointed down, the length of it parallel to her body. I watched as Officer Jake walked over to Gaysie, his face serious. As they spoke, Gaysie nodded, then shook her head in short, vigorous jerks.

"Absolutely not!" Her voice rose above the crowd.

Micah lay down on the typewriter keys and covered his head.

The crowd went quiet. Officer Jake put his hands on his hips and turned to address them.

"Thank you all for coming. As you know, this is an informal search party for Wilbur Truesdale, who hasn't been seen for a few weeks now."

"Officer Jake was here last night," Micah whispered.

"And you're just telling me this? Micah! What did Officer Jake say? Did he accuse her of a crime? Did he read you your Miranda rights?"

"I'm not guilty, I swear," Micah said.

"And that's all?"

"I was trying not to listen," Micah sniffed.

"Micah!"

"Spread out in a line and go slow," Officer Jake yelled.

"It's starting!" Bitty said excitedly.

Micah began typing.

"This isn't a foot race," Officer Jake yelled. "We'll start in the back of Ms. Myrtle's house, but under no circumstances are you to search Gaysie Cutter's property."

My reaction was the same as the crowd's.

"Why in the world not?" I exclaimed.

Jimmy crowed, bouncing up and down.

My eyes flicked to the tacky fluorescent NO TRESPASSING signs stapled on her house and fences. I had long thought she was either paranoid or guilty. Maybe it was both.

Micah said nothing, miserably plunking down keys. An unhappy ripple moved through the crowd as Dr. Long called out.

"We should be searching everywhere." He tipped his head at Gaysie. I liked Dr. Long. He was always polite and kind to Vienna when he visited, even when she acted out. "With all due respect, Ms. Gaysie," Dr. Long said, "we should leave no stone unturned. We all love Wilbur!" He spread his arms wide. "We just want to find him, the same as you."

She began to speak, her voice hard and superior.

"No one shall set one foot on my property. With all due respect," she added, nodding at Dr. Long. "I've searched under every rock on my property and everywhere in between. This is my cornfield, my life's work. You'll not ruin it by having the whole town of Crow tromping through it." The announcement smacked the crowd with dissatisfaction, but Gaysie's voice rose above the rest again.

"I will say it again: YOU WILL NOT SEARCH MY HOME!" she yelled. "YOU WILL NOT SEARCH MY YARD OR ANY OF MY FIELDS unless you have a warrant, which you do not have."

A tall, weathered, and tough-looking man folded his arms and stepped forward, a black eye patch over one eye.

"A pirate," I whispered.

"All adults are pirates," Jimmy whispered back, his face hardening.

"What you got to hide, Gaysie? I'm givin' up my whole work morning, and we can't search the place Wilbur's always at? You gonna stand for this, Lytle?" The man's voice was low, hard, and gravelly, like a truck moving slowly across granite rock.

Officer Jake Lytle looked between the two of them.

"No search warrant," I whispered to Micah, who was typing at a furious pace. "Rookie mistake." I shook my head pitifully.

"Officer Jake said he'd get one if he had to," Micah said tearfully.

"Again!" I said. "Information you're not sharing with me!"

"Guys," Jimmy said, shushing us with his hand.

"We need your *permission*?" The pirate spit on the ground. Jimmy sat transfixed in the window, his hand on the zip line.

"I already told you, Hank," Gaysie said, her voice loud. "I've been over my own property. Every single inch of it."

"Then what do you care if we double-check?" the pirate exploded. "Who do you think you are? Don't like it? Go ahead! Go ahead and shoot me!" I looked across the crowd. It was obvious that Gaysie was alone. I felt a small pang despite myself, thinking of what my father had said earlier. The pirate took a step forward. Gaysie raised the gun. The crowd gasped. I covered my mouth, saw the white flash of her bandaged hand.

"Don't you dare try to bully me, Hank Quintel." Gaysie's voice rose.

"Quintel!" I whispered. "Is that . . . ?"

"Jimmy's dad," Micah said, furiously typing.

"The plot thickens," I whispered.

"She hates him so much, she wouldn't spit on him if he were on fire," Jimmy said, unable to tear his eyes away from the scene. Oh, he sure was stoic standing in that window-sill, as still and strong jawed as I'd ever seen him. But I also noticed a small, nearly imperceptible tightening of his fist.

"Jimmy," I breathed. "You have a *dad*?" I had a million theories about why Jimmy mostly lived with Gaysie, but he rarely spoke about home and never included information about parents.

"Everyone has a dad."

"But—"

"Shh!"

"You gonna shoot me?" the man yelled, raising his hands in the air.

"She's gonna shoot him!" I whispered loudly.

Micah typed faster.

"Save him!" Bitty exclaimed.

"Ah heck," Jimmy said. He put both hands on the zip line and pushed off with both feet. He sailed across the backyard, over the heads of a hundred people, and landed beautifully at Officer Jake's feet. It was a most spectacular distraction. "Stop it, Dad."

"Boy!" the pirate barked. Jimmy trudged over and stood before him. The pirate slapped Jimmy's face hard. Bitty and I flinched and grabbed each other.

"You putrid piece of scum," Gaysie said, her voice venomous. The SNAP, I thought, was coming!

Micah was at my side, shaking his head. "You see, don't you? Why Jimmy . . . ?"

I clutched his arm. I looked from Micah to Jimmy, my heart in my throat. I saw.

My father alone stepped forward and put a hand on Gaysie's shoulder. My mouth dropped open.

"Won't do us any good to provoke a shooting. Come on, Hank. Let's cooperate. Gaysie, please." The pirate stepped back.

Gaysie lowered the gun, chin held high in proud triumph.

"Enough," Officer Lytle said briskly. "There's no evidence of a crime yet. Ms. Cutter is not a suspect, and we'll just have to do the best we can. And, Mr. Quintel, if you strike that child again, there *will* be charges, and they won't be against Ms. Cutter." The pirate bristled but lowered his eyes.

We watched the crowd organize into a line, spread out on either side of Gaysie's fields, and begin to slowly walk, eyes roving from side to side. Jimmy walked back toward the house.

Some of the searchers carried garbage bags and flashlights, even though it was the middle of the day.

"It does make her look guilty," I whispered, glancing

at Micah and flipping through my law book. "I saw this show once, about a search party finding a dead body in the woods. It was rotten! Decomposing. But they identified it with dental records."

"There's a lot of decomposing in this backyard, but not Wilbur." Jimmy was back, standing in the doorway, a red handprint splayed across his face. We were silent as he casually walked back over to the window.

"Jimmy," I whispered.

He shook me off and went back to his window.

"They should have dogs," I said, looking out the window. "Sniff him out."

Suddenly Micah flung himself on his bed, covered his face with his cape, and began to cry.

"Micah! What's the matter?"

Jimmy looked at me. "Wilbur is our friend, so try not to be so happy about finding his dead body, okay?"

I sat by the window, stung, remembering that Micah and Jimmy loved Wilbur like family, and of course they wouldn't want to believe that he was dead, much less killed by Gaysie. It's not that I wanted to either. Not really. I just knew it was true in my gut.

Micah sniffed loudly as he cleaned his glasses with his cape.

"I'm real sorry, Micah."

He nodded and wiped his eyes.

I thought of Gaysie and the blood on her clothes, her finger lying beside the tractor that no one besides Wilbur ever touched. Her history of mysterious "accidents." But when I looked at Jimmy and Micah, their faces did not recognize the same thing I felt. How could I make them see without ruining everything between us?

I turned back toward the window and spied Officer Jake walking toward the house with my father. Straining hard to eavesdrop, I heard my father say, "foul play."

"I don't think that's what happened here, Jed," Officer Jake said. "Most likely . . . hurt, disoriented, something . . ."

"Have you dusted the Blue Mistress for fingerprints?" I yelled, then crouched on the floor below the window.

"She's practicing for a lawyer," Bitty said.

"We *know*," said Jimmy.

"Gwyn?" I heard a voice call up. "Guinevere!"

Oh sugar sticks! I peeked out the window to see my father, standing next to Officer Jake, peering up at us.

"Hi, Daddy!" I called lightly.

"You've got Bitty with you?"

"Of course I do!"

"Go home now," he said. "Go out the front door and go home."

"But . . ."

"Now."

"Yes, Daddy," I said, smarting.

"Hey, Sherlock," Jimmy called as I left the house. "If they're not gonna get the fingerprints, why don't we?"

I stopped and turned around. "Jimmy Quintel, I'm sorry I ever called you stupid!"

I didn't walk home. I skipped.

CHAPTER 17

IT WAS BRILLIANT, I ADMITTED while attempting to unearth an ancient forensics textbook at the library. The text was so old that dust covered the outer pages, and the library card showed that it hadn't been checked out since 1983. Crow was obviously lacking in supersleuths.

Unfortunately, the chapter on collecting fingerprints described the requirements of chemicals and a lab. Using the library computer, we searched the interlibrary database until I found just what we were looking for: *Fingerprinting for Amateurs*. They had a copy a few counties away. I pressed "print."

"Even if you get prints off the Mistress," Jimmy whispered, "what's it's gonna prove?"

"You said Wilbur didn't let anyone touch the Mistress. So if we find two sets of fingerprints, then we'll know something." Gaysie, of course. It would point to Gaysie.

Ms. Priscilla peered at us from around her desk.

"If you touch the Mistress," Jimmy whispered, "Wilbur will haunt you from the grave. . . ."

"He's not dead!" Micah wailed. Jimmy stopped laughing and slung his arm around Micah's shoulders.

"I was just joking, dude."

Ms. Priscilla's expression turned alarmed. "Can I help you kids with anything?"

I shoved Micah behind me and handed the *Finger-printing for Amateurs* book printout to her. "Book request, please."

She gave it a once-over and nodded slowly. "Science experiment?"

"Exactly," I said. "Bitty and I—we just love science!"

"Especially when it's going to deliver a guilty verdict!" Bitty contributed.

I laughed nervously and patted Bitty on her head. "Precocious little thing."

Thankfully, Ms. Priscilla smiled. "Bless your hearts. I love to see girls interested in science. Your father must be very proud."

I smiled angelically.

"I should be able to get this in within a few weeks."

"A few *weeks*?" My angelic expression turned to dismay. "Any chance it could be a rush job? I'm real anxious to get my . . . science experiment started!"

Ms. Priscilla beamed. "I'll do my best, Guinevere."

A few days later the calendar turned its page and brought the glories of fall in earnest: pumpkin patches, hayrides, and Nana's homemade applesauce. The cooler, dry wind seemed to nearly blow the very thought of Wilbur away for everyone but us. Winter on the plains was coming, and the town became busy with farm equipment, snowmobiles, and snowplows. There was still lots of talk in Petey's Diner and

Arnie's Supermarket, but Wilbur didn't turn up. Nothing had come of the search party, and I overheard my father tell Nana that there wasn't probable cause for a search warrant. But while people shot strange, mistrustful glances Gaysie's way, Midwesterners were also a cheery, optimistic bunch. Wilbur would show up, and we'd all have a good laugh. Only Gaysie did not express this sentiment. She gave no indication we would ever see Wilbur Truesdale again. And she did not buy another coffeepot, as if she already knew he wasn't coming home.

We needed to get fingerprints in a New York minute, but every day I checked in with Ms. Priscilla, the how-to book had yet to arrive. In the meantime, I read the dusty forensics book and tried to keep tabs on an investigation that had become as exciting as dry toast. Rumors said Officer Jake had sent out a missing person's notice and was pursuing leads, but really, there were no leads. Wilbur Truesdale had simply vanished.

There were other distractions too. Vienna wasn't progressing as much as my father had hoped. Family dinner hours with Vienna not remembering anything longer than she ever had, led my father to lengthy and brooding silences. Then there was Nana. I had tried my best, but I was simply not the acquiescing child she had hoped for. Compromise of any sort came to a halt when Nana laid out matching flowered dresses for me and Bitty, who shocked me by prancing around the bedroom in her new frills.

"I don't even know who you are anymore!" I hollered at her.

Nana did one of those bless-her-heart gestures. "I bought this one especially for you, Guinevere," Nana said. "It has the pretty blue—your favorite color."

"I would rather die."

Her face crumpled slightly, guilting me into "just trying it on."

I walked into the kitchen to find Nana washing dishes by hand. Nana had an aversion to all modern conveniences. They were downright offensive! She marched up stairways instead of taking the escalator, opened doors instead of using the automatic ones, and lifted the garage door instead of pressing a button. It was actually shocking she wasn't still cooking over a campfire in a pioneer dress.

"Isn't she precious as pie?" Nana said when I stood in front of my father.

"You look very pretty, Guinevere," he said.

"I'm hideous," I said, glowering that he took Nana's side. "And I don't know why we can't get a dishwasher."

"A dishwasher," my father said, folding his paper and raising an eyebrow.

"I bet I'm the only person in the whole world that has to ask for a microwave for Christmas."

"I have a surprise for you," my father said smoothly, ignoring my outburst.

"I can burn the dress?"

"No. Lolly is coming. She'll be here for Halloween."

"With Moose and Tomato?"

"No way around it."

"Is she coming for Vienna or me and Bitty?"

"For all of us!"

"Yippee!" I shouted, skipping down the front stairs with Bitty.

"And don't forget your piano lesson after school," Nana called after me. I stomped to school, resenting how she *purposely* blackened my mood, not realizing until I was halfway there that I was still wearing the hideous flowered dress.

"Not one word," I said.

"Nice dress," Jimmy said, taking off on his skateboard. "You should wear one more often."

"I should?" I looked down at myself, stunned.

"Whatever. Watch this new trick. It's called the Girlfriend Getter." He took off toward his homemade ramp.

He skated fast, his overgrown Mohawk flopping. Flying up, he grabbed the tail of his board, then came falling down to earth. This time though, he didn't land neatly like he always did. Bitty screamed.

"Are you okay?" I asked, squatting down beside him.

"I didn't know you could crash!" Bitty said.

"It doesn't hurt," he said, even though he was wincing. He rolled over, his elbow bleeding through his long-sleeve T-shirt.

"Guess you better work on the Girlfriend Getter."

He grimaced, his eyes narrowing. "I hate girls. Except for Bitty. I don't hate Bitty." Jimmy gave her a smile and pulled his boots up.

I frowned at his preference for Bitty until I noticed his boots. "Jimmy, are those . . . Wilbur's?"

"I don't know. They were by the back door at Gaysie's. I needed 'em."

At the look on my face, Jimmy had the decency to look chagrined.

"I'm comin'!" Micah yelled, coming down the front stairs while shoving his lunch box in his backpack. Today he was wearing a light blue sweater with green bunnies all over it. His jeans were tucked into an old pair of large cowboy boots.

"Are those Wilbur's too?" I asked darkly.

"You like 'em?" Micah asked proudly. "They used to be my dad's." My sarcasm dried up.

"Hurry up," Jimmy said, helping himself to the last bite of Micah's toast.

Gaysie came out, and my heart banged along with the banging of the door behind her. Her hand was obviously getting better, as she carried a full milking pail of white cream with it. Her towering frame shadowed the entire porch.

"Willowdale Princess Deon Dawn will have company next time she decides to trample all my flowers," she said. "We have just acquired our very own milking cows, though none with such a pedigree as yours."

"We need money," Micah said. "We're gonna sell milk and have our own dairy." I eyed Gaysie. Money was often the cause of murder.

I also observed the pail she carried. Fingerprints everywhere. It occurred to me that if I got prints off the Mistress they would need to be matched to another set of Gaysie's, taken from another surface.

My eyes drifted upward to a necklace around Gaysie's

neck I hadn't seen before: a golden cross, large and spar-kling with fake diamonds.

"My mother sent it," Gaysie said, noticing my gaze. "It seems we're both feeling feminine today." She raised her eyebrows at our dresses. "Bitty, you look just like your mother did fifteen years ago."

I sighed loudly, wanting to wiggle out of the stupid dress again.

She continued. "But, Guinevere"—she smiled—"you act more like her."

I stomped all the way to school.

In gym class Micah and Jimmy had a fight. It was because of that Creeper, Travis Maynard. We had avoided him like he was contagious since the night he followed us home. But today he grabbed the kickball and appointed himself cap-tain. Our oblivious gym teacher, Mr. Zabriski, nodded his head like this was a good idea.

While waiting to get picked last for kickball, Micah carefully tied his bunny sweater around his waist.

"We don't want you, we'll play down one," Travis said, dismissing Micah with a look. Ever since the orange soda incident Travis had found any reason at all to push Micah in the hall, flick his ear, or growl at him like a rabid dog—always without a teacher to witness. "Let's go." The two kickball teams broke up, Travis's team kicking first.

"You can be on my team," I whispered to Micah.

"No," Travis said roughly. "He can't play. Roll the ball," he said, turning to Jimmy, who was pitching for us.

I stood still. Micah's eyes met mine. Then he looked at Travis's huge shoulders and strong, curled hands.

"I didn't want to play anyway," Micah said with a shrug. He sat down against the wall and pushed up his glasses. He looked like a lost bird.

Travis watched me, daring me to interfere, his beady snake eyes narrowed in small slits. "I said roll the ball, Quintel!"

"Get up, Micah," Jimmy muttered. But Micah did nothing.

"Roll the ball!" Travis yelled a third time.

Jimmy walked over, reached down, and pulled Micah to his feet. "Come on, kick a home run."

But Micah, in a rare show of defiance, turned and marched away.

Travis said something about Micah being a sissy, and before I knew what was happening, Travis and Jimmy were throwing fists at each other, Mr. Zabriski was blowing a whistle, and none of us got to play kickball at all.

"Gwynnie, what happened?" Bitty asked when I met her outside in the hallway.

I shook my head. "Jimmy was protecting Micah." But I somehow knew at that moment, that there would come a time when Jimmy wouldn't always be able to protect him. And perhaps the reason Jimmy wanted Micah to stand his ground so often was because he knew that too.

I squeezed Bitty's hand. As we headed back to class, I wondered, Was there anything Jimmy wouldn't do for Micah? Did that also extend to Gaysie? Would he do anything to protect her, too?

CHAPTER 18

MICAH AND JIMMY WERE GROUNDED for a few days after the gym incident, which wasn't fair to Micah, but Gaysie said since they did everything else together, they could share the punishment. It proved serendipitous. I'd been so preoccupied with my case that I hadn't been paying enough attention to my other eavesdropping.

Bitty and I were attempting to put together a puzzle with Vienna, while my father spoke to Annabelle.

"Don't be discouraged," Annabelle was saying. "It's only been a few months. Surely you didn't think she would suddenly remember everything again?" Her voice was gentle, but admonishing. I stole a glance at my father, who looked a bit beat up after a long day looking at teeth and then attempting to teach Vienna how to meditate. Meditation supposedly helped boost neural pathways, but Vienna wasn't exactly taking to quiet and focused breath. Instead, she continually burst out into uncontrollable laughter.

"Jed," Vienna said. I turned to see her putting the last piece of my father's face together. Nana had ordered the puzzle from a photo company that made puzzles out of family pictures—it was my father's latest experiment on memory.

This puzzle was made from a picture taken right after Bitty was born. I watched Vienna's eyes closely. She was curious about her and Jed, but her eyes did not register recognition of the baby Bitty or little Gwyn.

I noted that Vienna had put almost everyone together but me; I was the most incomplete.

"Cute," she said, pointing to the baby.

"That's me," Bitty said, pleased and smiling as she helped Vienna find Jed's shoulders.

"No, silly! That's a baby."

"And who's that?" Bitty asked, pointing to me as a child.

Vienna avoided the question by flicking a puzzle piece off the table, just to be obnoxious. I refused to pick it up. I ignored her, making my eyes glaze over as I focused on the adult conversation.

"Anatomically, there's nothing wrong with Vienna's heart," my father said. "It's a rhythm disorder. You'd think that would be trickier, but it was the damage to her brain . . . We're doing the memory exercises, the video simulations, getting her more exercise, learning new things. We moved all the way here, I've introduced her to so many old friends, taken her to familiar landmarks, and still . . . I can't help her. I can't seem to . . ." He cleared his throat and began packing up to go home. "There's been progress, of course. One must have perspective."

Yes, I thought grudgingly, watching Vienna. Was she putting puzzles together faster? Was she holding the pieces a little less awkwardly? Were new neural pathways being made? My father thought so, but I wondered if he was only seeing what he wanted to.

Annabelle had moved closer, tossing her long black hair down her back.

"I'm always here for your family, if you ever want to talk." She touched my father's arm and smiled up at him under her dark black lashes. I watched my father's face soften as he studied the pictures on Vienna's windowsill.

"I'm sorry, Gaysie. I'm sorry, Gaysie. I'm sorry, Gaysie," interrupted my intent listening. I turned to see Vienna fingering some dried-out flowers Gaysie must have left days ago.

"I'm sorry, Gaysie," Vienna said again.

I walked over to her and smelled the flowers. "Why are you saying sorry?" I asked. "It's Gaysie who has things to apologize for. Don't be sorry!"

"I'm sorry, Gaysie."

"Why?" I demanded more forcefully. My father and Annabelle glanced over at us, so I lowered my voice. "Vienna?"

Bitty skipped over. "Don't be sorry, Vienna. It's okay."

Vienna's eyes welled with tears. "I'm sorry, Gaysie." Then her face went blank, and I knew she'd already moved on. But what had made her so upset? What was she apologizing for?

"You should have seen her," my father said, still staring at Vienna's pictures, not noticing the outburst. "She was really something."

Six years ago, extraordinary efforts were taken to save

my mother's life. My father, the scientist, had pleaded for a miracle.

I was wicked and hateful for thinking it, but as I looked at the uncompleted puzzle, her yellow room, the Care Bear, at Annabelle smiling so kindly at my father, I wondered if we wouldn't have all been better off if we hadn't gotten our miracle after all.

CHAPTER 19

LOLLY'S IMPENDING ARRIVAL, TWO DAYS before Halloween, sent Nana into a tizzy of nervous energy and forty-eight straight hours without sleep. She also banned me from discussing or mentioning anything to do with Wilbur until after Lolly left.

"We've just never had dogs in the house," Nana said, surveying the living room, mentally picturing hair on sofas, dirty paw prints on clean kitchen floors, and chewed-up living room couch cushions. Nana was brilliant at imagining the absolute worst-case scenario.

"You'll love them so much, you'll want to keep them."

She pointed a finger at me. "Don't you even think about it—you have your cow!"

"Lolly's gonna love Willowdale," I told Nana when we brushed our teeth that night. Bitty nodded in agreement as Nana wiped the small dots of water off the mirror while we brushed. "She might not have ever seen a cow in her life!"

"I'm sure she's seen a cow," Nana said. "Everyone has seen a cow."

"No, Nana, in New York City there are no cows. I bet Moose and Tomato have never seen a cow."

"Where will the dogs sleep?" Nana worried.

"With me and Bitty in our beds!"

"Don't you even think about that, either!"

Skipping home the next afternoon, Bitty and I checked in with Ms. Priscilla about the fingerprint book.

"Trick or treat?" she said with a smile, two hands behind her back.

"Treat?" I asked excitedly.

She proudly handed me *Fingerprinting for Amateurs.* Bitty and I ran all the way home to start reading.

Lolly stepped out of the car an hour later. She was wearing her favorite blue-and-white-striped seersucker dress. She held out her arms and hugged us tight. It was so familiar, so comforting, that Bitty and I couldn't help but burst into tears.

"Let me get a look at you," Lolly said, holding us out. "Hair all combed, dressed so nice. What's happened to my little girls?"

"Nana," Bitty and I said at the same time. Lolly laughed, showing her white teeth, the deep wrinkles in her face accentuated.

"I missed you," Bitty said, clinging to her.

"Oh, honey, not as much as I've missed you all and your mama. Is she here?" Lolly looked past us toward the house.

"Lolly," I said, not wanting to share her yet. "You've got to meet Jimmy and Micah and guess what else? We *walk* to school. It's whole mile of nothing but corn!"

"You've certainly not lost your gift of gab, have you?"

I grabbed Lolly's hand and skipped toward the house, admiring Nana's magnificent effort; even the fall mums looked better than yesterday. Nana came outside with a newly ironed shirt and freshly pressed pants, smiling warmly, like she hadn't been cooking and cleaning for days.

Behind her came my father and Vienna, who was walking slowly with her disjointed step. Vienna stopped. Lolly reached for Vienna and gave her a long, enveloping hug.

"Vienna, do you remember me? Well, of course you do, honey. I can tell you do." Lolly stroked Vienna's hand for a few seconds before Vienna grabbed her shoulders and held on tight.

"Lolly?" Vienna said. "Lolly. Lolly . . ." Lolly pulled out a tissue from her pocket and wiped Vienna's eyes and nose.

Vienna lurched her head free. "I can do it."

Lolly smiled. "Yes, you can."

I could tell by the look on my father's face that he was pleased. After all those years together, Lolly had imprinted on Vienna's brain like Micah had on that goose's.

"Do you know who Lolly is?" my father asked.

"My nurse."

"Do you remember where Lolly lives?"

"New York."

"Very good." My father beamed. But I knew they'd been practicing.

"You are looking good yourself," Lolly said, grabbing my father for a hug. "This small-town life agrees with you!"

"I'm hungry," Vienna said.

Lolly turned and clasped Nana's hands. "So sweet of you to have me and most especially for letting the dogs come too."

"Oh, it really is my pleasure," Nana said, peering around Lolly to get a look at Tomato and Moose, who were peeing on the mums.

I had to hand it to Nana. She kept that perfect hostess smile right on her face.

I still had to go to stupid piano on Thursday, even though Lolly was visiting. Surprisingly, even though I detested being in Ms. Myrtle's house, I looked forward to what she had to tell me about Vienna. Some weeks she was more forthcoming than others. For instance, last week I learned that Vienna was often the ringleader of mischief. Ms. Myrtle said that Vienna had once convinced all the neighborhood children to climb into Ms. Myrtle's tree with her. She had taught them such convincing birdcalls that Ms. Myrtle thought that an unusual species of fowl had taken up residence outside her window. She had called the fire department, only to discover half a dozen children up in the branches. Even though Ms. Myrtle didn't like me, and I wasn't a piano natural, I comforted myself with the fact that I might have potential to give a decent birdcall.

When I got there though, she just mumbled at me to sit and play. After one disastrous piano rendition of "Dinah, Won't You Blow," she fell asleep and, disappointed from the lack of new information, I left.

As soon as I got home, I knew something was wrong.

Nana was wearing her good pants, but she was kneeling on the grass and waving kitchen scraps.

"Thank goodness you're home," she fluttered. "The dogs are gone. You've got to find them!"

"How am I gonna do that?"

"Use that great detective brain of yours!"

"The Creepers," I said, recalling how they had tauntingly barked at me after school. Now I knew why. "Dognapping is just the thing Travis Maynard would like to add to his résumé."

"What are you talking about?" Nana asked.

"Bitty!" I yelled. "Come quick! We've got a mission!"

We rode around our school to spy on the Creepers, who were playing basketball behind the building, but not holding any dogs. When they saw us, they started to laugh, bark, and howl.

"Mutants!" I said, riding away fast with Bitty. We looped back around to Main Street, and when we reached Vienna's care center, I was surprised to see Vienna slumped on a bench with her hands wrapped tightly around Lolly's.

"What's the matter?" I asked.

She looked up at me, tears spilling down her cheeks.

"I just found out my dad died."

"Honey, he died many years ago," Lolly said, patting her hands. "You just can't remember because you have a brain injury."

"I do?"

"Have you seen Moose and Tomato?" I whispered to Lolly.

"What? Aren't they here?" she asked, alarmed.

"We'll find them," I said quickly. "Where's Daddy?"

Vienna began to cry again. "I just found out my dad died."

I sat next to her and wiped her cheeks, the tears warm and wet and familiar on my fingers.

"Jed?" Vienna said suddenly, pushing past me. Her tears stopped. "Jed!" she screamed. I fell abruptly back onto the bench, seeing my father and Annabelle walking down the road.

"*Who* is that?" Lolly asked, smoothing Vienna's blond hair.

"The new nurse," I answered.

"She's pretty," Vienna said. "She has big bosoms."

"Totally inappropriate!" I snapped at her.

She frowned, her lower lip out like a child's.

Bitty ran to greet our father, but she tripped, hitting her hands and chin hard on the sidewalk. There was a second of silence before Bitty let out a high-pitched scream that made the hairs on my arm stand straight up.

Vienna began laughing like she was witnessing an entertaining circus performance.

"Stop it!" I said. But Vienna didn't stop. She kept laughing as Bitty cried.

"Stop. NOW."

"Vienna, shhh," Lolly said. "Bitty is hurt."

Vienna laughed harder. My brain knew she couldn't help it, but at that moment I wanted to slap the laughing right off her face. Instead, I pinched her hard on the arm.

"Ow!" Vienna grabbed her arm but at least she stopped laughing.

Annabelle reached down and lifted Bitty up, kissing her cheeks.

"Gwyn," my father said, frowning. I noticed he was wearing new work boots, like some sort of Iowan farmer.

"Gwyn!" Vienna said, pinching me back even harder.

"Ow! We have to go find the dogs," I said, taking Bitty from Annabelle, while rubbing my pinched arm. "They escaped."

"That Gwyn girl is a meanie!" I heard Vienna say as Bitty and I walked away. If I hadn't been so angry I would have taken this as good news; Vienna had remembered something I had done for longer than thirty seconds.

"Honey," Lolly said, "Gwyn and Bitty are your daughters."

Vienna started to cry again. "Guinevere, Elizabeth, and Gus."

"Come on, Bitty," I said, kissing her chin and patting her hair. As we rode our bikes, I tried putting a hand over my ears until we were out of earshot, but even then Vienna's voice found its way through the Iowa wind—a laugh, a cry, a sharp burst of recognition.

Nana was standing on the porch when Bitty and I arrived home in the dark, peering down Lanark Lane to where Jimmy and Micah were coming, each one holding a dog. The dogs wagged their tails and barked excitedly when they saw us.

"Praise be," Nana said. I looked at her, surprised. My father said Nana had once been a devout woman, but now she never spoke about God. I suspected she was holding a big, fat grudge.

"You found them!" I yelled at Jimmy and Micah. "Whoa, you guys are dirty."

"Guinevere," Nana said, opening the door to go into the house with Bitty. "All thoughts need not be shared."

"They were . . . down the road," Jimmy said as soon as Nana and Bitty were inside. He sounded hollow.

Micah nodded, ghostly white.

They looked at each other, shifting in their shoes.

"What?"

They hesitated.

"What!"

"We saw Wilbur's ghost!" Micah burst out softly.

"What do you mean?"

"I mean . . . ," Micah began.

"No," Jimmy said. "We just saw someone on the tractor and thought it was . . ."

"Wilbur's ghost," Micah said, his eyes huge.

I looked down at Jimmy's feet. "Probably because you are wearing his boots!"

"Jimmy, it's true!" Micah said.

Jimmy said. "Come off it! It wasn't Wilbur."

"Who, then?"

"We don't know," Jimmy said. "He was gone by the time we got out there. But Wilbur couldn't jump, and he definitely couldn't run away so fast."

"I'm going to faint," Micah whispered, breathing like an asthmatic.

"It wasn't a ghost and don't you dare faint!" Jimmy said.

"Maybe it was a Creeper?" I asked.

"No. He was old. Like—as old as your dad."

"Did you say *old*?"

We turned at the voice, Micah shrieking.

It was my father, still wearing the boots from earlier.

"Sorry to scare you, Micah."

"I didn't mean real old!" Micah said. "Just kind of . . . old."

My father laughed again. "You boys hungry?"

They shook their heads.

"Well, it's good to see you. Say hello to Gaysie for me. Gwyn, dinner?"

I nodded and waited until my father was inside to resume our ghost discussion.

Micah and Jimmy exchanged a glance.

"What else?"

"The ghost looked an awful lot like your dad," Jimmy whispered.

I laughed. "Does my dad look like he drives a tractor? Anyhow, I just saw him at the care center. Maybe it *was* Wilbur's ghost, and he's trying tell us something." I felt a deliciously spooky feeling coming over me.

A blackbird cawed overhead. Micah shrieked and fell to the ground, covering his head. I looked up and saw Bitty in the window, gazing at the sky.

"Fly away, birdies," Bitty said from behind the upstairs glass window, flapping her arms. "Fly, fly away."

"Gotta fly," Jimmy said. "Later."

I went inside, washed my hands before dinner, and sat down.

"Where's Dad?"

"Taking a quick shower," Nana said. "He was filthy."

"Filthy?" I asked. My father was never filthy.

"Must've been helping someone out on his way home. In Crow, that's what neighbors do for one another. Bitty!" Nana called. "Time for supper."

My blood ran cold, my heart pounding against my rib cage. I tried to think logically. Nana was right about neighbors helping one another out. But what if that neighbor was Gaysie? For all I knew, maybe my father did know how to ride the Blue Mistress. For all I knew, he told me everything—until he didn't.

I stared at my father when he came into the kitchen, his hair washed, combed, and parted neatly. He wore his usual khakis and button-down shirt and looked like my father again, nothing like a ghost on a blue tractor.

CHAPTER 20

I BECAME SHERLOCK HOLMES ON HALLOWEEN night, my absolute most favorite holiday. I wore my grandfather's old, brown tweed driving cap and carried a fake plastic pipe. I tried to talk Bitty into being my sidekick, Watson, but instead she dressed as a princess. In, like, pink stuff.

Jimmy showed up as a zombie wrapped in white toilet paper, with black makeup encircling his eyes and mouth. Micah wore a chef apron and a little white cap. In his hands he carried an apple pie.

"Made it myself," he said proudly.

"Mmmm," I said, pinching off a piece of crust. "Share with me later?"

Micah smiled from ear to ear.

Music played on Main Street, while jack-o-lanterns glowed and local businesses kept their lights on, handing out treats. My father, Lolly, Nana, and Vienna set up Halloween outside the dental office. Except they handed out toothbrushes and floss. My father kept one hand on Vienna's shoulder at all times and said to each person, "You remember my wife, Vienna?"

She sat in her wheelchair because she tired easily, dressed as a toothbrush, to match my father's toothpaste costume. Lolly stood behind her, dressed as a nurse.

"Vienna," I said nervously, wondering how unpredictable she might be. I touched her hands lightly. "This is Jimmy and Micah, my friends." I smiled in an extra friendly way to show her we were friends.

Vienna nodded, her eyes dancing.

Lolly smiled. "I've heard all about what good friends you boys are."

"Vienna, they come with Gaysie to visit you," I added.

"Where's Gaysie?"

"At home," Micah said. "She doesn't like Halloween."

"I love Halloween!" Vienna said. "Where's Gaysie?"

"At home," Micah said again.

"She's so ugly," Vienna said, wrinkling her forehead.

"Never mind," I interrupted, not wanting to hurt Micah's feelings.

"But I'm her friend," she said. "I'm a good friend, right?"

"Yes, you are," my father said, patting her arm.

"Mom and I went to see her in the hospital. I said I'm sorry."

"Oh my!" Nana interrupted. "It's Halloween, for heaven's sake. Go eat candy!"

"Go eat candy!" I exclaimed. "Did Nana just say that?"

"No. Yes." Nana looked flustered, and I paused. What was wrong with her? Did it have to do with what Vienna just said about Gaysie and saying sorry? Was there really something to it?

"I like candy!" Vienna yelled, tapping on my arm. "Candy, candy, candy!" And the moment was gone again.

I rummaged around and gave her my only banana Laffy Taffy. My father frowned, taffy being a dentist's worst enemy. Vienna played with the wrapper, tried to open it with her fingers, then her teeth, and finally threw it on the ground out of frustration.

"I like your costume, Mrs. St. Clair," Micah said, opening the taffy for her.

Vienna grasped his hand, gazing into his eyes like she'd never seen him before in her life. "Mrs. St. Clair?" she murmured.

"Bye, Vienna," I said just as Annabelle appeared behind my father. She was dressed as a red devil with red lipstick. Red horns sat atop her long, shiny, dark hair. She was the most breathtaking devil anyone had ever seen.

"Come on," I said, elbowing a drooling Jimmy and Micah.

"Have fun," my father called.

"I know, I know, we'll be careful," I said before Nana could open her mouth.

"Happy Halloween!" Bitty yelled, skipping along after me.

"Just look at your girls going off by themselves!" I heard Lolly say.

I looked back, my father the toothpaste juxtaposed between a toothbrush and the devil.

Jimmy peered down into his pillowcase. "Great treat," he said, holding up the toothbrush.

"He's a dentist," I said. "He can't give you a candy bar. And even raisins will cause . . ."

"I don't care I don't care I don't care!" Jimmy yelled, sprinting ahead of me.

We ran down Main Street, seeing bunches of kids from school. Penny and her friends were Crayola crayons, and Travis and the Creepers wore black trench coats and goblin masks. When they saw us they began to bark.

"Avoid, avoid, avoid," I muttered, steering a clear path away from them. But Micah found himself face-to-face with Travis Maynard. Travis lifted up his mask.

"What is that? A pie?"

"Don't even think about it," Jimmy said.

"Give me a bite," Travis said.

"No," Jimmy said.

"It's okay," Micah said. "You can have a bite."

"Sweet," Travis said. He looked at his hands and felt his pockets. "I don't have a fork. Just give me the pie," he said, lifting the pie out of Micah's hands.

"Like Jimmy said—don't even think about it!" I pulled the pie back.

"Give it," Travis said. We tugged back and forth until I saw Officer Jake walking toward us. I let go. Travis fell backward, and Micah's beautiful pie went with him, smashing all over his black coat, neck, and face.

"Why am I not surprised?" Officer Jake said, hands on his hips. "Travis Maynard stealing a pie." He looked down at Travis and shook his head as Travis sputtered, wiping apple pie out of his eyes, nose, and mouth.

"You all go finish having a fun evening," Officer Jake said to us. "I'll deal with this."

"Enjoy the pie, buddy," Jimmy whispered to Travis.

"Watch out for your little dogs!" Travis yelled after us.

I grimaced, wondering if Moose and Tomato were roaming Crow again, thanks to the Creepers.

"Don't be sad, Micah," Bitty said as we walked away.

He sniffed. "It was my best one. I made it extra special for you and Gwyn, with extra cinnamon and my best picked apples of the tart variety."

We comforted Micah the best we could, making him laugh when describing the apple goo all over Travis's face.

I immediately forgave Officer Jake for his past behavior until he condescendingly winked at me when we passed him again later on and asked if I had any more tips for him, as if I hadn't given him a genuine suspect.

Toward the end of the night we held out our bags for the staff at the care center, whom we had become fast friends with. They smiled and chattered about Vienna, her excitement for Halloween, and her love of candy. They doubled up on our candy distribution and waved good-bye as we headed past the town cemetery.

"Let's walk through," Jimmy said casually. "There's something we've never shown you."

"No, Gwyn," Bitty said, clutching my arm.

"Come on!" I said excitedly, drawn to the old headstones, crypts, and stone birds.

I felt that delicious, spooky feeling again as we wandered past graves, leaves crunching under our feet and a sliver of a moon shining down upon us.

"What do you want to show me?" I asked Jimmy and Micah.

They stopped in front of a white granite stone with an

angel engraved on it. The plot was well cared for, with flow-ers tastefully trimmed back. I read the name on the grave-stone and nearly sunk right into the ground.

The stone was for a ten-year-old boy named Myron Myrtle.

"Myrtle," I breathed. "Not . . . Myron was Ms. Myrtle's *boy*?"

"You didn't know?" Micah asked.

"No one ever said the words 'Myron' and 'Myrtle' together!"

"I'm never going sledding again," Bitty said.

"Gaysie's been here, hasn't she?" I asked.

"Oh sure," Micah said. "She and your dad even brought Vienna. But Vienna doesn't like it so well."

Why would Gaysie and my father take Vienna to a gravesite? To remember? I shivered.

"Come on," Jimmy said. "Best day of the year. Let's get more candy!"

My insides twisted into miserable knots. I felt so fool-ish! I had spoken to Ms. Myrtle about her boy as if he were grown up and alive.

I stumbled after my comrades, out of the cemetery, try-ing to shake off the feeling.

We finished trick-or-treating down the street before parting ways. I gave Jimmy and Micah a thumbs-up sign.

"See you at midnight," I whispered.

Because tonight, you see, was the night we were finally getting our fingerprints.

• • •

Four hours later, at eleven forty-five, I was reluctant to wake a snoring Bitty up. As she was the world's heaviest sleeper, I had to make a decision: risk a noisy wake-up scene or let her slumber in peace. I would be faster alone, and snoring was a great cover, if someone should happen to check on us. I prayed Bitty would someday forgive me for what I was about to do.

I climbed out the first-floor window and landed on Nana's juniper bushes. I paused, looking at my father's dark window. He had not come home from the care center yet. If he had, he would have come to us.

I stalled, conflicted.

What if he came home while I was gone? Or what if we ran into each other while walking down the street? The air was getting cold. Winter was coming. I would have to risk it.

I ran to my bike parked behind the barn, dog jerky in my pocket to keep Moose and Tomato from yapping. But when I turned on my headlamp, I saw the kennel doors were wide open. Empty again.

Darn those Creepers!

Then again, if I got caught, the dogs could be a red herring. I pedaled down Lanark Lane, the only light shining from my headlamp and the occasional glimmer of the moon in an overcast sky. The cold wind whipped at my face. It felt like snow. We had to complete our mission tonight.

The clementine house was entirely dark. Passing underneath Gaysie's window, I heard a noise like a stick snap. I paused. All was quiet again except the wind in the trees and overgrown cornstalks.

I held my shaking hands tight and gulped as I found the milking pail on the porch. I used my jacket to grab it and hid it behind the barn, completing my solo task before waking my friends.

At 12:08 a.m. I threw a pebble at Micah's window, but it missed and hit the house.

No one appeared. I began to climb the tree closest to the house in the darkness, the trunk and branches black and overpowering with shadow. For once in my life I was glad it was dark, glad I couldn't see how high off the ground I was. *This is easy, I am not afraid, I am a good climber*, I said over and over, trying to trick my brain. *Don't be a scaredy-cat like Nana!*

Balancing on a branch, I threw another pebble at Micah's window before shining our signal: three quick light flicks from my flashlight.

No response except for the sound of Gaysie snoring loudly enough to shake the window frames.

Suddenly, a light went on in the upstairs bathroom. I almost fell out of the tree when I saw a white face with big, black-circled eyes.

Jimmy!

I slid down the tree, jumped down, and performed a somersault across the grass, the contents of my backpack making a loud turnover noise.

"What took you so long?" I asked when Micah and Jimmy tumbled out of the house.

"Sorry," Micah yawned, patting my shoulder. "I fell asleep."

"I didn't think you'd really come," Jimmy said. He turned and started walking quickly toward the cornfield.

"Are you wearing . . . Wilbur's shirt?"

"Gaysie gave it to me, said it didn't fit him anymore," he said over his shoulder. "But I put his boots back by the back door. So he can have 'em when he gets back."

"And so he won't haunt us anymore," Micah said.

"Ah, Micah, hush up!" Jimmy said. He led the way as we walked single file down the corn path. White clouds moved overhead, illuminated by a bright moonlight, and old cornstalks crunched under our feet. We halted by the river, where Wilbur's Blue Mistress had sat for months now.

"Don't touch anything," I whispered.

The wind moved the cornstalks, creating a sound of someone constantly walking toward us. Micah looked around, the whites of his eyes wide.

I pulled out the needed items I'd read about in our fingerprinting book: Nana's baking cocoa powder, my father's camel hair paintbrush, tape, and construction paper.

Pulling on Nana's too-big disposable kitchen gloves, I carefully climbed up onto the tractor and sat. The wind picked up my hair and blew at my face. How wonderful it was to be so high and free, how different from New York. How eerily quiet! I could see why Wilbur liked it.

"Cocoa powder," I called down.

Micah fumbled the box, but managed to hand it up. I shook cocoa onto the steering wheel.

"Are you sure you know what you're doing?" Jimmy asked doubtfully.

"Of course I do," I said confidently. "If protected enough, prints can remain on objects for years." I pulled back the thin plastic atop the tractor. Hopefully, the paltry covering had protected the Blue Mistress. *Fingerprinting for Amateurs* said that if there was a sticky print, the cocoa powder would stick. If this worked, and I was interviewed on television for breaking the case, Ms. Priscilla would be the first person I thanked.

"What was that?" Micah asked, looking behind us.

"Probably the ghost," I whispered.

"Just hurry up," Jimmy said.

"Wilbur never let anyone on his tractor," Micah shivered. "And you're up there . . ."

"You still think his ghost is watching us?"

"We changed our mind," Jimmy said. "It wasn't a ghost, because that would mean Wilbur is dead and he's not."

"Micah," I whispered, "Gaysie said she died once. Does she know what ghosts look like?"

He looked up at me and scrunched up his nose.

"I don't think she really sees ghosts. More like angels."

"Sees?" I asked. "Like, she still sees them?"

"Kinda."

"Stop talking about ghosts!" Jimmy said, handing up my father's camel hair brush. I carefully dusted away the excess cocoa powder. It had felt like a long shot, but there it was! Some cocoa was still sticking to the steering wheel.

"Tape."

Very carefully, I stuck it onto the cocoa powder.

"Paper."

I peeled off the tape and stuck it to the orange construction paper.

"Now what?" Jimmy asked.

"Lolly will take this back to Georgia Piehl—the prosecuting attorney in New York. I'll tell her it's a rush job. Time is of the essence." I'd heard that in a movie once.

The wind blew and again we heard the rustling sound. It stopped, then stirred.

"Let's go," Jimmy said softly.

I pulled the tarp back up and jumped down. Adrenaline made us move, but whatever was behind us, real or imagined, was moving faster. Micah tripped and fell to the ground.

I pulled him up and we began to run again. Suddenly, there was something at my feet.

Micah let out a scream that prompted a domino effect, sending all of us into hysterics. I screamed so loudly it echoed across the entire field. But when I looked down I saw two twin fur balls.

"Moose! Tomato!" I cried.

"Oh," Micah said, scooping both the dogs up and sniffling with relief.

"I need to take them home," I said.

"An excellent idea," a voice said behind us. We screamed again. She had appeared from nowhere, a giant looming over us.

"Children."

"Ma!" Micah yelled, taking a step toward her.

"Go inside."

Micah dumped the dogs in my arms and obeyed, running with Jimmy to the house. Gaysie turned, looked out toward the field before zeroing in on me.

"What are you looking for, Guinevere?" Her voice was low. My mouth opened but nothing came out.

"Hmm?" she asked, taking a step toward me. I took a step back.

She stopped walking.

"I . . ."

"What *exactly* are you looking for?"

"I'm looking for Wilbur!" I said boldly. "I'm wondering why *you* aren't!"

"Are you, now?"

"Yes!"

Gaysie rocked her large body as she looked out into the dark night. "Guinevere, be careful. Sometimes the answers you think you're looking for aren't the answers you find."

She turned toward me, her long scar accentuated by the moon.

I was unsure what she meant. What other answers could I be looking for? Was she just trying to throw me off her scent?

When I remained mute, she said my name. "Guinevere?"

"Yes?"

"Go home now."

I ran quickly to my bike, Moose and the fingerprints in my backpack, and Tomato down my jacket.

On the road I glanced back, where all I could see was

the giant shadow of Gaysie Cutter, who appeared to be slowly following behind.

Ahead of me was nothing but the dark, black road. When I coasted I could hear it, though. That rustle again.

The image of ghosts made me pedal faster. The closer I was to home, the more panic I felt to *get inside the house!* I dumped my bike behind it and shoved the dogs in their kennels. Moose growled.

"Shh," I said. He wiggled his head around, wrestling with something in his mouth.

"What have you got there?" I whispered. I reached toward his mouth and pulled on something wet and slimy. Fabric of some sort. Grimacing, I stuffed the wet glob in my pocket, threw the dog treats in the kennel, and securely latched the locks. I turned to the black night. The rustle came again.

"Stay away," I whispered fiercely. "Don't you dare come any closer."

I felt emboldened by my own words, and the fear abated as I backed toward the house, until I heard it again.

I sprinted to my bedroom window, noting that my father's room was still dark.

"Hurry, hurry!" I whispered as I shoved myself through, my feet dangling for mere seconds as I imagined the ghost of Wilbur Truesdale reaching for me, grasping my feet. . . . Tumbling in, I slammed the window shut harder than I had meant to, slipped off my shoes, and fell into bed beside Bitty. I didn't dare breathe.

I stayed awake for a long time, adrenaline coursing

through my body as I repeatedly glanced at the window. *Adrenaline*, I practiced in my head, *is produced in times of stress by the adrenal glands, which sit atop the kidneys. Inhale. There is no threat. Exhale.*

There was the rustle. *Wind through cornstalks.* But there was no corn in here.

It sounded like it was right outside my window.

I leaped back to the window and locked it.

Just in case.

But as I did, something caught my eye. I squinted. There, standing with his hands in his pockets, was my father. His back was turned to me as he stared at the giant, hanging moon.

At first I felt a flood of relief, but then a cold shiver rocketed through me. He wasn't in costume any longer. His shirt was hanging out of his jacket. It was torn, reflected brightly against the glow of moonlight. My eyes widened as I felt in my pocket for the soggy fabric I had dug out of Moose's teeth. My mouth went dry. Moose had torn my father's shirt. Had he been at Gaysie's? Why? When?

He did not come to our room that night, either because he was too tired or because he knew I was already there.

CHAPTER 21

OVER A BLEARY-EYED BREAKFAST, NANA commented that Halloween had really done me in. "You look like you stayed up half the night."

I had filled Bitty in and had sought her forgiveness this morning, but she still gave me an unforgiving, murderous look.

My father silently read his science journal as if he hadn't been standing outside in the moonlight in the middle of the night with a torn flannel shirt. I fingered the torn fabric in my own pocket, now dry and soft.

After breakfast I crept into my father's room to rifle through his laundry basket. No torn shirt.

"May I help you?" my father asked from behind me. I jumped a mile.

I thought about saying I was helping Nana with the laundry—but he'd never believe it.

"I . . . you didn't come say good night last night."

He tilted his head at me. "I didn't?"

We stood and stared at each other until Nana called us to say good-bye to Lolly.

I nodded and scooted past him, feeling a sadness I had never felt before; my father and I were keeping secrets from each other. But there had to be an explanation for his behavior, a reason he was looking more and more suspicious with the Gaysie and Wilbur business . . . but no, never! I couldn't even think it.

I cornered Lolly as she was packing up the car and handed her the envelope containing my letter and the fingerprints. I hadn't told a soul the second part of what I had done, not even Bitty. I had fingerprints from the tractor, but also from the milking pail I'd seen only Gaysie handle with all nine fingers. They had to be a match.

"Could you please get this to Georgia Piehl?"

"*The* Georgia Piehl?"

"Yes," I said. "It's a matter of life and death." Which was totally true.

"Well, when you put it that way," Lolly said. She looked at me closely. "What are you chasing, Gwyn? Your father told me about a missing man you seem pretty intent on finding."

"Please, Lolly? It's real important."

"Ms. Piehl's office is only a few blocks over from me," she mused. "I think I can manage that."

I nodded, abruptly wistful for the walks we used to take in the loud and busy city, the large screens advertising the latest musicals, and the sound of a cabbie laying on a horn in the middle of Manhattan. Oh, and the hot dogs. Man, I missed those hot dogs.

Meanwhile, Nana came down the walkway with enough packed food for a small village: apples, pot roast sandwiches, crackers and cheese, and individually wrapped slices of pumpkin pie.

My father accompanied a gum-chomping Vienna.

"Hungry," Vienna mumbled. "I'm hungry." We had just eaten, so she wasn't really hungry, but her brain didn't register that. Gum helped. I unwrapped another piece for her and let her spit her old piece into my hand. It was warm and smelled like bad breath. Vienna grasped my hand tightly, smashing the gum into my palm.

"A successful visit," Lolly said, smiling at Vienna. "You remembered me. I'm excited to report back to your neuro doctors in New York. You even remembered Moose and Tomato." What Lolly didn't say was that Vienna had failed most every other memory test that involved recalling any events past the age of thirteen. "I'm thinking Crow is going to work some magic for all of you," Lolly said.

My father smiled. "Not magic, Lolly . . ."

"I know, I know"—she waved at him—"it's all about the brain and neuro this and all that. You make me proud, Jed St. Clair. As persistent as a hound dog—and Gwyn." I smiled proudly at the resemblance between Dad, Gwyn, and hound.

Lolly knelt in front of Bitty and me, her eyes wet and shiny.

"You be good girls," she said. "You've got such a good nana, and this is a sweet little town to grow up in, much better than the city. If I had half a mind, I'd move here myself."

"Please, Lolly!" Bitty said.

"Please, Lolly," Vienna echoed, blowing a small gum bubble.

I looked at her hopefully, even as I thought how disappointed Annabelle Ziers might be.

"Oh, Guinevere," Lolly said, smiling. "You keep reading your books. It's made you the smartest snapper I know." I threw my arms around her, smelling her warm, vanilla scent, already missing her. "I love this girl," she said, putting both arms on my shoulders, looking at me like she wanted to say something more.

Instead, she picked up Bitty. "You're getting so big—I won't be able to pick you up next time! You keep using your words and standing up for yourself."

Lolly hugged Vienna, who smiled amiably, not realizing Lolly was about to drive a thousand miles away from us.

She honked twice and drove away, with Bitty and me running after the car. She stopped at the one stop sign on the street. I ran to the open window.

"Don't forget," I said, "to deliver my package—and be careful. Reveal this information to no one."

"I'll deliver your package, Guinevere. But listen to what I'm saying. Whatever you're hung up on . . ."

"It's a mystery," I said. "And I'm helping."

"Listen, honey," she said sternly, "you and your father are both looking for someone you might never find."

"What do you mean?" I asked. "My father isn't helping me at all. I'm doing it alone."

Lolly smiled, her eyes growing dark and troubled.

"Honey," she said more gently, "some people just never come home."

CHAPTER 22

I TRIED WAITING PATIENTLY FOR MY fingerprint analysis. It was excruciatingly difficult, as patience was a particular weakness of mine. I valiantly bit my nails down to the roots. In the meantime, I completed more puzzles with Vienna, walked to and from school, and tried to keep close tabs on the comings and goings of Gaysie Cutter. Each time I passed the clementine house, I saw Ms. Myrtle's, whose home I hadn't visited since before Halloween. She was very sick, Nana said, and would likely not last through the winter.

But just before Thanksgiving she rallied, and I climbed the stairs for a piano lesson. I was anxious, hoping to finally ask her about her son, Myron. But when I saw Ms. Myrtle, I noticed her wrinkled face looked like dried fruit leather. She seemed to have shriveled since the month before.

I sat on the bench. In front of me was a piano book I hadn't seen before. Inside was the name *Vienna*, the handwriting loopy, feminine, and written in a faded green ink. Next to her name was a smiley face and a *Hi, Vivi voo voo!* in different ink and handwriting, signed with the initials *M.M.*

"*M.M.*," I said. "Myron Myrtle."

"They were good friends," Ms. Myrtle said weakly.

"Vivi voo voo!" I said, stifling a laugh.

"Vivi voo voo," Ms. Myrtle whispered. "Yes, sometimes he called her that." My arm hair stood up with goose bumps, just like the hair on Mr. Thompson's scaredy cat. The pages had notes throughout, holding the ghost of a young girl I had never known. I let myself fall into the trance of Vienna's hands sliding over the pages, learning how to play the same songs as me. And then a funny thing happened. Perhaps it was the proximity to crazy Gaysie next door, but all at once I was in a different time and place, a place where I *did* know a Vivi voo voo. It was as if she were sitting next to me on the piano bench, grinning, whispering a secret in my ear, giggling as she waved from a high tree branch, running fast down Lanark Lane, shrieking at the sight of a cow, being scolded by Nana for coming home so dirty.

My heart seemed to explode as I realized something: I would have *liked* this girl. And somewhere in that narrative was Jed St. Clair as a kid, waving his arms for her to come out and play with . . . Gaysie Cutter. I shuddered, my daydream screeching to a halt.

My heart shrank back to normal, maybe even a bit smaller. I felt cold and dark as I began my scales and arpeggios, wondering how to bring up the subject of a drowned boy.

After a torturous lesson involving the metronome and Ms. Myrtle waving her hand close to my face, I played my one memorized piece, "The Playful Pony."

After three rousing renditions, I turned around to see her slumped over in her chair.

"Ms. Myrtle?"

I was struck with the terrible thought that my bad piano playing had actually killed her.

"Ms. Myrtle?"

I arose from the piano bench and walked a wide circle, slowly approaching her. My mind reviewed my CPR training. Tentatively, I put my fingers on her neck.

She gave a giant croak and raised her head. I jumped back.

"Sorry . . . I thought you were . . ."

"Dead?" she spat out. "Out of luck!" She pointed to the piano. "Play!"

I played my one song yet again, vowing to never pump her chest or administer breaths even if she needed it. After the last chord, I touched Vienna's music one more time, wondering if the old witch would let me have it. I turned around slowly, gulping and sitting up straight.

"Ms. Myrtle?"

She wasn't looking at me or even listening to my piano lesson. She was gazing out the window, a faraway look in her eyes.

"I'm . . . sorry about your son," I began. "I didn't know."

"I haven't always done right by her," Ms. Myrtle said.

"Who do you mean? Vienna?"

Ms. Myrtle slowly shook her head.

"Tell her . . . tell Gaysie." Her voice was crackly and tired when she looked at me with her old, sagging, yellow eyes. "That I forgive her."

My eyes widened.

"For what?"

But Ms. Myrtle closed her eyes and said no more.

I walked down Lanark Lane deep in thought, not even racing the cows that trotted behind the fences all the way home. What had Gaysie done to Ms. Myrtle that would need forgiving? My hunch was Myron. It had to be what had happened to Myron.

CHAPTER 23

FOR VIENNA'S BIRTHDAY WE GAVE her Micah's story as a play. I was Queen Guinevere, Bitty my loyal subject. Micah wore his purple cape as King Arthur, and Jimmy rode through her doorway on his skateboard, dressed in a knight costume made of tinfoil and wearing a black eye patch. I wondered if he'd snatched it from his pirate father.

"Happy birthday, Vienna!" we shouted.

Vienna was lying on her bed in the care center, dressed in soft, stretchy pants and a blue sweater. Her eyes lit up as she touched my long white cape made from a white bedsheet.

"I'm Guinevere, the queen," I whispered conspiratorially.

"Ohhhh!" she said in a soft whisper voice. "Guinevere."

"You love Queen Guinevere," I reminded her. She nodded enthusiastically.

"This is Jimmy and Micah," I said. "And remember Bitty?" Vienna gazed at Bitty's short blond curls before fingering her own. I noticed her darker roots, wondering if she would go gray like Nana.

Then I noticed her bare left hand.

"Where's your ring?"

"Ring?"

"Oh no," I said, turning to Jimmy and Micah. "She's lost her ring again."

"Oh no," Vienna mimicked.

"Where is it?" I demanded.

"Be nicer," Micah whispered to me.

"Be nicer," Vienna said.

"Let's find your ring before Jed gets here," I said, using my coaxing baby voice. "Then we'll give you a play."

"Jed?" she yelled, struggling to sit up. "Jed!"

"Think very carefully, Vienna. Where is your ring?" I took off my cape and put it on the end of her bed.

"Not telling." Her sky blue eyes danced. She reached down and fingered my cape before suddenly throwing it up on the ceiling fan. "Ha ha ha!" she laughed.

I leaped up, grabbed my cape, and stupidly put it back on her bed. "Vienna."

"I'm sorry," she said.

Vienna watched with wonder as we began to tear the room apart. I crawled on the floor, lifted books and magazines she didn't read, and rifled through all her drawers. We looked in corners, on slightly dusty windowsills, and under her mattress.

Vienna waited until I turned to look at her before she threw my cape back up on the ceiling fan. She clapped her hands and fell back on her pillow, laughing.

I refused to even look up. "Vienna. Focus. Where is the ring you wear on your hand?" She lifted my hand to her mouth, kissed it, and bit it, hard.

"Ow!" I yelled, pulling away my hand. "Where's the

ring!" Impatiently, I picked up the fork on the tray beside her hospital bed and pushed around cold scrambled eggs that sat next to a half-eaten slice of toast. No ring.

"I'm hungry," she said.

"Eat your eggs, then," I said, pushing them toward her. She opened her mouth and I put a bite of eggs in.

"Cold," she said, letting them dribble out onto her chin.

"That's disgusting. Stop acting like a baby."

Micah put his hand on Vienna's shoulder. She tilted her head to rest on his hand and stuck her tongue out at me.

I looked under the crumpled napkin on her tray, in the empty juice cup, in her socks, pockets, and the red JanSport backpack she had used in middle school.

"We need the ring!" I said, picking up her pink Care Bear. "And you can't have Love-a-Lot until you tell me where it is!"

Vienna kicked her legs and screamed at me.

Suddenly, the door opened and in walked Gaysie Cutter. She wore a large flannel shirt, jeans, and big, black, men's work boots like Wilbur used to wear. I gulped.

"Hello, Vienna!" she said, putting down a large bouquet of leaves, sticks, and holly, before beginning to sing "Happy Birthday" in a loud, operatic voice. Vienna smiled and clapped her hands. "Is it my birthday?"

I stood between Vienna and Gaysie. What was *she* doing here?

"What's wrong with you?" Gaysie demanded, coming close to my face. "Why is your cape on the ceiling fan? Preperformance ritual?"

"No! I'm looking for her wedding ring," I burst out. "She hides it or throws it away a lot, even though I keep telling Daddy to stop putting it on her hand! And it makes him really sad when she does it." I suddenly wondered if someone had come in and stolen it. Vienna could be easily bribed with candy.

"I always hated wearing my ring too," Gaysie mused. "I took it off two weeks after my wedding and never put it back on."

"She loved her ring," I said hotly.

"I'm hungry," Vienna said.

"No, you're not," I said crossly. "You just ate breakfast! You only think you're hungry because your brain is messed up!"

Her face contorted into a great pout as she yelled, "I hate you! I hate you so much, jerk face!" She picked up her food tray and tipped it onto the floor just as Annabelle came into the room. Vienna began screaming her bad words at me, but I set my face into stone and continued to dig through the trash, the pink Care Bear under my arm as punishment. Gaysie stood still, watching me.

Annabelle hustled over to Vienna and tried to calm her down, but Gaysie physically moved her out of the way.

"Here, honey," Gaysie said briskly. She began to brush Vienna's hair and talk in a soothing voice. "Vivi voo voo, let down your hair."

I snapped to attention. "Vivi voo voo," I said. "That's what Myron used to call her."

"Myron," Vienna whispered.

Gaysie looked at me, surprised. "Yes, we all did. Kind of a funny pet name."

"Myron!" Vienna said, beginning to look upset.

"There now, Vienna," Gaysie said. "Let me tell you the story of a girl, young and bright, adventurous and smart, sometimes a bit of a know-it-all."

I paused.

"Who?" Vienna said, calming down.

"Why, you know who! Her name was Vienna."

I exhaled.

"Have you looked in the bathroom?" Gaysie asked without looking at me, still brushing Vienna's hair.

"Why are you so ugly?" I heard Vienna ask as I went into the bathroom. "I've never seen anyone as ugly as you."

"I seem to have gotten the short end of the stick in the beauty department. Plus, crashing through the ice and into the river didn't help, did it?"

I sat on the edge of the tub, alert, listening.

"I'm sorry," Vienna said.

"You don't need to be sorry, Vienna. Accidents happen."

"It's my fault," Vienna whispered.

"No, it's not," Gaysie said firmly. "We had good times, didn't we? Even if it didn't work out so well in the end."

I bit my nail. Poor Vienna. She was confused, sad about the accident that claimed the life of her friend, taking the blame.

"Look in the toilet!" Gaysie yelled to me. "Wonderful way to get rid of something."

"You are so weird," I whispered, wondering if Gaysie had done just that when it came to Wilbur. Was she flaunting her guilt in front of me? But I looked down at the closed toilet lid anyway, slowly opened it, and peered in. Nothing.

"Look down that deep, dark hole," Gaysie yelled.

"Deep, dark hole," Vienna echoed.

Jimmy and Micah came to the bathroom door. I scrutinized the hole, getting closer with my face, trying not to breathe.

Something.

There *was* something way down deep. I held my breath then plunged my hand down into the small hole and grasped it. I brought my hand up. I was holding Vienna's diamond ring, dripping with toilet water.

"Sick," Jimmy said.

"Awesome," Micah breathed.

"How . . . ?" I asked.

"She always knows," Jimmy said, tapping the side of his head. "She just knows."

"Well, hello, birthday girl," I heard my father call.

Relief flooded hot through every vein in my body.

"Jed!" Vienna screamed. "Jed! Jed! Jed!"

"In the nick of time," I said, quickly washing the ring and my hands with lots of hot water and soap.

We went out into the room to see my father kissing Vienna on her forehead, her face aglow. Gaysie continued to brush Vienna's blond, shiny curls.

I walked to Vienna's bed and gave her Love-a-Lot.

I hesitated, but then put the wet ring in my father's hand instead of on her finger.

"Gaysie found it," I said, conflicted on whether or not to feel slightly more grateful.

"I most certainly did not!" Gaysie boomed.

"She did. She told me where to look."

I turned reluctantly to face Gaysie, who was looking at me, chin raised.

"Thank you," I said stiffly.

"Gaysie Cutter saves the day," my father said. "Not the first time, and probably not the last."

He looked down at the wet ring in his hand, shoulders drooping ever so slightly before slipping the ring into his pocket.

After that day he never put it on her hand again.

I jumped up and took my cape off the fan. Vienna giggled.

Miracles happen every day. And I'll tell you what, not going crazy was one of them.

We walked to Petey's Diner for Vienna's birthday lunch because it was next door to the care center and because it was her new (and old) favorite place in the world. Really, the whole world. It had food and it had Jed.

Petey was a large man who had a shiny, bald head and a loud laugh, and Nana called him "a meathead," but not to his face. He was always wiping his greasy paws on the dingy white-and-red-checkered apron around his big belly, which looked like it never made it to the washing machine. You can imagine what Nana thought of that.

Annabelle came in after Bitty, Jimmy, Micah, and

I were sitting down on the barstools. Jimmy practically drooled.

"You're ridiculous," I said.

"Lucky you," Jimmy said. "That could be your new stepmother."

"She'll never be my stepmother and don't ever say that again, Jimmy Quintel!"

"I—"

"You must be real stupid if you don't know I already have a mother."

"I didn't mean . . ."

I settled back into my chair, my hands shaking.

"You should feel lucky," he said, shoving a french fry he found on the counter into his mouth. "You have a nice mom. *And* you have Annabelle, too."

"Well, you have a mom . . . don't you?"

He looked at me and considered.

"If she had a choice between me and anything else, she'd choose anything else."

It was the biggest admission he'd ever made.

"Ah, Jimmy."

"Ain't no thing," he shrugged. Of course I didn't believe him. It *was* a thing. I had learned a lot because of my mother—some good, some bad. But perhaps the thing I had learned to do best of all was hide how I really felt about the person who was supposed to love me most.

Petey set our milkshakes down with a flourish, rubbing his big belly with pride. "Atta girl," he said when I finally smiled. "And look who's coming through the doors—the birthday girl!" Vienna was hanging on to my father's arm, slow and uncoordinated, but upright.

Gaysie trailed behind, equally uncomfortable in public, lips pursed, chin up, hands held tightly together. That's when I noticed the blue flyer on the wall by the door: HAVE YOU SEEN WILBUR TRUESDALE? it said in bold letters with a picture of Wilbur on the Blue Mistress. Gaysie barely glanced at it, like she didn't care at all.

"My wife is having a birthday," my father announced, helping Vienna into a booth seat. She alternated between grabbing for my father's hands and kissing his cheek. I saw Dottie and Lavinia in the back, old friends of Nana's, give a wave and call, "Happy birthday."

"Ah, Ms. Guinevere, did I tell you how glad we are you came home to Iowa?" Petey asked me, calling my attention back to the counter.

"You can tell me again," I said.

Petey laughed. "Funny, like your mom. You know, I knew her way back when. Prettiest girl in the whole town. Everyone said your dad was the luckiest guy in the world before . . ." His voice trailed off as he grasped for words.

"Well, I'd say he's still pretty lucky," Gaysie said loudly, as the silence stretched uncomfortably.

My father chimed in, "Well, I sure am!"

Nana came hustling into the diner then with cake and apologies for being late. Dottie and Lavinia hurried over and kissed Nana on the cheek, nodding stiffly at Gaysie.

Annabelle sat next to Vienna to help feed her, across from Gaysie, who dwarfed even my father.

"I have to go to the bathroom," Bitty whispered.

I went into the stall with Bitty, and a few minutes later we heard a door open. I peeked through the crack to see Dottie and Lavinia. Dottie pulled out a lipstick, opened her mouth into an O, and began to apply a shiny pink.

"Vienna's birthday," she said, patting her silver hair on both sides. "Still so sweet and pretty. My goodness."

"I'm surprised to see Gaysie out in public with them," Lavinia said flatly. "It's just an appalling reminder for the rest of us."

Dottie waved her hand. "A reminder of what?"

"Dottie!"

"I mean, I know what you're talking about, but at some point we have to move on. They were all just kids, and you know how kids are."

"Well!" Lavinia said. "Jed has a true heart of gold. See the way he dotes on his wife and includes Gaysie, bless his heart. But I don't know why he allows his children to play with hers."

"Gaysie's harmless. Though I am surprised Nancy allows it."

"Exactly," Lavinia said, blotting her lips together. Bitty put her hand on the flusher, and I shook my head. "Jed's a saint," Lavinia swooned. "Can you imagine living with a wife who doesn't know who you are?"

"Roy says Jed should have checked under the hood a little more with that one."

"Oh, Dottie!"

It wasn't his fault, I wanted to say. No one knew Vienna's heart was a ticking time bomb. But I suddenly wondered, if given the choice again, would my father have made the same one?

The bathroom door creaked open.

"Nancy Eyre!" Lavinia said, quickly. "What a wonderful idea to celebrate Vienna's birthday here. I remember her sitting in a booth like it was yesterday!"

"I'm looking for the girls. Gwyn? Bitty? Are you in there?" I unlocked the door and led Bitty to the sinks. I scrubbed especially well, rubbing my hands together.

"Good girls," Nana said, smiling and raising her eyebrows expectantly. "Did you say hello?"

"Oh, hello," I said, turning back to a speechless Dottie and Lavinia. "I hope you have a *very* good day." I smiled so sweetly that Nana beamed and let us have an extra scoop of Moose Tracks ice cream with our cake.

CHAPTER 24

"SOMETIMES I STILL WAKE UP and reality is like a sharp pinch on my arm," my father said to Annabelle. My father was not the spill-your-guts type of person, but he sure liked talking to Annabelle. We were at the care center the next week, and Vienna was napping, her arms wrapped tightly around Love-a-Lot. She wore a soft red Christmas sweater that made her cheeks bright, even though the holiday was weeks away. I was reading my Peter and the Starcatchers book while eavesdropping.

"Sometimes," my father said, "I wonder if I'm going crazy. I actually pause and think—*Am I dreaming, or is she always going to be this way?*"

The words on the page blurred. It was the first time I could ever remember hearing even a smidge of doubt in his voice. I carefully glanced at Bitty while she drew pictures using new smelly markers Annabelle had given to her. Outright bribery had worked brilliantly on my little sister. I stole a peek as Annabelle reached over Vienna's sleeping body and patted my father's hand.

"You're so good to her," Annabelle said softly.

My father exhaled, his whole body wilting.

"I'm sorry you didn't know her before. She was the

small-town, sweet-tempered girl everyone adored—most of the time, anyway," he laughed. "She was incredibly bright, curious, and loved learning. She was a lot like Gwyn that way."

I let my heart soften when he spoke about her this way, imagining her as I had the day I read her notes in the piano book.

"She loved children and children adored her. She was never mean. Not ever . . . until after. We all wonder," my father said, "how such ugly things can come out of such a beautiful head."

"It's common," Annabelle ventured, "with her type of brain injury."

"Yes," he said. "There were bound to be impairments, but . . ." I was so absorbed in my eavesdropping my book fell slack in my lap.

"She was such a wonderful mother, just adored her babies. She was, simply, the most amazing woman I ever knew."

"I just don't know how you do it every single day," Annabelle said.

"A few months after it happened, I came home to Crow, to get some of Vienna's old things so she could see and remember. Gaysie Cutter came to see me."

"Gaysie?" Annabelle asked. "That . . . woman that brings her flowers?" I forgot to be discreet and looked up. I had never heard this story.

"I forget you're new to town. Yes, Gaysie brings her flowers because Vienna always loved them, for as long

as I can remember. Anyway, she told me to give it time,"
he said. "She said that perhaps my idea of love would be
something I had to unlearn and relearn."

"Unlearn and relearn," Annabelle repeated. "And . . .
have you?"

"Well, I'm a realist and an optimist at the same time.
A man of science, a man of faith. I know I must adjust my
vision and still be hopeful. My idea of the old Vienna might
be a fool's dream, but you see I have to try, don't you?"

"And if it doesn't turn out the way you hope?"

He drooped slightly. "I don't know what it feels like
not to be fighting for her. And yet for all the years of studying and learning and pushing, the brain is still such an
incredible mystery to me. The heart, it seems, is far easier
to understand."

Annabelle looked at my father like Willowdale looked
at me when I came toward her with an apple.

My father gently leaned over to Vienna. He gave his
wife a kiss.

"It's been a long time," Annabelle said.

"It has," he answered. "It has."

CHAPTER 25

IN EARLY DECEMBER, JUST AS Crow was moving into high gear for Christmas, there was a candlelight vigil held for Wilbur Truesdale. Bundled in down coats, hats, and gloves, we stood in front of the gazebo on the town green, right in front of a giant lifelike statue of Santa Claus and a drop box for children's wish lists. As light snowflakes fell, Pastor Weare suggested that instead of gifts we ask for Wilbur's safe return. Micah shut his eyes and wished so hard, his candle blew out.

I liked the gazebo, decorated with twinkling white lights. Music played day and night, and the festive feeling of Christmas was so strong and comforting that Bitty and I had begun to visit almost every day after school.

I didn't write a Christmas letter and put it in the drop box for the Crow Service Club to read. I had my heart set on the one present no one could know anything about: the fingerprint results. Though I was sure Lolly had delivered my letter to Georgia Piehl, I had heard nothing back yet. The waiting continued to be excruciating.

On Christmas Eve, Nana said she had something to tell me. I leaned forward expectantly, searching her hands for signs of a white envelope with Georgia Piehl's return address.

"Guinevere," Nana said gently, "Ms. Myrtle expired last night. Bless her heart."

"Expired," I repeated. Nana made Ms. Myrtle sound like a Diet Coke past its prime.

"She passed away."

"Passed away?" I knew what that meant, of course, I just couldn't believe it.

Nana looked at me anxiously. "She *died*, honey."

Even more unbelievably, I felt my eyes fill.

"Who found her?" I became all business, rubbing my eyes as if I were merely tired.

Nana sighed. "Don't worry about that."

"Probably Jimmy or Micah."

"Let's not worry about that right now, okay?"

"Was she sitting in her chair?"

"Gwyn, I don't know!"

"I bet she was. I thought she had *expired* in her chair last time I was there, and I had to check her pulse!"

Nana looked at me with her mastered horrified expression.

I chewed on my cuticles, itching to go over to Ms. Myrtle's and have a look around. Nana would never allow it . . . unless . . .

"What about my music?"

"We can find you a new teacher, honey."

"No, I mean the music I used at Ms. Myrtle's was Vienna's. And . . ." I let the statement sit there like a slow-roiling kettle of water.

"Your mother's music?" Nana asked, her voice higher. She wanted the music and she wanted it bad.

I made a move for my coat.

"No," Nana said, her worry lines deep with thinking. "We can't just take it."

"Nana, if we don't, it will get thrown out." Brilliant. She had me on my feet and buttoned up before I knew what hit me.

"Heavens, how will it look for you to go in and just take piano music?" She twisted her fingers into my coat.

"Don't worry," I said. "I'm good at this stuff."

She gave me a look. "Guinevere, sometimes you really do scare me." And then she practically pushed me out the door.

Out of habit I knocked on the door before I turned the handle. The living room was as cold as the outdoors.

I sniffed, wrinkled my nose at the old smell, and looked around, wondering if death stank. Ms. Myrtle's chair sat alone in the corner, and I felt a wave of wistfulness for the tales of my parents, and even of Gaysie, sorry I hadn't asked for more stories and information, sorry I would never get the chance. And even though she was a frightful woman, I suddenly missed that she wouldn't be watching us grow up or sticking her head out the door to tell me to "hush up!"

How did it happen, exactly? How does one just *expire?* I imagined checking for rigor mortis, taking Ms. Myrtle's pulse, and shaking my head sadly. *There was nothing we could do.* After bravely calling Officer Jake with a time of death, I would recount the details for my interview with the local paper.

I walked to the piano bench and opened it up. It was empty. I frowned.

Glancing down the hallway, I took a step. A bedroom door was ajar.

I gently pushed it open. It was a child's room, in colors of blue and green.

On the floor was an empty prescription bottle, cat food spilled beside it. There was a twin bed, a small bedside table, and a lamp. On the bedside table was a familiar-looking book—my *Huckleberry Finn* edition. I grabbed it, pulled it to my chest. I must have left it here and she kept it. Why?

There was a small creak of the floorboards. I paused to listen, my eyes searching frantically for a place to hide. I heard nothing, but suddenly . . . cold, icy fingers touched my neck as a zombielike voice said, "Guinevere." I felt hot breath on my ear. I swirled, and, using my best uppercut, connected with skin and teeth.

"Ow!" my assailant shouted, holding his face.

"Jimmy!" I yelled.

"You didn't have to hit me!"

"Ow," I said, shaking out my hand.

He licked his lips, and I saw a red and swelling upper lip, a tiny dribble of blood running down his chin.

"Oh, Jimmy, I'm sorry. . . ."

He roughly pushed my hand away. "It didn't hurt!"

"What are you doing here?"

"What are *you* doing here?"

"I came to get my piano music. Did you know Ms. Myrtle died last night?"

He sat down on the bed, crossly feeling his facial bones. "Of course I know."

"How?" I asked, disappointed.

"Because Gaysie came over and took care of it."

I gasped. "Took care of it! She buried her in the backyard?"

"Of course not!"

"Ms. Myrtle warned me—she said she knew things about Gaysie that could get her in trouble. . . ."

"Ah, the old crab apple," Jimmy said, stretching his arms out. "She's always hated Gaysie, even though Gaysie is the only one who took care of her."

"Took care of her?"

"Sure. Who do you think mowed her lawn? Usually me—Gaysie made me! Or took her trash to the curb or went grocery shopping or moved her mailbox so she could reach her mail? And all Myrtle did was crab crab crab."

"Oh."

"Gaysie tells us to remember she's bitter from grief, never got over what happened." Jimmy shrugged.

"Because Myron drowned?"

"Yeah."

"Well, it is suspicious, isn't it? Gaysie lives, Myron dies. Why's that? And before she died, Ms. Myrtle said to tell Gaysie she forgave her. I haven't told her that yet. I'm not sure she deserves forgiving."

Jimmy looked at me. "What happened wasn't Gaysie's fault, you know."

"Says Gaysie."

"No, Myrtle was just mad Gaysie survived and he didn't. Myrtle never forgave Gaysie, and Gaysie says Myrtle likely hated us for living too. That's why she was so mean. It's Ms. Myrtle who should have said sorry. I never saw Gaysie be anything but good to her—better than anyone else was!"

My mind was taking this in, imagining four kids on a sled, two of them going under the ice. One of them surviving. Gaysie taking care of Ms. Myrtle, while Ms. Myrtle did nothing but hate her for it.

"Before," I said. "When you said Gaysie *took care of it*? What did you mean?"

Jimmy exhaled impatiently. "Like she checked on Myrtle every night, and last night she was dead, just sitting in her chair. Gaysie called the police just like she was supposed to."

"Does she do other things she's *not* supposed to?"

He actually had the gall to laugh at me.

"This was her son's room," I said. "She had my book in here."

"Old Ms. Myrtle brought lots of things in here she thought he'd like. Sometimes, when I was over, she would make me sit and listen to her read, like I was Myron or something. It's actually a real good book. I like that Huck Finn." Jimmy had a mischievous look about him.

"Jimmy, why are you even over here?"

He shrugged. "Gaysie made me check on her all the time. She wasn't that bad once you got to know her. Anyway, I figure that now she's dead, someone's got to eat the food in the fridge."

"Jimmy!"

"What?"

I dropped it, given I was there to steal music. "Where's Micah?"

"Gone. They went to pick up Candy."

"Yum."

"No, Candy is Micah's grandma," he said, making a face. "Like you've never seen a grandma before."

"Why didn't you go?"

"She can't stand the sight of me, and the feeling's mutual!"

"Well," I said, back to business. "My piano music is gone."

He shrugged. "Maybe the Creepers stole it."

"The Creepers!"

He rolled his eyes. "Nah. Why would the Creepers want your old music? Maybe Gaysie has it."

"Gaysie Cutter!" I stomped my foot on the floor.

"To give to you," Jimmy said. "Why you gotta hate her so much?"

I gazed out the window at the large clementine house next door, feeling pulled in two different directions. I wanted to run home, but I wanted something more than I thought I had: Vienna's piano music. Was it in Gaysie's house? I had a great, curious longing to see what else I might find. Specifically, in Gaysie Cutter's bedroom, the one place in the house I'd never seen.

My father often spoke about the body's response to stress: fight or flight. It's a physiological reaction to a perceived attack or threat. Like encountering a large, black bear in the woods or Gaysie Cutter finding me rummaging through her drawers. But I took a cue from Jed St. Clair: fight.

We walked out the front door, down the snowy front steps, but I impulsively turned back and grabbed the piano bench.

"What are you doing?" Jimmy asked.

"Taking it home," I said, poofs of warm air coming from my mouth as I lugged the bench to my bike and set it down. "But first," I said, looking at Gaysie's house, "I'm going to go get my music." Jimmy smiled and punched me in the shoulder.

"Always knew you were my kind of girl."

"Ow."

"Now we're even."

I rubbed my shoulder as Jimmy leaned against a tree. Above him hung a sign that read, IF YOU CAN READ THIS YOU'RE IN RANGE. If Gaysie caught me, she'd probably shoot me on sight, no questions asked.

"That's not all you're looking for, is it?" Jimmy said.

"Nope. Let's go."

"Not me. I've been in that house plenty. Go through the side door and up the stairs."

"I can't go alone!" I protested.

"You need a lookout man. I'll keep watch for you, but you gotta be fast. They've already been gone a long time."

"Don't let me down, Jimmy Quintel."

A funny look crossed his face, like he was either touched or embarrassed.

"Go on."

I ran across the snowy yard and into the kitchen, dismayed at my wet footprints streaking across the floor. Scrambling up the stairs to the second floor, my heart pounded as I ran down the dark hallway, past Micah's room, where his purple cape was tossed on his bed instead of around his shoulders.

I slowed outside Gaysie's room.

I didn't know what to expect, but it wasn't what I saw. Gaysie's bedroom was Fairy Land. The walls were painted a pale lavender, sprinkled with a light smattering of glitter. The curtains were a breezy, white feminine, held back with fairy clips. The bed was on the left, a girly canopy, with the same breezy, white cascading curtains. The closet was open, two hangers swinging slowly back and forth. She had several pictures on her dresser. One was a picture of her with a man I assumed was her husband, a baby Micah on her lap. Gaysie looked so much younger and happier, like she hadn't yet spent ten years of her life working too hard on a farm.

I picked up a picture of four children around my age, realizing that two of them were my parents. There was another girl and a boy in the frame. I could tell the girl was Gaysie, before she had a long purple scar down her face. She had a wide, open smile like she'd been laughing. And the boy? It had to be Myron Myrtle, with the same red hair as his mother.

I held it, studying it too long, before picking up a framed picture of Wilbur on the Blue Mistress. "Wilbur Truesdale," I whispered. "Where are you?"

I went down on my knees when I saw a piece of white paper under the bed: sheet music. And there was more than had even been at Ms. Myrtle's—sheets and sheets of music. I opened a Brahms book filled with chords and notes, where Vienna's name was written in her flowery, adolescent cursive. I startled when Jimmy made a rooster call: Gaysie was home!

I scrambled to go, but stopped when I spied a worn navy suitcase under the bed. I crawled under and touched it, feeling something hard and then something crackly inside. Did I dare? I'd come this far, hadn't I? Holding my breath, I unzipped it.

Reaching in, my hand touched cold metal. Slowly, I pulled out an old metal pocketknife and examined it. It was engraved with three small initials. I gasped and dropped it quickly, realizing I was leaving my fingerprints behind.

I reached into the suitcase again, pulling out small, folded pieces of paper that looked like notes you'd pass back and forth in class. They were obviously old, with faded handwriting on the outside, soft from wear, and in a myriad of colors.

"Gwyn!" Jimmy whisper-yelled from outside.

Frantically, I unfolded a piece of paper. The handwriting was familiar, and I realized why: Vienna. The note was silly, about what she had eaten for lunch that day. I quickly folded it and opened another one, again from Vienna. This one was more personal, with drawings of hearts and the inscription *J.S. + V.E. = Love.*

Jed St. Clair and Vienna Eyre.

"Gwyn!" Jimmy yelled.

Panicking, I shoved the notes into the suitcase and zipped it halfway.

Suddenly, there was a small creak, like the sound of a chair shifting under weight. *Creak.* I stilled.

A car door slammed outside, female voices floated in through the window. My left hand steadied my shaking right one, which grasped for the pocketknife once again.

Creak.

"Who's there?" I whispered.

I glanced up from under the bed. The hangers were still slightly swinging. If I had been more Sherlockian, I would have realized sooner that swinging hangers likely meant someone had recently touched the hangers; and it hadn't been me.

A scream rose in my throat as I looked around me from under the bed. I saw no shoes, no sign of an intruder. The thought crossed my mind that maybe it was Wilbur—kept prisoner in Gaysie's room! Or maybe it was a Creeper, come to exact revenge!

"Jimmy!" I heard Micah yell.

I had to escape, and it wasn't going to be through the front door.

The zip line. I had to get to the zip line. A cold sweat of panic flushed over me. I hated heights.

Suitcases banged on the pavement. A high-pitched and unfamiliar female voice rose through the air.

Go!

I rolled out from under the bed, still holding the knife.

It was old and looked hard to open, but maybe it would scare away whoever was there.

Creak.

Someone was behind the door. I could hardly breathe as I reached forward. Behind the door was a wooden rocking chair, slightly rocking. *Creak.*

Sitting in the chair was not Wilbur nor a Creeper. It was Mr. Thompson's cat. At the mere sight, I sneezed, then slapped my hand over my mouth—sneezing spittle contained DNA!

The cat raised its eyes at me, steady and unblinking.

"If only you could talk, cat!"

Wind blew in from a cracked window, making the hangers swing ever so slightly once again. The wind, not an intruder, not Wilbur.

"Come on!" I said to the cat. "Gaysie's home!"

He went back to licking his fur. *Creak.*

"Fine!" I hissed. "Save yourself!"

I ran to Micah's room and looked out the window to where Jimmy was hanging in the tree, waiting for me.

I lifted the window, cold air blasting right through me.

"Took you long enough," he said, holding the zip line handle out to me. "Go!"

I looked down. "I can't do it."

"Jimmy?" Micah called from downstairs.

"My floor is wet!" Gaysie roared.

I fell through the window, grabbed onto the zip line handle, clamped my mouth and eyes shut, and flew like a crow, all the way across the backyard. It was the coldest and most exhilarating ride of my life. Unfortunately, the knife slipped from my waistline, slithered down my pant leg, and fell out onto the white snow. The line swung low and fast, and I landed in a heap.

But Jimmy was running toward me, the knife in his hand.

"Come on," he said. We ran until we found a barn and hid behind it.

I put my face in my hands. I'd mishandled evidence and hadn't even gotten Vienna's music. Plus Gaysie would likely find out I'd been there.

"Stop your cryin', will ya? I'll take care of it." Jimmy rubbed his head uncomfortably.

I stood and looked out into the cold, barren field. Then I grabbed the knife from him with my shirt, took a step, and threw it as far as I could.

"What are you doing?" Jimmy yelled, standing up. "I just got that back for you!"

"I . . . I . . . I don't know! We can't carry it around—it could be the murder weapon!" Even as I said it, I was kicking myself. If it was the murder weapon, there was likely still some evidence on it—and I was throwing it into a corn-field.

"I'm not thinking straight," I said.

"Yeah, no kidding."

We turned at the sound of Micah calling Jimmy's name again.

"I gotta go," Jimmy said, glancing out into the field. "Go home, Gwyn." He took off running toward Gaysie's.

"Thank you, Jimmy!" I called. "Are you gonna get in trouble?"

He turned all the way, running backward, his long Mohawk flopping in the wind, grinning.

"Did you forget or something? I was born lucky!"

I let him go, feeling sick at heart, still seeing the initials *J.S.C.* on the knife.

I went to bed preoccupied. I thought of all the mistakes I had made that day, all the evidence I'd abandoned. I'd left behind my bike, the piano bench, Vienna's music, a knife. Nana was not happy I'd come home empty-handed. What a debacle. I comforted myself with my father's mindset talk: My failures would make me better the next time—and there would be a next time! Also: Vienna's notes were old, that knife with the initials was too. My father probably didn't have anything to do with that knife or Wilbur's disappearance! Then again, I had thrown the evidence in a cow patty in some field down the road, so how could I be sure?

In the morning, it was Christmas.

When Bitty and I went outside to look for reindeer tracks, my bike was leaned up against the porch. Next to it was the piano bench filled with Vienna's music inside, a red ribbon tied around the middle. On top was a note: *To Guinevere St. Clair. Your Friend, Gaysie.*

"How sweet," Nana said, taken aback.

Sweet, I thought. Sure, Gaysie was all sweetness.

CHAPTER 26

I N NEW YORK WE CELEBRATED Christmas, but it was always at Vienna's care center with Lolly, nurses, other patients, and take-out Chinese. Christmas at Nana's was vastly different. We had a spectacular, real tree with decades' worth of homemade ornaments. There were cutout snowflakes on every window, and gingerbread houses made of real dough. Pies were in freezers with handpicked cranberries; apple-sausage stuffing recipes were tested multiple times while bread rose on the counter. Aromatic soups filled the air, and two giant turkeys thawed in the sink.

Nana bossed and fretted even when the food was ready, the bathrooms and bedrooms sparkled, and our hair was brushed until our scalps hurt so much we hid the brush. I intuitively knew that, above all, Bitty and I were Nana's most important showpiece, having been rescued from complete savagery.

I was still smarting about my mistakes at Gaysie's house, but since no one came to arrest me after I broke in, stole a knife, and threw it away, I tried my best to enjoy Christmas. The morning was filled with squealing from Bitty, Vienna, and me as we ransacked our stockings, found goodies Nana rarely let us eat, and tore open carefully wrapped presents.

Nana's face lit up as we fussed over our new baby dolls and buggies, even though I secretly thought I was too old for such gifts. She even smiled when we opened our father's gift: a chemistry set. I plotted making an elixir to hypnotize Gaysie for a confession.

When the doorbell rang, I raced to the door, yelling for my favorite auntie, Macy. This was a big moment for our family, my father said. After so many years, how would Vienna react to her siblings all together in the same house?

But Aunt Macy was not at the door. My face froze to see Officer Jake standing on the front porch. His hands were behind his back. I knew it—I was going to jail on Christmas morning.

"Cold out here," he said, lifting his eyebrows.

I remained a statue. Nana came around the corner.

"Jake!" she exclaimed. "Land sakes, Gwyn, let him in!" She hustled over, practically pushed me aside, and grabbed his arm. "I know you're here for the bread pudding," she said, wagging her finger, "but it isn't ready yet."

Officer Jake smiled. "You know me well, but actually, I came as a police officer." He glanced at me.

"Go in the other room, honey," Nana said. I stumbled around the corner but waited.

I heard whispering and Nana gasping.

"Found in the field down the road," Officer Jake said.

I squeezed my hands into tight, little balls and held my breath.

"Jimmy Quintel—you know that kid? Hangs out with your little girl and Gaysie's boy?"

Jimmy! That rat!

Jake's voice was low. "Here I was, driving down the road, about to go home this morning when I see him walking down the road with no coat, no gloves, just holding a knife. He tried to hide it behind his back. Wouldn't say a word."

Jimmy! That saint.

"Nancy, it's probably nothing, but it struck me as a little odd."

"Why's that?" Nana asked. Behind the wall I shook my head. Honestly, Nana was no kind of supersleuth.

"Well, it was Jed's knife. Why would he be walking down the road with it? And I just can't shake this feeling. . . . Nancy, we've got a missing man."

"What are you saying . . . Wilbur?" Nana said. "You think this knife . . . ? Oh my goodness!"

He calmed us both down (me behind the wall, hyperventilating) by saying, "No, no, no . . ." Officer Jake lowered his voice, but I did hear a name: "Gaysie Cutter."

Finally!

I slid down the wall and held my hands over my mouth. A shadow appeared over me. I looked up to see Vienna. She crouched awkwardly in front of me.

"Are you in deep doo-doo?" she whispered.

"Your granddaughter," I heard Officer Jake ask casually. "Was she with Jimmy Quintel yesterday?"

Oh, Nana. She was in a state!

I was neither handcuffed nor arrested, but I was briefly questioned by Officer Jake. I admitted to zip-lining out of Gaysie Cutter's house on Christmas Eve, but I gave up no other information. Prosecuting attorney Georgia Piehl would have been impressed at my resolve.

I pleaded the Fifth when asked about the knife.

"Guinevere!" Nana scolded.

"It's my constitutional right," I said, folding my arms tightly across my chest.

"If you know anything," Officer Jake said, "it's also your obligation to tell me."

I considered this. "Our agencies would benefit from more collaboration."

"Go on."

"I found the knife at Gaysie's . . . then lost it in the cornfield."

"Why did you take it?" Nana demanded.

"I thought it might provide insight into the investigation. I was wrong."

"Investigation?" Officer Jake asked.

"Wilbur Truesdale?" I reminded him.

Officer Jake blinked and tapped his foot on the ground. "I appreciate your interest, but you need to stop this meddling."

I opened my mouth, offended. *Meddling!*

To add further insult, I was then driven down to Gaysie Cutter's like a common criminal. I would have rather spent a hundred more Christmases in a smelly care center with a loud television blaring, bad Chinese food, and old people pinching my cheeks than have to face Gaysie!

"There you are!" Gaysie said like she had been waiting all morning for me.

I stood trembling, my eyes downcast, planning what my tombstone would say, wishing I had said my final good-bye to Willowdale.

"Gaysie," Nana said. "I'm just so mortified. . . ."

Gaysie held up her hand. "It is I who is mortified! Interrupting your Christmas morning this way. Oh, Nancy, I apologize for not asking your permission. Leaving a knife out for a mere child to take, how clearly irresponsible and neglectful." She smacked both of her cheeks. "I promise you this—it will never happen again!"

"Well . . ." Nana began to look uncertain.

"I got carried away. The knife was her father's. How could she resist it? He gave it to me many years ago as a sign of friendship. You *will* forgive me, won't you?"

"Of course, but . . ."

"Guinevere, make sure to check inside the piano bench. I left something else for you."

I perked up.

"Now, please go enjoy the day—it's Christmas!"

Back at Nana's I looked inside the piano bench, underneath all the music, and found an envelope containing all the notes that had been in the suitcase, notes to and from Gaysie, Jed, and Vienna. Silly, inconsequential notes I knew I would treasure my whole life. On the envelope Gaysie had written:

To Guinevere St. Clair. This is what I know of friendship: Hold on to the people you love. Know what they feel like, smell like, and act like, so that when they're not there to hold on to, you remember. G.C.

I tucked it under my mattress and tried to forget Gaysie Cutter had done something nice for me.

The doorbell rang a second time that morning.

"My favorite little girls!" my auntie Macy said, opening her arms. Coming in behind her was her husband, Uncle Bill, and their three boys, Peter, Tommy, and Patrick. Bitty and I quickly found them delightful as their dirt, farts, and *ABC* belching made Bitty and me the saintly grandchildren. Aunt Joanna was the next to arrive with her husband and new baby, followed by Vienna's other sisters, Margaret and Alana. Nana's face began to transform into pure joy.

At dinner, Vienna sat next to my father, looking bewildered by the commotion and company. Bitty sat next to me, while Aunt Joanna sat across the table and discreetly nursed her baby under a blanket.

"I would like to propose a toast," my father said, raising a glass of homemade apple cider.

"Joanna," Vienna interrupted. "What are you doing to *that baby?*"

"Love, this is *my* baby."

Vienna wrinkled her forehead and opened her mouth, but my father continued.

"We've had some big changes in our family," he said. "And I want to say thank you to Nancy, who has opened her home to us, who is helping me raise my girls, and does it all with grace and love. Here's to our wonderful Nana." Nana, her eyes happy and shiny, waved away the compliment.

"Who are your girls?" Vienna asked curiously.

"Guinevere and Elizabeth," I reminded her.

"And Gus," she said.

"That was the cat."

"Where is Gus?"

Uncle Bill abruptly picked up the cider with a "Hear! Hear!" as rolls were passed and buttered, and heaps of stuffing, turkey, and squash consumed.

Joanna leaned over and asked Bitty and me, "Have you made new friends?"

Bitty nodded shyly.

"Micah and Jimmy," I said, my mouth full.

"Micah is Gaysie's boy?" Macy asked. I choked on a piece of turkey, my heart thumping at the mere mention of her name. Nana pounded on my back.

"Where's Daddy?" Vienna asked, looking around the table. She sat back and folded her arms like a two-year-old.

"Eat up!" Nana said. "Would you like a roll? I know you love my rolls."

"I want my dad!"

My father opened his mouth.

"He's not here," Macy said.

"When is he coming home?" Vienna demanded.

I looked painfully at my father, willing him to lie, just this once. *He's at the store* was so much easier than *He's dead* on Christmas Day.

"He's coming," Joanna said, winking at Vienna. "You know Daddy's always late!" Contented, Vienna dove into her mashed potatoes.

"How is, uh, the place where you live, Vienna?" Joanna asked, trying to disengage her baby from nursing and onto her shoulder to burp.

Vienna stared. "I just totally saw your you-know-what!"

The boys lost it. They fell off their chairs, their minimal table manners completely dissolving. I covered my mouth to keep from laughing out loud. Bill rapped Peter's head and grabbed Tommy's collar, his face red, trying to stifle his laughter.

"The care center," my father said, "is wonderful! We're adjusting, aren't we?"

"Whose baby is that?" Vienna demanded.

"It's my baby." Joanna turned to my father. "Will it ever be possible for her to live here? With her family?"

"You had a baby?" Vienna's mouth dropped open in shock. "I'm so telling!"

My father patted Vienna's hand and smiled.

"No, it's really not possible," I answered for him.

My father and I locked eyes. I had told the truth. He knew it was the truth. But it hurt him for me to speak it.

Nana sat very still and didn't take another bite. I stopped laughing and glared at Joanna; if she knew her mother at all, it was the meanest question she could have asked.

"Disgusting," Vienna suddenly yelled, spitting out Nana's mustard pickles. "I hate these."

There was an awkward silence until Nana, surprisingly, laughed. "You've always hated my mustard pickles."

Late that evening I pushed Vienna's wheelchair back to the care center. It was cold and felt like snow was coming, sharp and expectant in my nose hair. Vienna's head bobbed in fatigue.

"Did you have fun?" I asked my father.

"Certainly a lively dinner conversation, Guinevere." He patted my hand.

"Guinevere?" Vienna said, lifting her head. "I love Guinevere."

Guinevere. Of course she was speaking of King Arthur's Guinevere. Even so, I felt my spirits lift at the thought of her naming me after someone she loved.

My father reached down to hold Vienna's hand while he walked.

I wheeled Vienna past the handicap space in the parking lot and leaned down.

"Want to walk the rest of the way?"

She looked up. "Who's handicapped?"

"You are, Vienna. You had a brain injury, remember?"

Her eyes drooped, and I pushed her up the sidewalk in the chair instead. While my father chatted with a night nurse, I leaned down. "Vienna," I whispered, "did you really always want a girl named Guinevere?"

She blinked several times, like she was thinking. I helped her onto her bed, tucking the covers under her chin, and found Love-a-Lot.

"Vienna," I whispered to ask her again. But her eyes closed. She was gone.

While Uncle Bill got the boys to sleep, and Nana was delivering pie to the neighbors, I lay at the end of my bed, eavesdropping once more with my superior hearing skills.

I heard my father settle comfortably into his favorite chair, closest to my room.

"Tell me how you're doing, Jed," Macy said.

"Quite well, thank you."

"We're family, Jed," Macy said. "Tell me the truth."

"I'm serious. I'm grateful. Goodness knows, the girls can use a mother figure in their life. In New York, Gwyn was practically raising Bitty. Now she has something else to fixate on." He laughed dryly and lowered his voice, but I heard the word "disappearance."

I slipped off the bed and sat by the door.

"Gwyn is obsessed with the whole thing."

"Of course she is, Jed," Macy said. "She's the perfect combination of her parents—an inquisitive little spunk who always needs to be solving a puzzle."

My father laughed. "Vienna did all right today, don't you think?"

"Depends on your definition of 'all right.'"

I heard the chair creak as he stood. "You know, I'm reading this fascinating book. It's groundbreaking, amazing stuff! The notion that the brain can't be fixed is a thing of the past."

"Jed." Macy's voice was gentle. "This isn't a science experiment. This is your life."

"Want a leftover turkey sandwich, a little cranberry sauce spread on the bread? That's really my favorite part of a holiday." I heard the fridge open. My mouth watered.

"There would be no shame," Macy said quietly. "Vienna . . ." I could almost see her swallow guilt as if folding something quickly and tightly in her mind. "I love my sister. I still grieve for her. But there was just too much damage. I'm so glad you've moved here, closer to Mom, and I'm sure it's wonderful for the girls, but, Jed, she's never going to be the Vienna she was before."

"We've had this conversation before, Macy. We have agreed to disagree. Now, sandwich or no? You're really passing up a good thing here."

"That conversation was years ago."

"We went through the scenarios. I made the choice. I'm not trapped."

"Jed, all this stubbornness, this constant waiting, is so hard—think of the girls."

"Don't you think I think of my girls!" My father's voice rose sharply. "Every waking moment—every thought and decision is with them in my mind. I want my girls to know their mother." His voice suddenly broke.

"Jed, there is nothing holding you back from moving on except for your sense of obligation to a woman who doesn't even know . . ."

"Vienna would know," my father interrupted. "I could never leave her, because she would know, Macy. That's why."

He loved her, of course he did. Even as it hurt him and cost him every minute of his entire life. And he loved me and Bitty. I knew in my heart that this love was the sole reason, the overriding, against-all-odds rationale for everything he did.

He was also right. Vienna *would* know. Jed St. Clair was a boy she would never forget.

I heard the front door open. Nana. I leaped silently onto my bed like a deft cheetah.

"You fixed yourself a sandwich!" she cried. "I could have done that for you, Jed."

"I'm particularly talented at making a leftover sandwich."

"Would you like some pie with that? A glass of milk? My goodness," Nana fussed. "Macy? What can I get for you?"

I crawled under my covers, silent and invisible, tucked safely next to a snoring Bitty, but it was hours before I was finally asleep.

I awoke before dawn, reaching under the mattress for the envelope of notes. I read them all by the light of my headlamp. There was one note I read over and over again.

It was from Vienna to Gaysie. She wrote that she was so sorry. The sledding trip, she said, had been her idea and she was so, so sorry.

I looked out the window. The wind had picked up, blowing cold, dry air through the trees, pulling leaves from branches. The sledding dare had been Vienna's idea. And she remembered. This was why, even now, she kept saying she was sorry. She hadn't been misremembering or confused. The revelation made me unsure of what to feel or do next except to open another note.

It was a flattened paper fortune teller made from red origami paper. I reconstructed it the best I could. The names Guinevere, Elizabeth, and Gus were written as fortunes. What had Vienna been doing when she wrote our names? Guinevere and Elizabeth were queens and maybe they were like Gus—pets—or . . . had she actually written down what she wanted to name her future children?

I put the notes back in the envelope and tucked them under my mattress as any good supersleuth would do, and lay down and cried myself back to sleep.

CHAPTER 27

I SAT AT THE BREAKFAST TABLE, harboring a great disappointment: Christmas had come and gone, and Santa had let me down; the fingerprint analysis had not come.

"Do you think we should consider having Vienna live here with us?" Nana had inevitably asked my father before leaving with Bitty to deliver a butter-pecan tart to the care center. Joanna's question at dinner had lodged its way into the overused guilt center in her brain.

My father, having already had the experience of living with my mother both before and after The Vienna Episode, wearily opened a brain journal. "Pass the sugar, please."

"Nana doesn't keep sugar on the table," I said. "But Vienna would sure change that!" I grinned at him.

He looked sideways at me, slowly chewing his sugarless cereal. "Hmmf."

"Daddy? Why did you give Gaysie a pocketknife?"

He put down his paper.

"Because I thought Gaysie might like it. She did, too, used it all the time."

"When did you give it to her?" I held my breath. And how exactly had Gaysie *used it all the time*?

"I gave it to her when she was in the hospital, after the accident. A very long time ago."

"Oh."

"You look disappointed. Were you expecting a different answer?"

Actually, I was relieved. His answer seemed to lessen the likelihood of my father and Gaysie in cahoots over Wilbur's so-called disappearance. At least, when it came to the murder weapon.

But I had another question.

"She gave me an envelope full of notes from Vienna and Gaysie and you. I found a paper fortune teller with three names on it: Guinevere, Elizabeth, and Gus."

My father laughed. "Gus was her cat."

"I know." My nose wrinkled. "Did I used to be a pet, too?"

"Oh no. She always used to talk about the names of her children, but she was particularly stuck on her two favorite queens—Guinevere and Elizabeth."

I couldn't help but smile. I really was named after a queen, not a pet gerbil!

Since he was talking, I pressed my luck.

"Daddy? One more thing. Won't you please tell me about the sledding accident, and I promise I'll never ask again!"

He exhaled loudly. "What would you like to know?"

"Well, I think I know it was Vienna's idea to go sledding down that hill."

He took his glasses off and put them on the table. Finally, he nodded.

I clutched at my heart, feeling for my mother in a way I hadn't in a long time. She must have felt so guilty.

"But that doesn't make it Vienna's fault," my father said. "We all wanted to do it; she was just our leader. No one could have known what would happen. It was a very unforeseen and unintended consequence."

"And there were four of you on a sled?"

"Yes."

"Once you said Gaysie saved you," I said slowly.

"Gaysie must have seen something—she pushed Vienna and me off the sled right before hitting the ice. I don't know why or how, but she did. Heroic, I'd say, but no one saw it that way in the end, because someone died."

"Why didn't she save Myron, too?"

"Oh, Guinevere." He put his hands to his face. "If you could have only seen her face when she found out he was gone. . . . It's not something any child should feel responsible for. She couldn't reach him. It was a terrible, terrible time."

"So she didn't kill him on purpose?"

"Of course not! We were all responsible and yet we were kids. It was an accident. Accidents happen. I have tried since that point, to make something good come of it. I have tried very hard to be a good friend to Gaysie. She, in turn, has been one back. Someday," he said, "she will tell you the whole story."

"What whole story?"

"You've surely heard the rumors of her death. When she was pulled from the water along with Myron, she wasn't breathing. But here she is, living and breathing, with an experience that changed her life."

"Like dying and seeing ghosts?"

"Like I said. Someday she'll have to tell you the whole story."

"Daddy!"

He put his glasses back on and went back to reading the paper. "It's her story, not mine."

"Can I go to Micah's and ask right now?"

"No. His grandmother is visiting."

"I want to meet her."

My father grinned like *Alice in Wonderland*'s Cheshire cat. "I'm sure you will. She's a real treat."

"What's so great about her?"

"'Great' would not be my first choice of words. Gaysie is remarkable in many ways, but most of all because she's refused to become her mother."

"Well, then, her mother must be *real* bad!"

"I didn't say Gaysie never made mistakes."

I raised my eyebrows.

My father put his paper down again. "Who brings your mother flowers every week?" he challenged.

"Gaysie."

"Who takes care of your friend Jimmy? Who feeds, teaches, and keeps him safe?"

"Gaysie."

"Do you think there was anyone else looking out for Ms. Myrtle?"

I went silent.

"She has a gift, of finding the marginalized, the lost and broken . . . She's always stood up for the underdog. That's what you and Gaysie have in common."

Horror-struck, I made a face.

"You've tried to stand up to those boys you call Creepers. You're trying to find Wilbur." I gave him a quick look, but he kept going. "You stick by your mother and wouldn't let a gnat harm your sister. And what do you know of that Micah?"

"That he's the kindest boy I know."

"Exactly," my father said. "And you can thank Gaysie Cutter for that."

CHAPTER 28

WAITING TO GET DOWN THE street to Micah's again was a torturous twenty-four hours. I stewed about our Gaysie conversation. I knew from the minute I met her that Gaysie was bad, but . . . was she also good? Could a murderer still do all those nice things my father talked about?

It was the return letter from Georgia Piehl that pushed me over the edge. It sat plain among the red-and-green Christmas cards, in a long white envelope. When I touched it, it was still cold from sitting in the mailbox. It smelled gloriously of fresh paper and answers to questions.

I waited to read it by tucking the letter into the middle of my newly-won-back Huckleberry Finn book as Bitty and I ran all the way down Lanark Lane to Micah's. It was my finest hour of self-control. After all, inside was the likely key to my investigation. Were we able to get any usable prints off the Blue Mistress? Were they Gaysie Cutter's? And if they were, would I be one giant step closer to having my direct link?

Wearing a pink bandanna and pirate eye patch, Micah was in the front yard, building a snowman. He waved excitedly when he saw us just as Jimmy handcrafted a snowball and bombed it all over my face.

"Cod face!" I yelled, ice and snow stinging my skin and half blinding me. "I was going to show you something, but now I won't."

"It's about the case!" Bitty said, trying to wipe snow off my eyelids.

"What case?" Jimmy asked.

"*Our* case!" I said bitterly, spitting icicles out of my mouth. I pulled out the letter and waved it around. "From Georgia Piehl."

"The fingerprint lady?" Micah asked.

"The prosecuting attorney!" I said hotly.

"Let's go get some hot chocolate first," Micah said. "And you can meet my grandma—"

"Oh, Grandma," Jimmy groaned. We entered Gaysie's kitchen. I gulped, wiping snow off my eyelids and wondering if Gaysie would mention my previous break-in now that no cops were around.

"Hello there!" Gaysie said, standing in front of the stove, a picture of domesticity. It reminded me of late summer, when Wilbur would come to drink coffee with Gaysie and the kitchen was roasting, but cozy.

"She's wearing an apron," I whispered to Micah.

"Take off those wet boots and sit," Gaysie said, casting a sidelong glance at me. "I prefer we not run through the kitchen in this house with wet boots on."

I gulped.

"Put your mittens on the wood stove. Hot chocolate?"

I nodded uneasily. She was unusually amiable today.

I'm not anyone's dishrag! I remembered her yelling

once when Jimmy left his dishes in the sink.

But the greatest shock was when Gaysie turned around. Under her apron, her clothes were all wrong. They were ironed or something. Even her face looked different, with some poorly applied blush, her hair shorter and sprayed stiff.

"Guinevere and Elizabeth," she said, setting down steaming cups of cocoa, complemented with sprigs of something green floating on top. "Rosemary," she announced. "Girls, I'd like you to meet my mother, Mrs. Delacroix."

At that moment, a woman swept into the kitchen. She was petite with short, platinum-blond hair and a bleach-white smile, but I suspected possible veneers. Her light eyes were juxtaposed between pencil-thin brows and thickly coated black eyelashes. She looked nothing like Gaysie. With a tilt of her head she swished into the room, wearing tight white spandex, carrying with her an overpowering scent of an English garden. I sneezed.

"Bless you, darlin'," the woman said. Gaysie smiled pleasantly, but her jaw was perceptibly tighter.

"I'm Mrs. Delacroix, but you can call me Candy. I'm Micah's grandmother." Candy patted Micah's pink bandanna atop his head and snapped his pirate eye patch before turning to me and holding out her ring-adorned hands. She motioned me closer. I held my breath, waiting for, *The better to eat you with, my dear.*

Bitty, who would usually be clinging to the back of my coat, stood bravely beside me. I smiled inside. Perhaps an unintended consequence of knowing dear old

Gaysie had been toughening Bitty up. When we were within arm's length, Candy reached past me and touched Bitty's cheek. Her breath reminded me of stale cigarettes, and her red lipstick bled into the cracks around her lips, like Dracula.

"Who wouldn't know this face?" she murmured. "I'm so glad Micah's bringing home friends," she said, eyeing Micah's leg warmers and outerwear. "Darlin', what in the world are you wearing? Is that a *shawl*?"

"He can wear what he wants," Gaysie said, stealing a pointed glance up and down her mother's white spandex and plunging neckline.

I danced a little impatiently, the letter practically burning a hole through my hand.

Gaysie handed Candy a knife and a green pepper. "Would you please?"

Candy smiled at me, the knife in her right hand. "So. You're the girl who's friends with these boys."

I nodded.

"Men. Full of tricks and lies. I've known my share. My last husband—well! I could tell you stories."

"Mother," Gaysie said dryly. "You forget who this child belongs to."

"Oh, that's right!" Candy said, beginning to slice the green pepper with hard, choppy strokes. "The daughter of Jed St. Clair. I always said that man could sell ice to an Eskimo." She smiled. "You should be proud of your daddy. Jed actually made something of himself. People round here are content to be ignorant their whole lives. My Gaysie was so smart, she went off to college too, but . . . ," she said, her knife pausing. "Never finished."

"Had the farm to run," Gaysie said.

"I guess you do the best you can," Candy said. "Unfortunate that your Wilbur chose to disappear just when winter was coming." I watched Gaysie carefully. She gave nothing away.

"Well, it was so good to meet you," I lied, stepping away and taking Bitty's hand.

"Oh, cupcake, the pleasure was truly mine." Candy bowed toward me as I pulled Bitty out of the kitchen.

Micah wriggled out of his grandmother's grasp, and Jimmy followed after us, jumping up and hitting the doorframe on his way out.

I heard Candy say, "I have a theory that that boy is actually a monkey!"

We were down the driveway when I remembered I had forgotten my new hat.

I raced back to the door, thinking I could do a fireman-crawl across the kitchen floor to get it undetected. Instead, I stood unmoving at the sound of Gaysie's voice.

"Mother." Her voice was low and enunciated, a tone that sent shivers of fear clear through me. The room went still. "My boy loves his shawl. He knitted it himself, and if you ever, and I mean *ever*, speak to Micah that way again. If you ever so much as hint at his worth in such a way, I swear upon the feet of our Holy Father." I peeked through the doorframe and saw Gaysie bent down toward her mother's ear. "You will not step back into this house."

In her hands was the cutting knife. "Ever."

I left my hat on the floor, running fast to the playground, and climbed way up high into the rocket slide, where Bitty, Micah, and Jimmy sat waiting for me.

"Your mother is going to kill your grandmother," I said to Micah.

"Ah, that's old news," Jimmy said.

From off the main road came the Creepers. They slowed at the playground, not getting off their bikes. Jimmy put his fingers to his lips. The Creepers, not seeing us up in the slide, threw some rocks at the school before heading around the side.

"Ready?" I whispered, exhaling. I pulled open the letter, tiny bits of envelope scattering in the wind.

Bitty and Micah squeezed in closer to me, while Jimmy folded his arms. I began to read aloud.

> *Dear Guinevere,*
> *My name is Maggie Cho. I write on Ms. Piehl's behalf as she is very busy getting ready for trial. Ms. Piehl says to tell you how delighted she was to receive your letter and how much she's missed your imagination.*
>
> *Your questions are intriguing. I assume you are getting ready for a mock trial of your own or some sort of reenactment for school? You used the term "crime scene," and I'm curious what kind of scene you are re-creating. Nothing too bloody and scary, I hope!*

"Crime scene!" Micah exclaimed. "What the heck did you say?" I read on.

> I received the fingerprint sample you sent, and here's what I can tell you:
> Fingerprint evidence is extremely unreliable. Oftentimes the judge will not even allow it into the courtroom. That being said, you are right, fingerprint samples should be taken as soon as possible before destroyed or contaminated.
> The fingerprints you sent me aren't exemplar prints, meaning you didn't deliberately take them from your suspect like a school would, to hire teachers. Exemplar are easiest to see and label because the suspect is giving you a full set and carefully rolling a finger from one ridge to the other. What you sent are latent prints.
> In forensic science, latent prints are left behind accidentally, and you're lucky to get a full print of even one finger. You sent partials. A full print would hold up far better in your court scene.

"Is she for real?" Jimmy asked.

> Latent prints are left from touching something with sweat, skin oil, ink, paint, dirt, or blood. But there is great room for error when

making comparisons because the fingerprint
was taken under uncontrolled conditions. The
grooves and ridges of a print contain much less
clarity.

    I liked the drama you added by sending the
partial print in blood. That was something we
could pick up in the lab.

We all gasped. I lowered the letter and thought back to
the last day we had seen Wilbur alive. A very clear picture
of Gaysie sitting in the rocking chair came to mind. The
blood on her clothes, the wet laundry Micah had been made
to hang after she killed the floatie—with a knife! The hair
on my arms stood straight up.

"Blood! What's she talking about—blood!" Micah cried.

I began bouncing up and down. A bloody print was a
lead, wasn't it? Now, if I could get that blood tested, we
would even have DNA. . . .

I skipped ahead, reading to myself while Jimmy calmed
Micah down.

    Congratulations. Your suspect's prints from
the tractor did not match the prints on the
milking pail you provided. However, they were
in the national database and we were able to
make a match.

I almost dropped the letter.

"Gwyn?" Jimmy asked.

My entire body stopped working for a moment. My blood felt as cold as ice.

The fingerprints on the tractor were not Gaysie Cutter's. Ms. Cho wrote that my suspect was someone else. His name: *Jedidiah St. Clair*.

It couldn't be.

I had pulled a thread, and the whole thing was unraveling in the worst possible way.

"What's it say?" Jimmy demanded.

"I . . ." I shook my head.

"Blood!" Micah wailed. "Gwyn, what did you do?"

"Nothing! You were with me, remember?"

"You were the one that climbed on the tractor, Gwyn. Why didn't you tell me there was blood, Gwyn? Gwyn! Oh . . ."

Bitty began to cry as the tension between us escalated.

"It was dark. . . ." I stood and decided right then and there to come out with my theory, even if I didn't have the evidence I needed. Even if the letter pointed to my own father, I knew it wasn't him. "There was blood on Gaysie the day Wilbur disappeared and she was in the rocking chair!" I burst out.

"She cut her finger off," Jimmy said. "Of course there was blood. She'd been working . . ."

"Why was there blood on the steering wheel if she was lifting it from the bottom?"

"Wilbur wouldn't let her drive the tractor! He wouldn't let anyone on the Blue Mistress!" Micah looked stunned. Yes, it was a terrible, sickening feeling to be suspicious of someone you loved more than anything in the world.

"It's okay, Micah," Bitty said, patting his arm, looking scared.

"Well, what did the letter say about the prints?" Jimmy asked.

"They couldn't match our print," I said weakly. "My experiment didn't work." Had Georgia Piehl ever been in such a mess? Compromised? Forced to recuse herself?

"That's it?" Jimmy asked, his eyes narrowing.

I nodded and shoved the letter into my pocket, hoping they would never ask me about it again. There was a national database of fingerprints. My father had prints in the system because he was a dentist. He had worked in hospitals. But how and why had they gotten onto the tractor's steering wheel? He didn't even know how to start a tractor . . . did he? Then again, he'd grown up in Crow. Why *wouldn't* he know how to drive a tractor? His prints had to be a mistake, a coincidence of some sort. My father was not involved. He was not a killer—he liked Wilbur! But by all accounts, so had Gaysie.

"I don't believe you," Jimmy said, making a grab for the letter.

"Stop it!"

"Show me!" Jimmy made another grab, and this time he ripped half of it from my hands, tearing the letter clear across the middle.

"Oh, Jimmy," Micah said.

Furiously, I tore my half—the part with the true evidence—into a hundred pieces.

"There!" I shouted. "Now there's no evidence to convict anyone!"

"Gwyn, what—" Jimmy began.

I pulled Bitty with me and we slid down the rocket slide—right into the tire of the Creeper of all Creeps, Travis Maynard. His buckteeth were particularly dirty today.

"Hey, watch it," he said.

Bitty and I jumped over the tire, with Micah and Jimmy right behind us.

"Get out of here, Travis," Jimmy said.

"What's your problem, Quintel?"

"Micah and I decided it's time to give it up!" Jimmy said, ignoring him and following after me as I hurried away. "Gaysie didn't do it, and now you know it's true too."

I turned, hands on my hips.

"No, we're not finished yet."

"Yes, we are!" Jimmy took a step toward me. "Micah, you've got to take a side here."

Travis and his Creeper gang were now on the perimeter, lurking like hungry sharks.

Micah's eyes were as big as his glasses, wide and worried. "But, Jimmy, we're the four musketeers. It's all for one and one for all!"

"Fight, fight, fight, fight," Travis began to chant.

"Don't you care?" I spat out. "Wilbur was your neighbor and friend! He lived in the backyard and he's gone and the suspect is right in front of your face and you can't see it."

"Now he really can't." Travis Maynard lifted the glasses

off Micah's face from behind and threw them to another Creeper.

"Give 'em back!" Bitty shouted.

They laughed, playing keep-away.

I lunged for the glasses, tackling Travis Maynard to the ground just as he caught the glasses in his hands. I heard glass crunching beneath my stomach. Travis and I rolled apart as we stared at the broken glass. I felt my stomach for mortal wounds.

"Go!" a Creeper shouted. The cowards were up and running. I picked up Micah's very crooked frames, the glass in the right lens shattered.

"I'm so sorry," I said, holding them out to him. "I was trying to help."

He took them sorrowfully, and put them back on his face, squinting. "I know."

"But sometimes when you try to help, you ruin things," Jimmy said.

I ran away then, only slowing up for Bitty to catch me.

"Are we all still friends?" Bitty asked, looking up at me.

"Just run," I said. "It will feel better if we run." A herd of cows noticed us and began running beside us, inside their fence.

"Moo!" Bitty yelled delightedly back at them. "Moo!"

I thought that life would be so much more simple if I were a cow and not a lead investigator on the verge of losing her only case—and her only friends.

CHAPTER 29

PERSEVERATION WAS COMMON WITH A brain injury. It meant that Vienna repeated the same things over and over. Imagine having the most annoying parrot in the whole world, and you'd have Vienna living at your house. The only upside was the distraction from Micah and Jimmy being angry with me. In addition, Nana had gotten wind of me breaking Micah's glasses, and I was working off my debt with chores to help pay for a new pair.

My aunt Joanna's questions had guilted Nana into having Vienna for a few overnight visits. We had tried this twice before with Lolly doing double shifts, in New York, and it had been a disaster. But sometimes, my father said, love makes you do a lot of crazy things.

"This is my room," Vienna said, standing under the white doorframe of my bedroom as I washed the windows.

"Actually," I said, "it's mine now."

"This is my room."

You see, Vienna's brain didn't know how to get past something she didn't understand, so she said the same repetitive phrase over and over and over again.

"This is our room now," I said. "You get to share with Daddy."

"Daddy?"

"Jed. You get to share with Jed."

"Jed! Where's Jed?"

"He'll be home soon. Emergency dental work."

"Ohhhh."

She stared at me before looking around the bedroom again.

"Do you want to wash windows? It's so fun," I said, thinking of Tom Sawyer's brilliance. "In fact, it's a great privilege!"

"This is my room," Vienna said, not taking the bait.

I took her by the arm and led her down the hall to get her mind off it. She walked in small, shuffled steps, leaning on me for support.

My father had set up his room so Vienna slept in his bed and he slept on a cot next to it. Next to the cot and bedside table was his large pile of reading material. All on the brain, of course. The only decoration he'd bothered to bring from New York was a large Japanese pot that looked broken and glued back together. It was a shiny blue-green, and very unique, unlike anything else I'd ever seen.

"Vienna," I said, "tell me about Gaysie."

"Gaysie," she said. "I like Gaysie."

"Why?"

"I'm hungry," she said.

"Focus, Vienna! What do you know about Gaysie?"

"Oh, she's fun! But she can't run very fast and she has a big bottom."

"Vienna, remember Wilbur?"

Vienna lit up. "I like Wilbur!"

"Did Gaysie like Wilbur?"

"One time she stole his tractor!"

"*Stole* it?"

Vienna broke into peals of laughter, something I hadn't heard her do for a very long time. "Actually, it was my idea! I am a good driver—a better driver than Gaysie! Can we go ride it now?"

"No! Because we can't find Wilbur—he's gone."

"Gus is gone too," she said sadly. "Gaysie buried him."

"Where?!"

"In the backyard." Vienna's voice became a conspiratorial whisper. "She says not to tell!"

Then she tilted her head at me. "She's not supposed to keep burying things."

"Does she bury people, too?"

"She does?"

I sighed. How much could I really trust anything Vienna said?

She peered at my eyes. "Are you sad?"

"No! Just forget it."

"Where's Jed?"

"Work."

"I'm hungry."

"Vienna, I'm going to tell you a secret."

She leaned closer and clapped her hands. "Oh goody!"

"And I know you'll keep the secret because you won't remember this conversation in five minutes."

"Okay."

"Gaysie killed Wilbur," I whispered.

Her eyes became wide circles. "She did?"

"I'm sure of it. I just can't prove it."

Vienna scrunched up her forehead. "Me neither."

She smacked her lips. "I'm hungry."

I fell asleep on my father's bed that night, Bitty and Vienna flanked on either side of me. I awoke to Vienna talking to my father.

"Jed?"

"Be quiet," I said sleepily. She stopped momentarily before resuming.

"Jed?" I tried to cover the noise with an extra pillow over my head.

It was quiet. For ten blissful seconds.

"Jed?"

I heard the soft snore of my father on the cot next to us.

"Jed?

"Jed?"

"What? What is it?" my father asked.

Later my father would tell me that she liked to sit up and stare at him until he answered.

"Jed . . . Jed?

"Are you going to take me to breakfast?"

"Mmm."

"Where's Gwyn?"

I opened my eyes.

"Jed?"

"Shhh."

"Jed? What's for breakfast . . . Jed?"

All. Night. Long.

She didn't say my name again.

The next day we were all tired, and nobody brought up moving Vienna back home with us full-time. Not Nana. Not even my father.

On Saturday, Bitty and I fed Willowdale some hay, checked her water, and headed to Micah's house, hoping for a truce. It was the Saturday before going back to school, and we had planned on going along to take Candy to the bus stop. Nana was too busy with Vienna to have objections.

Candy was still alive when Bitty and I arrived, having survived Gaysie's threat, but there was a gulf of tension the size of the Mississippi between us all.

Gaysie loaded Candy's luggage on the top rack of her old gray station wagon, the back bumper tied on with bungee cord, the left side flopping up and down and hitting the road like a loud, clunking concerto. There was not a car in the world that was louder or uglier than that one.

Candy sat up front, her heavy perfume wafting to the back, making me feel nauseated. She began to talk about the long hours she would have to endure on the bus and the smelly, working-class citizens she was bound to encounter.

"Remember, Mother, we grew up on a pig farm."

Candy sniffed. "I refuse to dignify that comment. Do you ever find," Candy said, turning to me, "that sometimes three's a crowd?"

"No," I said. "It's really four, with Bitty."

"The first time I met Jimmy was when he jumped on me like a wild wildebeest," Candy said.

Jimmy was giving Candy the most spectacular silent treatment, looking out the open window like Candy wasn't even talking, his Mohawk blowing all over the place.

"He fell out of a tree. He didn't jump on you," Gaysie said. "You wouldn't guess it, but that Jimmy's got a heart of gold."

Micah patted Jimmy on the shoulder, and Jimmy smiled.

This was true. I gave Jimmy credit for Micah's survival. Micah wouldn't be standing with both legs tucked into silver, curly laces or wearing purple capes or bunny foo foo sweaters if it wasn't for Jimmy. And for the first time, really, I realized what Micah did for Jimmy. Micah was soft and sweet, and I think he kept Jimmy from being too hard. I thought of the handprint on his face. Maybe Jimmy would have become a Creeper without Micah. I dismissed the thought that Gaysie had played a role in any of Jimmy's better qualities.

"Guinevere is a girl who appreciates her friendships," Gaysie said. "I like that!" She proceeded to cross three lanes of traffic without looking, the entire highway laying on their horns in protest. My stomach lurched.

Upon arrival, Gaysie opened her mother's door. Candy carefully poofed her platinum hair and walked to the back windows.

"Micah, I love you," Candy called, blowing kisses.

"Bye, Grandma," he called, waving.

"You remember, Micah," she yelled. "You remember

that YOU. ARE. A. BOY. Don't you forget it!" she said, pointing her long finger at him.

Micah looked confused.

We watched Candy give Gaysie a hug, then suggest a new hairstyle, before she walked away in her leopard-print purse and white spandex pants, leaving Gaysie standing alone on the curb in her ratty jeans and flannel shirt. A stranger mother-daughter match I never saw. Gaysie got in, the car groaning under her weight. She rubbed her reddish-purple scar before finally putting the car into drive.

"Don't forget Micah," Jimmy cackled, punching him in the shoulder. "You. Are. A. Boy."

"Ouch," Micah said, rubbing his shoulder. "I know I'm a boy! Why does she keep saying that?"

"Your grandmother has very little imagination, that's why," Gaysie said. She glanced at me. "You're looking a little green—sit in the front." I climbed over, sitting as far away from her as possible, and held my stomach. A mile from the bus station Gaysie exhaled deeply and drove with her eyes closed a frighteningly long time until roaring, "Hallelujah! She's gone!"

I had a revelatory thought: Between Candy, Gaysie, and Vienna, maybe Vienna wasn't such a bad choice after all.

"My," Gaysie said. "What an eventful day. Jimmy, you get your body parts back in the car this very moment!" But I hung my head out the window as Gaysie laughed. "Oh, oh, oh," she said. "Stop it! I have to pee. What in the world will you tell your nana?"

"I don't think we should tell her anything," Bitty said.

This made Gaysie laugh harder until she suddenly swerved over to the side of a long road flanked by cornstalks, her face deadly serious. I looked around us. We were truly in the middle of nowhere.

I stole a glance at Gaysie, my hand over the door handle.

"I invited her to come, you know," Gaysie said. "Because there comes a time in your life when you have to make peace with your past, good or bad, all of it.

"My mother was not a kind person," Gaysie said, hitting the steering wheel, her knuckles white. "But I have to make peace with it, and you know what? I think I might almost be there. Thank you, Guinevere, for helping me do that!"

"Me?"

"Why, yes, your moving here has brought back memories of a wonderful time of life for me. I've realized that I'm actually quite a lucky woman. Not everyone is given the gift of friendship."

I couldn't help but be a little bit pleased. But I also felt a little sad for her, and suddenly proud of the way my father not only defended Gaysie Cutter, but befriended her—as misguided as he might be.

She inhaled and shook out her big arms like she was shaking off fleas. "Guinevere, I'd advise you not to wait as long as I did."

"For what?"

She raised an eyebrow. "To make things right in your heart. Life doesn't always wait for your own personal timetable."

Gaysie started the car again and swerved onto the dirt road. "My mother. Even Wilbur couldn't stomach her," Gaysie said. "Great balls of fire, I miss that man."

I glanced at the backseat, where Jimmy, Micah, and Bitty sat. We had not spoken of Wilbur since our fight, but it was coming to a head—I could feel it. Like Gaysie said, life doesn't always wait for our own personal timetable.

CHAPTER 30

FOR DAYS AFTER CANDY LEFT, Gaysie sat in the old living room rocking chair. It was just like when Wilbur disappeared. Back and forth she rocked, not saying a word, as if she were rocking all of the sad and bad out of her life. She kept her hands in her lap, her eyes closed, her lips pursed tightly together, and every once in a while she would whisper vehemently, "I am *not* my mother. I am *not* my mother!"

Micah said Gaysie always needed about a week of Candy detox. After the detox Gaysie shook herself out like a dog, rose from the rocking chair, and looked out the window.

"Spring is coming early," she said, eyeing the sky. "And so is rain." She turned around to face us. "Guinevere, one of the things your mother likes most is rain. When it starts, you should take her out to play."

She turned to Micah and Jimmy.

"And to you I issue a warning! Once the rain begins, you are *not* to go down to the creek, do you hear? I've been having dreams again. As you well know, children die from being stupid." She gave us all her hairy eyeball until we nodded. "This town is not at all prepared for a flood, and it could well be the apocalypse!" We watched

Gaysie march away toward town in search of sandbags.

Much as I hated to admit it, Gaysie was right: Spring was early and the rain came. I loved rain like I loved mysteries, Willowdale, and textbook anatomy—it was that good. We stomped, jumped, and waded in large puddles in the backyard. We made forts to protect us from the impending apocalypse.

Gaysie was also right about Vienna liking rain. Many an afternoon, my father brought her to play with us outside, and this is when I enjoyed her most. Dancing in the rain, I could almost see her more as my friend, not my mother. She laughed more, and though her movements were clumsy, she was playful and funny, not yelling and irritable. Her blond curls became heavy and longer with dripping water, making her look like an impish elf with an uncanny resemblance to Bitty. Also, for the first time, Bitty had school friends over. Since I knew I'd always have favorite-playmate status, it was a nice sort of relief. Watching us, my father looked almost completely happy.

Not everything about the rain was peachy though. Rain melted the snow so quickly that the frozen ground couldn't soak it up fast enough. And when it began to flood, nobody talked about anything else but rain, rain, rain.

When I complained of the monotonous rain chatter, my father reminded me that Crow was a farming community whose survival depended on weather cycles.

Finally, when Bitty and I were drawing up Noah's ark plans, the rain eased. We then had a new problem: The Crow River began to rise.

"Remember when school was canceled because of the flood?" Vienna asked Nana.

"Yes," Nana said, wringing her hands, watching out the window.

"I remember too," my father said. "Bad business. Whole farms were washed away. Doesn't happen often, but it looks like this might be our year."

I began sleeping with two life jackets under my bed.

School was canceled. Shops emptied, dental appointments were dropped, even Petey's Diner had a sign that said GONE FISHIN', which was funny since Petey always said he was too large to sit in a boat. Sandbags arrived from Des Moines, and when we ran out of sandbags, and the fields next to the river began to fill with water, the governor announced on television that Iowa was in a state of emergency. Nana did not share my excitement.

Like Gaysie, she spent hours watching the river out her kitchen window. One evening Gaysie came to check on us, to make sure we were prepared for the end of the world. She stomped her feet happily on Nana's entryway floor, dirt and water splattering on the floor and walls before Gaysie went on to the next neighbor. My eyes burned after her. The flood may have been a diversion, but I hadn't forgotten about Wilbur, like she apparently had. Was she joyful or worried that evidence was being washed away or washed ashore from her backyard?

"Gaysie Cutter has always done best in a crisis," Nana said, looking after her. "I don't know what most of the people in this town will do if their fields wash away, but Gaysie is not someone I worry about. I'll say this: Gaysie Cutter's a survivor." She sighed to indicate a dire situation and to spur my imagination into a wild torrent; our whole town was going to be washed away in one big tsunami wave.

Without any prodding from my father, Nana stiffly suggested we all go to church together, including Vienna.

"Should I bring the duct tape?" I asked.

"Guinevere!"

Nana wasn't the only one thinking of church. The entire town showed up except for one person: Gaysie. I was sorely disappointed, as her dramatic way of "channeling the Lord" was far more entertaining than Pastor Weare's.

"Why is everyone here?" I whispered to Nana. We'd gone to church a few times, but never with so many others.

She looked down at me in surprise. "The flood, that's why." She used a hymnal to impatiently fan herself.

"So it's just 'cause we want something?"

She looked at me again and didn't answer.

"The Lord *giveth*!" Pastor Weare cried.

"And the Lord *taketh away*!" Nana said under her breath, her eyes closed, her head bowed.

Spiritual conviction was lost on only one person.

Vienna loudly chewed her lollipop to get to the gum in the middle. Small pieces of crystallized green sugar fell onto her lap, as she carefully fingered and nibbled on the candy. She licked her fingers noisily and wiped the sticky slobber on her wheelchair handles.

"If Crow washes away, let's make a deal," I whispered

to my father. "You can take Vienna back to New York, and I'll take Willowdale and Bitty to the Alamo. Deal?"

He patted my leg. Deal.

Just when it was getting exciting, the crisis waned, the flooding slowed, and the sun began to shine. Crow began the very slow process of drying out.

We were hanging out of Micah's window looking at Gaysie's backyard, a mess of calf-deep water, broken cornstalks, ruined flowers, and an odd assortment of holes and junk.

"Look at that old blanket floating over there," Jimmy said. "Wasn't that Ernie's?"

"Ernie?" I asked.

"My favorite parakeet," Micah said. "Died last year."

"It'll be like dinosaur hunting," Jimmy said, looking through my binoculars.

"Do you think we buried José deep enough?" I asked.

"Deeper than the goose," Jimmy answered.

Nobody said it, but I wondered if we were all thinking the same thing: With all this unearthing, would Wilbur Truesdale finally emerge?

Gaysie was too busy and tired to comment on her unearthed personal cemetery. We didn't see her for days while she sandbagged with the men in town. When she came home she yelled from downstairs, "I've peeled my clothes off down here. Hide your eyes 'cause I'm comin' up!"

Micah remained at his typewriter, but Jimmy, Bitty, and I dove for cover under Micah's bed.

"I've worked to the bone," Gaysie said, stomping up the stairs. "And I'm dead tired. I'll be in bed for the next three days," she said, passing by. "Do not eat any raw bacon and do *NOT*, under any circumstances, wake me." We took a deep breath when we finally heard her bedroom door shut. She suddenly flung it back open and yelled, "Unless the house is burning down . . . Micah?"

"Yep!"

"And I mean really burning down!"

"As opposed to just kind of burning down?" Jimmy yelled back, still under the bed with me.

"You're a pain in my arse, Jimmy Quintel!" The door slammed, a bed creaked, and almost immediately, Gaysie's snores echoed through the house.

I turned to Jimmy under the bed, our noses just inches apart.

A wicked look came across Jimmy's face.

"It's time."

"Time for what?"

"Meet me down by the creek in fifteen minutes," he said, pushing me out from under the bed. He took a flying leap out the window and sailed across the backyard on the zip line.

"Jimmy!" I yelled, running to the window.

"Shh!" Micah said. "You *do not* want to wake up Ma."

"Sorry," I whispered.

"Micah," Bitty said. "Nana and Gaysie said not to go down there. What's he doing?"

"Jimmy found us some boats," Micah said. He looked

up from his typewriter. Even through a broken right lens, I could see the fear.

But Micah stood. And this, you see, was always his greatest strength and weakness. Micah would follow Jimmy anywhere.

"He made good on his plan. He's gonna sail us to the Mississippi."

We wore our rain boots as we tromped through the wet and muddy field, Micah holding up his long purple cape. I saw no recognizable human corpses, just fields of ruined, wet crops intermingled with odd miscellaneous items: a baby blanket, a small spoon, a ruined photograph, a dog bowl, and an old clock. Apparently, Gaysie had buried more than pets, and she sure hadn't gone down six feet!

I was halfway across the field when I saw it sticking out from the ground: Gaysie Cutter's coffin.

I ran to it, putting my hand on my heart. "It's here!" I said to Micah. "It's really here. Micah—you might not want to be here for this." Using my hands and an old hand tool I found in the ground, I pushed away dirt to reveal the whole of it.

"You're right, I can't look," Micah said, turning himself and Bitty around.

I wasn't ready to see Wilbur Truesdale in this box either, but I forced myself anyway; that's what lead investigators had to do. Without a lid, you could see all the way in if you dropped to your knees. Slowly, I opened one eye. It was filled with dark mud, small rocks—and one piece of Wilbur Truesdale.

"His hat!" I exclaimed. "It's Wilbur's hat!" My hands shook. Wilbur Truesdale had been in this box.

Micah turned and started shaking his head. "No, no, no. This doesn't mean . . . He could have dropped it! It could have blown off his head or off the tractor or . . ."

I considered this. Micah was right. It didn't prove anything, and yet Wilbur's hat *in* the coffin? It was more than a coincidence.

We heard Jimmy make a rooster call from the creek.

"Maybe you're right," I said for Micah's benefit. "Come on, we have to tell Jimmy."

Closer to the river, we saw the jagged edges where the bank line had fallen in, leaving giant tree roots exposed like giant, hairy spider legs.

"To the mighty Mississippi!" Jimmy yelled. He was balancing on two large pieces of thick floating Styrofoam, one foot on each piece. They were broken apart and irregular in shape, but big enough for two people to sit on each. He kept the Styrofoam close to the bank by holding on to a large tree root bursting out of the ground.

"Where'd you get 'em?" I asked, impressed.

"They came with some farm equipment a few weeks ago. Guess what—they float!" He grinned proudly at us, flicking his Mohawk from his eyes.

"Rafts," I breathed.

Micah pushed up his glasses and trembled.

"Jimmy," I said, taking a deep breath. "We can't go! Gaysie and Nana will wring our necks. And we found Wilbur—his hat, I mean. It was in the coffin."

"But no Wilbur?"

We shook our heads.

"Well, then," Jimmy said. "Looks like he's not dead after all. Gaysie Cutter just buried his hat. Now, get on."

"Jimmy!"

"Then, don't come," Jimmy said lazily. "I'll sail to the Mississippi alone. And I'll find Wilbur myself."

I had to give it to Jimmy—he sure knew how to goad me.

"Jimmy, you can't just set sail and find missing persons!"

He shrugged, then made a movement like he was leaving us behind.

"Wait!" I said, lifting one foot onto the Styrofoam.

"Gwyn," Bitty said, grasping my arm.

"Bitty sails on my boat," Jimmy said, balancing between the two pieces. "She's the lightest and I'm the heaviest."

"No way. Bitty's with me."

"Listen," he said. "You want to tip over and drown or do you want to get to the Mississippi?"

Micah shuddered.

"It's okay, Gwynnie," Bitty said. "I'll be okay."

I looked doubtfully at Jimmy. "You have to promise me . . ."

"I promise. Double dog cross my heart."

Bitty tentatively put one of her pink mud boots on the raft. The Styrofoam was sturdier than I expected, staying afloat and not tipping an inch with Bitty's weight. I looked down into the water, the river so high and swollen I was surprised I couldn't see the bottom any longer.

I pushed Nana's objection far from my mind.

"Ready?" I asked, looking back at Micah.

He had a look on his face.

"What's the matter?"

He didn't answer, his face pale, his purple cape wrapped protectively around him.

"I . . . we . . . we could drown!" he burst out.

"Micah," Jimmy said, standing like a captain. "So you're not going to *live* 'cause you're afraid to *die*?"

I looked at Micah's face. I remembered how in the horridly humid summertime he never swam, even when it was a hundred degrees. He was afraid to wade in the creek when it came to only our ankles. The water now was probably over our heads. And it was moving.

"You won't drown, Micah," I said. "You just won't."

"How do you know? It happens, you know."

"Because," I said, "we can't die yet. You wear a *cape*, Micah!" I faced the water and yelled, "Today we set sail to the great ends of the earth!"

"To Neverland!" Bitty yelled, bouncing up and down.

Micah smiled then. "Remember when you knighted Jimmy, Gwyn? Remember what you said?" He straightened his cape and lifted his face to the sky. "It is better to die with honor than live as a coward!"

"Err-er-er-errr!" Jimmy crowed at the top of his lungs. He was playing Huck, but I thought he sounded just like Peter Pan.

CHAPTER 31

WE WERE INVINCIBLE. THE WATER swirled beneath our rafts, but couldn't touch us. It pushed all our cares behind and hurled us toward an exciting new land. Jimmy faced the river like a warrior, his black hair blown back in the wind, pure exhilaration on his face: the boy who was afraid of nothing.

I was exhilarated just watching Jimmy balance on his Styrofoam raft, remembering how he once said he was going to sail away and never come back. But that was a long time ago, before he really knew me and Bitty. Now here we were, sailing toward the mighty Mississippi together.

Micah sat cross-legged at first, his hands clenched on either side of him, trying very carefully to balance both our weights. Only after drifting a long time without falling off and drowning did his clenched hands relax.

"Micah," I said. "He doesn't really think we're going to sail to the Mississippi *and* find Wilbur, does he?"

Micah looked at me, hope in his eyes. I thought of our move here, the Hail Mary pass. Yes, I supposed that I could believe in Micah and Jimmy's quest too.

The small creek opened up at times but always narrowed again, keeping our two rafts together. We used long

278 • Amy Makechnie

Moses sticks to propel us forward by pushing off the sides of the bank, but after a while we lay down in the early-spring sunlight and just let the current take us. I lay close to the edge of the thick Styrofoam raft and reached out my hand to touch Bitty's, who lay on Jimmy's raft next to me. She giggled as we tried to keep our fingertips together and squealed at the shockingly cold water.

We were given a slow and thorough tour of Crow, from the river's standpoint. The flood had tipped trees, eroded riverbanks, ravaged fields. The farmers, though, were beginning again. Tractors were out, men and women consulting. For the first time since moving here, I felt a surge of pride for a small town I was beginning to belong to.

It was only when we moved farther toward the edge of Crow's town limits that the creek widened slightly and the water began to carry us faster.

"Dingle!" Jimmy shouted, pointing to the next town's welcome sign, barely visible from the creek. Reluctantly, Nana came to mind.

"Hey, Huck," I yelled. Jimmy stuck his long staff in the water and dragged it along the muddy creek bottom until we caught up.

"How far are we really going to go? We're going to have to walk back, you know."

"You're not chickening out now, are ya?"

"No! It's just that the Mississippi is really like five hundred miles away and . . ." But Jimmy wasn't listening. A blade of grass fell from his mouth, his eyes catching something behind me.

"Jimmy?"

I turned my head. I saw nothing at first but then—flashes of moving clothing behind trees coming quickly toward us.

"What the . . . ?"

Micah stood, straightened his glasses, and wobbled on the Styrofoam.

"What do you know? The Creepers," Jimmy said. "They followed us here." A rock ricocheted off our raft.

"I knew they'd get me someday," Micah moaned.

"No, Micah. Never!" I said, eyes narrowing.

Bitty, on the raft with Jimmy, bit her lower lip as she stirred the brown water like a vat of witch's stew.

Jimmy pushed off the riverbank with his staff just as Travis and the Creepers caught up to us. They tried, but there was no hiding their jealousy at the sight of us floating down the river. I smiled and waved like a pageant queen.

Travis leaped into the water toward us.

"What are you doing!" I yelled.

His hideous sneer turned to panic as he began to doggy-paddle helplessly.

"I can't touch!"

Reluctantly, I lay on my stomach and held out my arm. He heaved himself onto our raft, soaking us and nearly tipping us over.

And then he sat, knees pulled to his chest. We stared at each other.

I was sitting on a raft opposite a Creeper.

"Thanks?" he said awkwardly.

The raft bounced. I turned forward, Micah scooting closer to me.

"Jimmy!" I yelled, and pointed over to the bank where we could get off. He nodded. But moving back over to the left proved harder now as the current pushed us over to the right and a heavily wooded forest, with no route home. Bitty kept her eyes on me.

"Jimmy!" I yelled again. *You promised.*

Jimmy pushed Bitty behind him.

"Get us closer, Micah," I said. "We have to get Bitty."

"He won't let anything happen to her," Micah said. "He'd die first." And suddenly, that's exactly what I was afraid of.

"Come here, Bitty," I said, holding out my hand.

"What are you doing?" Jimmy said.

"Come here," I repeated. Bitty reached out, fingertips touching mine.

"Gwyn," Jimmy said. "Don't do that, you'll sink. I got this, Gwyn."

Jimmy's raft bumped a large rock in the middle of the creek, forcing it into a fast spin of river water. I dropped to my knees, tried to control the panic creeping into my veins. Micah shook with fear.

Over the sound of rushing water Jimmy yelled, "Get off up ahead!"

We looked up the river. Glancing at Travis, I was filled with resentment; we would have gotten off earlier if the Creepers hadn't interfered. My eyes met Jimmy's, his promise held fast there. I wanted to believe him.

The sound of a large gush of water pulled my attention back. I looked up ahead.

What was once a simple and shallow creek was now a full-fledged river, wide and fast, the high water rolling us quickly forward.

"Swirls," Micah whispered. "She talked about the swirls."

I was going to contradict him until I saw a small white cross at the base of a giant oak tree. Around the cross were overgrown winter flowers, and new green shoots popping out of the earth. A memorial for Myron. Gaysie had done this for her childhood friend. I was sure of it.

Jimmy glanced back at me. We were headed toward trouble.

I had learned how desperation turned a person outside of himself, made someone do something they never thought they could. There was power and strength in the world. There was force and brutality that crushed the weak. When pushed up against a wall, the weak could either stay still or push back.

"Whoa," Travis said, his voice trembling. "I don't swim, I don't swim, I don't swim."

I looked at my little sister again. *Bitty Baby.*

We floated faster, tried in vain to stay together. Finally, our chance came as we neared the left side of the bank. Jimmy grabbed a large tree branch that was sticking out of the water. Our rafts bumped together and stalled.

"Go," I said to Micah. The water, fast and bumpy, moved us up and down, splashing onto our faces. But he did it. With a little awkward bunny hop, Micah's legs and cape carried him up and across the water, and he landed on the bank of the river.

"Go!" I yelled at Travis. But he sat, scared and immobile.

Our chance was lost within seconds when Jimmy's tree branch snapped, and our rafts moved swiftly downstream again.

"Gwyn!" Micah yelled, "Jump off!" But I couldn't leave Bitty. I pushed off, still on the raft with Travis. Micah ran along the shoreline beside us, his cape flying behind him. He tripped in the mud, splashing his broken glasses with black goo, and clambered back up.

My raft hit a rock, circled, and hit Jimmy and Bitty's.

Bitty was on all fours, holding on to nothing, her fingers trying to curl into the Styrofoam, pure panic on her face.

"It's okay, Bitty baby," I called.

"Gwynnie," she said, tears swimming in her eyes.

"I can't swim," Travis said again, the look in his eyes so different from his usual demeanor.

The river swirled, pushed us forward, and our once-unsinkable rafts felt light and inconsequential. Jimmy's face held intense concentration, but still, no fear.

Suddenly, he dropped the big Moses stick into the water.

"Here we go," he said.

Up ahead, across the entire width of the river, was a line of large rocks. Before the flood, the rocks would have made a path across, but now only the dark, wet tips were visible, slowing the avalanche of water for a second before it diverted around them.

"We're gonna hit hard," Jimmy yelled, balancing like he was on his skateboard about to ollie up a curb. "Climb on and, whatever you do, don't go over the rocks—there's a waterfall. I got Bitty." I had no time to argue.

Jimmy was right. We hit the rocks hard. I tried to climb as the foam broke into pieces, flipping and tossing us mercilessly into the river. The cold took my breath away as I plunged down, the freezing water coming through my skin and all the way to my bones. The water swam over the edge of my rain boots, soaked the lining of my socks, and froze my toes. Touching the bottom of the river, I rocketed up to the surface and grasped the slippery rocks to see Micah hopping onto a boulder and attempting to edge across the rocks toward us, slipping every few inches.

"Gwyn," Micah said, reaching me, both lenses of his glasses now completely gone as they sat crooked on his face.

"Get Bitty," I half coughed, half cried, water coming out of my nose and mouth.

He crawled three feet farther to my right. I turned my head and saw Jimmy's hands emerging from the water, pushing Bitty up onto the rocks, where she perched like a bird. Micah pulled her up and held her tightly as she screamed for me.

My body was so cold I could barely pull myself out of the water, but I did.

"Jimmy," I said, my whole body shaking as I finally sat up on the rock.

"Micah," Jimmy yelled, his teeth chattering like an anatomy skeleton as he tried to climb out of the water. "We need help! Get Gaysie." What was he talking about? Gaysie was miles away!

"Gwynnie," Bitty said, shaking and crying hard as she tried to balance across the wet, slippery rocks in front of me. "Help me." I tried to stand.

Then another voice shouted, "Help!"

I looked over my shoulder to see Travis climbing over Jimmy in a panic, trying to get out of the water. I reached out to help, but wobbled and fell, slamming my shins down on the rocks. It hurt so badly I cried out in pain. Jimmy and Travis thrashed in the cold. I reached out again, but instead of pulling Travis out, he pulled me in. I struggled under his weight, tried to wiggle out of my jacket and kick my rain boots off. The current was so strong, it propelled me into the rocks again, this time connecting with my head.

Micah yelled my name, and then Jimmy was beside me. With all of his twelve-year-old power, he pushed me upward. I grasped the rocks with my entire upper body, my arms and fingers numb with cold.

I was so tired I could hardly move. I wanted to be warm, to stop fighting. But it was the moment that I realized I could either lie down and die or try a little harder.

So I clung to the rocks with every bit of strength I had.

Travis, panicking, put his arms and full weight around Jimmy's neck. They went under.

"Jimmy!" Micah screamed. Jimmy came up, gasping.

"Go," he chattered brokenly at Micah. "Gaysie. Get . . . Bitty . . . across."

Micah set his face in determination and took off his cape.

Using it like a life preserver, he threw one end in the water and yelled for Travis and Jimmy to grab it. Travis grasped it, pulling himself out while Jimmy swam to me.

"Gwyn, hang on!"

The water lapped up and hit my face, my fingers and hands slipping as I tried to lift myself out of the water again, the cold, dark river that was becoming a part of me—hungry, like wolves lapping at my face. My hands were incapable of holding on any longer. I slid off the rocks again and went down. Down, down deep.

Everything grew darker. I looked up from the bottom of the river. It was like a slow-motion scene, and I was hearing Vienna play the piano. What was the song? "The Playful Pony"? The music began to fade as I became weaker, the fight leaving me. Deep bubbles escaped from my mouth.

But then there was a hand. Floating gently. It was white and wrinkled and bloated, reaching out to help me. I grabbed it but it didn't grab back. I pulled hard, then screamed, the last of the oxygen bubbles coming out of my mouth. I inhaled water through my nose and mouth as I dropped the hand of Wilbur Truesdale. I could not see his face, only his hand and arms, the flannel shirt he always wore. His spirit was clearly gone but somehow his body lay under the cold Crow River.

Wilbur's splayed fingers touched my leg and, though

horrifying, I was distracted by Jimmy's feet thrashing in the water. I instinctively knew that Jimmy was going to have to make a choice: Save himself or me.

It was my father's voice that came to me, and then his deep, dark, thinking eyes reminding me to use my brain. Yes, my brain was what was going to save us. I focused on a rock in front of me. It was angular, had a place to hold, perfect for my hand. I grabbed it.

As I pulled myself up again, the hood of my jacket was caught on another rock behind me, only inches from the surface.

I pulled upward, but my hood kept me anchored in the deep.

Words came to me in puzzle pieces . . . *oxygen* . . . *brain* . . . *Mama*. I needed air. My father wouldn't be able to handle another loss. Nana. Bitty needed me! And Vienna. She would know Gwyn was gone, wouldn't she? I swam, kicking my arms and legs, but I was losing to the deep that had once claimed Myron, a boy I would meet only in heaven. Darkness was growing as the sound of the water became louder in my ears.

The kicking legs of Jimmy disappeared, replaced by a bright light. It was coming for me.

But then a dark shadow interrupted, moved between me and the light. A hand came through the water.

It was a very large, meaty hand. Different from Wilbur's. It reached for me with authority. It was alive. It was strong, calloused, a farmer's hand. I could hear the voice even under the water. It was not a request.

"Take my hand," the voice said. "Guinevere St. Clair, take my hand!"

My eyes focused in on the hand. There was a missing finger.

I took it. It yanked me up hard, the hood of my coat tearing as I was hauled out of the water. The hand dragged me across the rocks, my sopping socks and heels hitting the jagged but smooth stones.

I was cradled like a baby, hair and water wiped from my eyes. A large mouth opened and closed above me. Veins bulged on a forehead, along a red-and-purple scar. I couldn't move my face, my mouth, or body. But when Bitty threw herself on me, a warm relief came. She was safe. Micah grabbed my hand, sobbing, hot tears falling like sizzling embers on my frozen cheeks.

The light shifted toward the river.

I turned my head. It was Jimmy I last remember seeing, on the other side of the rock barrier, as the current carried him away from us.

Floating dead on the water.

CHAPTER 32

I AWOKE COLD, IN THE HOSPITAL, listening to whispered reports I could barely make out. Did they know that Wilbur was in the river?

What was long anticipated as my great triumph, wasn't at all. Jimmy was gone.

Every time I opened my eyes, I saw Gaysie Cutter's face above me on the river. So I kept my eyes closed and shut my brain off like a faucet, so I wouldn't remember. For the first time I envied Vienna's blank memories.

Within two days I was discharged from the hospital and carried to my bed so I could "rest up and get all better." But I hid my eyes from daylight like a vampire. The longer I lay, the more tired I felt. Guilt was coming for me like a runaway train. They said I was like Vienna, and now I really was. Wasn't it she who had wanted to go down on that sled with Gaysie? And wasn't it me, who first suggested sailing to the Mississippi?

Dreams were nightmares. Not whole stories, but broken images of Styrofoam, Jimmy, struggling, trying to save me, cold river water, legs thrashing, deep gasps of air, an unforgiving current. The last one—of Jimmy being taken—it gutted me. My resentment toward Gaysie grew into a hard, cold stone. Jimmy had loved her, needed her. Why had she not given Jimmy her hand instead of me?

And, of all people, how could Jimmy give up the fight? He was a quitter, and I hated him for it!

"Gwyn," my father whispered as he held me tight. Even as I was shutting down, my father was not letting go. *One last miracle*. One more time.

He began talking about the brain. He said I was in shock, but it didn't feel like shock. It was like a bitter poison taking over, nothing else. I should have let Jimmy practice cutting my hair, like he wanted. I never should have yelled at him by the rocket slide.

My father brought Vienna to sit next to me, either to keep me company, or to vex me into saying something.

"Are you sick?" Vienna asked. In her hands she was holding the puzzle of our family.

When I didn't answer, she leaned closer.

"Tell me a story. I like Guinevere and Arthur. Or Peter Pan." When I said nothing, she got bored and stood up, shuffled closer, and peered down at my face.

"This is my room," she said. Before I could stop them, tears were trickling down my face. I commanded my brain to make them stop, but they kept coming down, down, down my face and chin, dropping small drops onto my shoulders and running cold down the back of my neck.

"Why are you sad?" Vienna asked, her own eyes filling.

"I'm sad Jimmy left me!" I whispered ferociously. "I'm sad *you* left me."

The last sentence shocked even me. But now I really

understood: Life wasn't as good without some people in it, no matter how hard you tried.

I closed my eyes, so tired. It seemed I'd been running for so long now. Trying to run away from her while being pulled to her like a magnet. Again and again.

She draped one arm over my body and fell asleep, snoring quietly in my ear. I didn't shake her off. It was the first time since I was four years old that I had cried in my mother's arms. At any other time, this would have made me somewhat happy.

"I was trying to sleep," Gaysie said to the room. I didn't want to hear her, but she spoke in her annoyingly loud and enunciated voice so I would have to listen.

"God knows I needed the rest after all that sandbagging, but I kept having this dream about you, Guinevere, the same dream I'd been having for months. And a voice came to my mind—*Go to the children!*"

I lifted my eyelids at her, watched her become animated as she recounted.

"I was Samuel hearing the voice of the Lord!"

I startled as she banged forcefully on the desk in my room.

"The voice came to me again," Gaysie said. "*GO to your children!* It woke me up right in here!" She pounded on her chest with her fist. "I've said it before and I'll say it again—when the spirit moves you, you move!"

I opened my eyes all the way, blinked from the light. Bitty and Micah sat on my bed, while my father slumped in a chair in the corner, his face pale and haggard. Vienna, holding Love-a-Lot, sat in a chair next to Nana. I turned my head to Gaysie, who was speaking directly to me.

"I was struck with an almighty fear! Seeing you all gone, I knew you had gone to the river." Micah hung his head, and I waited for the reprimand but it didn't come.

"The whole town was watching crazy Gaysie driving the Blue Mistress along the river. Those boys you call Creepers told me they'd seen a raft sailing down the river and that Travis Maynard jumped in after you. I knew exactly what had happened!

"I found you at least two miles up the river after you'd hit the rocks." Gaysie's voice broke as she cleared her throat and began to hum. There was an audible sigh as Nana closed her eyes.

"Gaysie," my father said, "if you hadn't been there . . ."

"No," she said. "Like I told you, I was told to move. That's all I did, same as you did on Halloween night, following after them to make sure they were safe."

My father! Following us. Standing in the moonlight, the torn shirt from the dogs.

"Look who's awake," he said. I knew he was looking at the pupils of my eyes, the color in my face, trying to gauge my brain's neural connections.

"Gaysie saved me," I said, surprised at how soft my voice sounded.

My father nodded and fell to his knees beside the bed. I had spoken.

I could hear the commanding voice. *Take my hand! Guinevere!*

Gaysie, my archnemesis with the missing finger, had saved me from certain death.

Micah spoke as he stared out the window. "Jimmy saved us too."

CHAPTER 33

FOUR DAYS AFTER JIMMY DIED, Nana went to church to pray for me and the soul of Jimmy Quintel.

My father lifted me out of my white sheets and covers and carried me outside, where the sun was shining, a light spring breeze lifting my hair. It was a beautiful morning that would have normally delighted me. Instead, I sat on the stairs, weakly clutching the railing. I didn't want to see the sky, the hayfield across the street. I didn't want to be reminded of Micah and Jimmy coming down Lanark Lane with a cape and a skateboard. It was an unnerving feeling, being alive in the world without Jimmy in it.

"Would you like to go for a walk?" my father asked.

I shook my head.

"Where do you hurt, Gwyn?"

Another head shake.

"Your heart?"

I nodded.

"You feel it's broken?" I leaned against him silently, until he finally carried me inside and tucked me back into bed. But he raised the blinds in my room to let the light in, and opened a window.

"Why did you follow us on Halloween?" My voice was

so soft it was barely a whisper. I figured since I was about to perish I might as well get the answers I had been seeking.

"I saw you leave when I was coming home from your mother's. I suspected it had something to do with finding Wilbur."

"Daddy. Your fingerprints were on the Blue Mistress."

"My fingerprints?"

"Georgia Piehl sent me the results."

He raised his eyebrows.

Was he protecting Gaysie? Or was it even worse than that?

"You obtained fingerprints they could match in a lab?" I heard the note of pride in his voice. "Guinevere," he said, "I was on the tractor because I suppose I became a bit suspicious myself."

"Suspicious of *her*."

I'll admit, my heart had softened mightily toward Gaysie. She *had* saved my life, after all. Though I reminded myself she had also almost tried to kill me the first time we met. Suspicions that Gaysie had something to do with Wilbur's disappearance and death still nagged at my brain. I had to find out. And I'd do it for Jimmy.

"I've asked myself a million times—how wide the truth really is and how much is mine to know. I didn't find anything that night except my precocious Gwyn."

"But she did it, didn't she?" I asked, agitated. "There was blood on the steering wheel."

"From her finger, I imagine. I must have touched it. Let's rest now. Your body and brain need to heal."

But I knew better. I wasn't going to heal. I was going to die.

"You aren't going to die," he said as if reading my very thoughts. "You know why? Because you don't die from a broken heart. Let me show you something," he said, going to his room and bringing back the weirdly broken Japanese pot.

"Remember when I got this?"

I nodded.

"Do you know how it's made?

I did not.

"It's Japanese kintsugi art. See how the cracks are repaired with a golden lacquer? It seals the cracks but doesn't attempt to cover them or make the pottery look new. Instead, it purposely accentuates the damage. This type of pot is highly sought after, and some people even purposely break their pottery to apply this art form, transforming their ordinary bowls and vases into high-end art. Many consider the vase to be more beautiful than before."

"But it's broken."

"Yes, Guinevere. And it can be beautiful again."

I could see why my father liked the cracked pot. It was pretty and uncommon. It was also the story of our lives. And my father was living proof, wasn't he? You didn't die from a broken heart.

Still. A broken pot. It might be beautiful again, but it's never quite the same as before, is it?

When Nana came home from church, she wheeled in Vienna, who was sucking on a cherry lollipop.

"That's her third," Nana said. "I thought they were supposed to keep her quiet."

"No?" my father asked.

"No! She swore twice, dropped her gum on the floor, and belched in the middle of the prayer! Of course it had to be Dottie who stepped on her gum."

My father stifled a laugh.

Nana threw her hands up in the air. "Dottie said it was *just fine*, ha!"

Bitty piped up. "Vienna was very loud and asked why Dottie had skunk hair!"

Nana sat on the bed next to me and exhaled.

"Gwyn, Penny and Charlie from your class at school were in attendance, and so many children told me to tell you hello." She touched my leg gingerly. "Your teacher, Mrs. Law . . . even those boys you call the Creepers." *The Creepers.* I blamed them for what happened, and I'd hate them even more if I had the energy.

"Then at the last moment Gaysie Cutter and Micah walked in, right down the center aisle. I never thought I'd see the day."

"She was wearing a big bird on top of her hat!" Bitty said.

"Yes," Nana said. "A bright green suit and a hat so large she looked like she was going to the Kentucky Derby with these giant green-and-blue peacock feathers."

"She prayed like this," Bitty said, clasping her hands together, shutting her eyes tight, and rocking back and forth.

"Bitty," Nana said. "Honey, go take off your jacket, wash your hands, and get ready for lunch." When Bitty left, Nana lowered her voice as if I couldn't hear her.

"They found his body."

"Jimmy!" My father stood quickly.

"No, not Jimmy," Nana said. "Wilbur. He was in the river. He'd been dead—for quite a while."

My hands clutched the white sheets. It had been real. Wilbur was dead.

"Pastor Weare announced that?"

"Certainly not. I heard afterward, in the foyer. Jake and the other officers recovered his body while looking for Jimmy. He had a small head wound, but he'd been dead a long time. They think Wilbur must have had a heart attack or fell and hit his head. Remember how his tractor was parked so close to the river? His body was caught up near the rocks, up at Crow Landing, where it catches all the trees and debris . . . where the children were. I shouldn't have been angry with him for not showing up to till my vegetable garden! Oh, I feel just awful."

"Ah, Wilbur," my father said, his voice sad.

"Yes," Nana said, her voice wobbly.

Nana felt my forehead. "She's got a fever, Jed. We need to bring her in again."

"I'll call Dr. Long," my father said, rising.

"I was thinking about Jimmy," my father said, when he came back into the room. "They haven't found him yet. Wouldn't it be something . . ." His thought trailed undisturbed, hopeful like a child's rising soap bubble.

Nana stomped it down hard. "No. Gaysie and the kids saw his body on the water. He's gone, Jed."

"They saw his body on the water, floating," my father repeated. I could hear the way he was pondering that, like when he was looking at a model of the brain and asking us questions aloud, like he was trying to make it fit together. "Why would he be floating?"

It was unreal, the way they could talk about my friend Jimmy and finding his body.

"I should help," my father said. "But I can't leave her." I felt his fingers touch mine. "I ask for so much, and I already got my miracle. How can I ask for more?"

"Ask for Jimmy," I said, my voice coming out as a whisper. For the first time since coming home, I felt a small hope. Was it possible that it was such a simple thing? *Just ask.*

"What, honey? Did you say something?"

But when I tried to say it again, my tongue was thick and my mouth unable to move.

"I asked Gaysie to help me head up the summer perennial show," Nana said, changing the subject.

"She sat by us at church today, huh, Nana?" Bitty said, coming back into the room.

"She will always sit with us," Nana said, patting her chest. "Bless her heart."

Later, when I was wrapped in Vienna's old quilt, I sat outside on the porch swing with Gaysie. She was so large I was tipped precariously back and upward. At any moment I expected the porch swing to come crashing down.

I clung to the chain for dear life as Vienna, who was sitting on the other side of me in her wheelchair, watched Micah and Bitty pet Willowdale. Micah hung on the fence next to Bitty, a yellow sash tied around his head.

Gaysie stopped rocking, watching them. "You taught me something, Guinevere. You were right. His sweetness *is* his superpower."

Known for her impeccable timing, Vienna chimed in. "I'm hungry."

"I've been thinking about Jimmy," Gaysie said. "Vienna, do you remember that fabulously obnoxious boy with the skateboard and Mohawk?"

Vienna looked at us blankly.

It was then I did something most appalling: I began to cry right in front of Gaysie Cutter. How could anyone forget Jimmy Quintel?

"Let me tell you about heaven," Gaysie said matter-of-factly, over my tears. "Jimmy's such a lucky boy! Heaven was a place I never wanted to leave." She rocked, straining the screw in the porch ceiling even further.

"You died and they brought you back?" I said, wiping my face. Epinephrine was shot up in Vienna's heart the day she died too. The paramedics had worked on her, had put electrical paddles on her chest, and given her CPR.

Gaysie shook her head. "Oh no, they didn't! I came back because I chose to."

"How?"

"Myron and I hit the ice and crashed through. I've driven myself all kinds of crazy reliving that moment. We both became trapped, couldn't get out from under the ice." She shook off the memory with a giant jiggling of her arms.

"And then what?"

"Eventually I was lying on top of the ice with the great light above, asking to leave this earth. I said no one loved me."

"What did the light say?"

"It said that even if it was true, I had to learn to love myself." She paused. "God knows I'm trying."

"It was Vienna's idea, wasn't it?"

Vienna began to sniffle.

"Now, Vienna, don't be silly," Gaysie said matter-of-factly. "You know full well I wanted to sled down that hill too."

"But you took the blame," I said.

Gaysie shrugged as the swing made a perilous creaking sound.

I began to make a contingency plan if the swing fell.

"But there were many silver linings from that horrific day. For instance, I've never forgotten the light."

"What about . . . the dead people you saw?"

"Well, you see, they weren't dead at all! I saw my friends. Vienna and Jed and Myron. I realized I wasn't as alone as I sometimes felt. I also saw a piece of my future: four children who would need me. That was all it took. When I saw them, there wasn't anything I wouldn't do to get back. I was in the hospital for months, and it was very hard. Gall bladder, spleen, skull, face." She pointed to the long, hideous scar down the side of her face. "My brain was swollen to twice its size. It's unexplainable why I don't have brain damage. Though I suppose that's debatable, isn't it?"

"I'm hungry," Vienna said again. Gaysie reached over and took one of Vienna's hands so that both of their hands were lying in my lap. "After the accident I was broken for a very long time, but life becomes okay again when you have people who love you. Even if things aren't the same."

My hands were covered by the hands of a woman who didn't know she was my mother, and my archenemy. Maybe I was going to need a new one.

I glanced at Vienna, chomping on her gum. She giggled, squeezing her pink Care Bear.

"Tell me a story," she said. "I like Guinevere."

So I told her a story, not about Guinevere the legend written in books, but about the real girl, the Guinevere St. Clair who happened to be a lot like her unforgettable mother.

CHAPTER 34

THERE'S GOING TO BE A funeral for Wilbur," Officer Jake said. I was in bed, but found my eaves-dropping skills undiminished. "Coroner said it was his heart, wore out from old age. His head was banged up a bit like he fell and tumbled right into the river." He sounded relieved to speak of death due to natural causes instead of something more sinister.

"We've got to start thinking about a service or memorial for Jimmy, too."

"But he hasn't been found," my father said, like Jimmy was a lost puppy instead of a dead boy. "You can't have a service if there's no . . ." *body. He meant "body."*

"I said we've got to start thinking. With the flooding and strong current, we may never find him, Jed. He could be all the way to the Mississippi by now, pinned under some rocks somewhere. . . ."

A teacup rattled noisily on a saucer.

"This is the kind of thing that can pull a community together or pull it apart. I want to be ahead of it, let people start grieving together," Officer Jake said. "The Quintels don't have the money for a proper funeral. They won't ask for help. . . ."

"We'll take care of it," my father said.

"If everyone pitches in . . ."

"All of it," my father said. "We'll take care of it."

Officer Jake sighed. "Heard your little girl wasn't doing so well, Jed, but I'd like to talk to her, take a full statement, and try to understand what happened out there."

"She can't talk, Jake," my father said. "She's barely . . ."

"Just for a minute."

"Not yet," my father said firmly.

I sunk lower in my white sheets, no longer crisp and cool. I breathed in the warm, comfortable air and let the pale lavender-scented cotton fall across my face. I finally knew what had happened to Wilbur, but it didn't make a bit of difference.

Dr. Long came again, but I refused to talk to him.

He stared at me gravely while examining my facial color, gauging my reactions, pinching my cheeks, holding my arms up and letting them drop limply back onto the bed. He turned on his small flashlight and shone it in my eyes until I closed them.

When he left, Bitty stood at the foot of my bed holding her doll Annie Bessy. I beckoned her with my eyes, suddenly missing her as terribly as a phantom limb. This realization was terrifying; that my brain could still recognize the absence of someone. I'd been through this before. I could not, would not, think of missing Jimmy.

Vienna wandered in holding Love-a-Lot as Dr. Long's voice floated into our room.

"I can't do much else for her. There's physically nothing wrong. But it's obvious she's barely functioning. Her heart sounds fine, and I know you've had both the girls checked out—but maybe we're missing something. You should consider taking her into Des Moines and hospitalizing her, to see what can be done. I'm sorry . . . There have been cases like this. Sometimes traumatic events damage a child so much, that they . . . change and never quite recover."

And then something remarkable happened. For the first time since we moved to Crow, Nana began to howl, like she was having a full-fledged adult meltdown.

I perked right up. Nana knew full well that there was nothing wrong with my heart, so why should she be affected by such a ridiculous statement? *Uh, Nana, I was the fastest girl runner in New York, a climber of trees, an up-and-coming, world-famous lawyer!* That Dr. Long—how dare he mention my heart to Nana after everything with Vienna? That was as good as telling Nana I was already dead.

In his perfected, coping voice, I heard my father calming Nana down.

Bitty turned her head to me and put her hands on her hips, her lips turned down in a powerful pout. Sweet Bitty rarely bossed me. "Gwynnie," she said sternly.

"Gwynnie," Vienna mimicked.

Nana unleashed another loud yowl.

Bitty tapped her foot on the floor. "Move it, tootsie."

Vienna clapped her hands like it was the funniest thing she'd ever heard. "Move it, tootsie! Move it, tootsie."

Using my upper body, I raised myself into a sitting

position. My legs went over the bed and my bare toes dangled. Slowly, I inched forward until my toes touched the cold wooden floor, and I stood without help for the first time in days.

Putting one foot in front of the other, I slid one stiff leg across the bedroom floor, down the hall, and into the kitchen. Slide, push, slide, push.

Bitty smiled. Vienna clapped all the way down the hall. Dr. Long, Nana, and my father turned.

"Ha ha ha," Vienna said, behind me. "You need a hairbrush!"

Nana's eyes opened wide. My father rose.

I fixed my eyes on Dr. Long.

"Don't you make my nana cry!" I yelled at the doctor. "Don't you dare. There's nothing wrong with my heart, and I'm not going to die until I'm darn good and ready!" Except I didn't say "darn."

I never saw my nana so happy to hear me swear in all my life.

"Nope," my father said. "My Gwyn has never had a weak heart."

CHAPTER 35

THE LATE-AFTERNOON SUN HUNG ORANGE over wet, brown fields. Soon, it would touch the horizon line and pretend to fall off the edge of the flat plains of Crow. A black night would come as a hopeless feeling sometimes does.

And then slowly, I knew the unconquerable sun would begin to rise out of the dark. This is what I clung to, that life might go on.

But the sun hadn't fallen yet as I sat on the porch in my white nightgown and bare feet. The white nightgown was from Nana, who would prefer that I die in something sweet and respectable versus the ratty pajamas I'd brought from New York. *It happens*, I remember a woman once saying with an unemotional shrug of her shoulders as I sat in a hospital waiting room many years earlier. People leave us. They shouldn't, but they do. *It happens.*

I wasn't going to die though. I knew that now. I couldn't. Nana, Bitty, Micah, and Willowdale Princess Deon Dawn—they'd never forgive me. Vienna would miss my stories. Gaysie would be very disappointed in my lack of gumption. And my father, well, every dentist needed a decent lawyer on staff.

Bitty had brought Willowdale to the front porch to see me, but unfortunately, she was more interested in eating Nana's tulip bulbs.

Micah sat on Nana's porch like he'd been there the whole time I'd been in bed. I'd lost track of the time, how many days had passed, how long he might have sat waiting for me.

"Hi, Gwyn," Micah said. "I've been waitin' for you to come out."

We sat in silence for a few moments.

"I'm sorry about Wilbur," I finally said.

"Yeah. Do you think he's with him?" Micah asked.

"Who?" I asked, knowing exactly who he meant.

"Do you think he's watching us like an angel?"

"Jimmy, an angel!" I almost laughed out loud at that one.

"I just wish I knew where he was," Micah said.

"Me too."

"I wrote him a poem on my typewriter," Micah said, pulling out a crumpled piece of paper.

"Let me hear it."

Micah pushed up his glasses, which I suddenly noticed were new. He smoothed his flyaway duck hair and began to read dramatically, like Gaysie would have.

For Jimmy, from Micah. Your best friend
forever.
Once there was a boy named Jimmy.
He came for breakfast, stayed for dinner.
And when we played

he sometimes let me be the winner.
He found a raft
and let it ride
All the way to the Mississippi

"Go on," I said.

"That's it so far. I can't find a word that rhymes with 'Mississippi,'" Micah said.

"That's a real good start, Micah," Bitty said.

Micah sniffed back a sob. "He always said he was going to leave Crow and never come back, but I didn't really believe him. And now I don't have a best friend—or a barber."

"I'll cut your hair," I said.

"And I'll be your best friend!" Bitty smiled hopefully.

Micah attempted a smile.

"Ma says that Jimmy's just waiting on the other side of the river."

We sat forlorn, seeing him so clearly in our minds, riding the raft.

"What does that mean?" Bitty asked.

"She means that Jimmy . . . will be waiting for us one day."

As we sat on the front steps, the wind began to blow. My matted hair blew up around my face. I inhaled and closed my eyes.

"Tell me a story?" Bitty asked, sounding like Vienna.

"I don't have any more stories."

"Please? One with Jimmy in it?"

"No."

"Please?"

I sighed, with no intention of bringing Jimmy into the story. But he came anyway. He was skateboarding and flying off a tall skateboard ramp, landing splendidly at our feet as he tossed his black hair out of his eyes. He crowed like a Lost Boy because he was one now, and he was happy that way. Now he would never have to wear a tie, go to school, or clean his room. He was perfectly happy in Neverland and sometimes rode a magical white unicorn. He was the leader of a gang of other Lost Boys who never had to grow up either.

Jimmy knew every yo-yo trick, wasn't afraid of the dark, haunted the Creepers, jumped out of windows, and could even fly. I spoke so fast, with such animation that I could hardly breathe. Micah and Bitty leaned forward, Willowdale stopped mid-chew—caught on my every word.

Micah stared off into the distance, his mouth slightly open.

Unfortunately, I had made the story so real that Bitty stood up and began to scream Jimmy's name.

"Oh, Bitty—" I began.

Micah stood with her, tripped down the front stairs, and began yelling Jimmy's name too. They were like two wild coyotes yowling in the night.

Willowdale mooed noisily.

"Jimmy!" Bitty screamed, closing her eyes tightly.

I stood, reached for her hand.

"Jimmy!" Bitty screamed again, opening her eyes wide and jumping off the steps.

"No, Micah," I said. "Don't let her."

But Bitty wouldn't listen. She wriggled free of me and

began running down the road like she could actually see that white unicorn. Micah took off after her. I stood in my white nightgown, squinting.

There was a boy walking down the road. He was not riding a magical white unicorn. He was hobbling and wore a crooked smile on his face, but he looked real, with a black, unkempt, overgrown Mohawk. He began to walk faster.

I grasped the cold porch railing as Bitty and Micah ran until they were upon him. They smashed into the boy, the two of them enveloping, almost carrying him from behind. I walked down the front steps and onto the road with my bare feet, feeling the sharp pebbles and the dirt.

He was dirty, his clothes were ripped, and he looked like he hadn't slept for a year.

"Are you the ghost of Jimmy Quintel?" I asked.

He held out his hand to me. I grasped it as Micah cried next to him, Bitty jumping up and down. I squeezed Jimmy's hand, thin and calloused with skin over real bones. It was real—as real my own hand. I squeezed real hard.

"Stop crying, Micah!" he said weakly. "Stop being such a baby." But he said it affectionately as he put his arm around Micah.

"We thought . . ."

He shrugged and said, "Did I miss my own funeral?"

"No!" I shouted.

"Shoot. Not as good as Huck and Tom, but still, it's pretty good, huh?"

CHAPTER 36

JIMMY WAS TREATED FOR HYPOTHERMIA, minor cuts and bruises, and malnutrition. We didn't see him for two whole days, and then one day Jimmy came riding down the road on his skateboard, right back to Gaysie's.

He was something of a celebrity at school. Mrs. Law still took away his skateboard, but she smiled when she did it. We had a new understanding with the Creepers. We weren't exactly on speaking terms, but they started playing kickball with us at recess. All the girls wrote Jimmy notes and cards, and the boys gave him things like a football, a duct tape wallet, and their snacks. Yeah, our Jimmy was living large, and I didn't begrudge him one bit.

Jimmy said he found himself floating atop the water. He opened his eyes and all he saw were blue skies and a big river. When his raft eventually caught up with him, he took it as a sign. He decided he'd sail to the Mississippi and never come back. But after a while, he said he got bored without us, said it wasn't any fun riding the river alone. Getting home, though, was a difficult trip. Surviving on squirrel nuts and a duck egg, he walked the long way home.

I knew he was telling a tall tale. I'd overheard my father talking to Dr. Long. Jimmy had hurt his ankle and back going over the waterfall. He lay beside the river for days before he could move again, very nearly dying from starvation and hypothermia. It was a wonder he got home at all. But I let Jimmy tell us his story.

"Did you hitchhike?" I asked. I had always wanted to hitchhike.

He looked at me like I was deranged. "Gaysie would have killed me!"

"Jimmy," Micah asked. "Are you saying you missed us? That's why you came back?"

He smiled his crooked smile. "Nah, I'm not sayin' that at all."

Our routine slowly went back to what it had been, with a few changes. Nana was different, like she had survived the worst and come out okay. It didn't change her completely, of course. Like my father always said: "Neurons that fire together, wire together." She still followed me around with a jacket and a piece of floss, but she was a tad bit more relaxed, like she was resigned to future shenanigans that would surely come with raising a child of Vienna St. Clair.

We went to school and lingered at Micah's, just like before. With renewed vigor, Gaysie worked in the fields, stomping around in her big men's boots until one day she drove the Blue Mistress again. Seeing her out there, I felt the curiosity rising once more: There may have been an "official" explanation about Wilbur's death, but what exactly did Gaysie Cutter know about it? How was she so sure, right from the beginning, that he wasn't coming back for a cup of coffee or a plate of dinner? Had she seen him hit his head and fall in the water or . . . had *she* hit his head? I tried to control my imagination. *A direct link, facts. Nothing circumstantial*, my father would say. And anyway, did I even want her to be guilty anymore?

We watched Gaysie out in the field. Mud churned violently into the air, spinning onto her pants, boots, and hair.

"Wilbur would like her using the tractor," Micah said, twirling around in circles, his hands out wide and free.

"What's she doing?" Bitty asked. She was wearing a blue hat Nana had knit, her blond curls sticking out underneath.

"Putting everything back in the ground," Micah said, stumbling wildly around, trying to steady from his twirl.

We watched the Blue Mistress stop, hover, then scoop up a large vat of mud.

"The floods washed her whole cemetery up," Jimmy said.

I shook my head. Officer Jake sure wasn't much of a law enforcer, letting her do this.

Gaysie was grumbling when she walked toward us sitting on the porch. She sat heavily in her rocking chair. It gave a mighty creak as she wiped her forehead with the back of her dirty hand.

She glared at Jimmy, who was walking the porch railing like a tightrope circus performer.

"Jimmy Quintel, when you died, it was like a giant vacuum sucked all the happiness out of Crow."

Jimmy smiled and kept tightrope walking.

"Did you ever think you were going to die?" I asked.

He shrugged.

"Well, you almost did," Micah said. "You went over the waterfall."

Gaysie took a deep, noisy breath. "Jimmy, it was a terrible time. Now, get off my railing before you either break my porch or your neck."

He spun in the air as he jumped off the railing and somersaulted across the grass.

"As long as I've lived in Crow, nobody, and I mean *nobody* has gone over that waterfall and lived to tell about it," Gaysie said.

"How'd you do it?" I shuddered, remembering the swift and unforgiving current.

"I just had to wait," he said, "until it took me over to the side."

"You have to go where the current takes you," Gaysie said. "Don't I know it."

"Yup," Jimmy said. "And then I grabbed a tree branch that was hanging over the water like this . . ." Jimmy jumped back onto the porch railing and then jumped up to hang from the roof.

"Probably the smartest thing you've ever done in your life," Gaysie said. Jimmy beamed, looking like he'd just won first prize at a rodeo. "He's had more accidents than you can shake a stick at," Gaysie said, drumming her fingers. "But I always said, Jimmy Quintel was born lucky."

Jimmy let go of the roof, splaying himself onto the grass, letting the sun shine on his face.

"Please don't ever die again," Micah said.

I heard the sound of trucks pulling into Ms. Myrtle's driveway.

It was a cleanup, clean-out moving business. Someone had bought the property and was tearing down the whole house to build a bigger one. Workmen had come all week, throwing away all the innards, sparing nothing. Carpet, curtains, pots and pans, the goose cage, Myron Myrtle's old toys—all of it thrown right into a giant maroon Dumpster parked on the new spring grass. But when they started taking the piano down the front stairs I let out a yell.

"Wait! That's my piano." I sprinted across the grass.

"You gonna have a bonfire?" a bald, sweaty man asked.

"This is not firewood! It's a musical instrument," I said. "It was my . . . it's mine!"

"Be my guest," Baldy said, wiping the sweat off his brow. "But you gotta get it out of our way." He walked back inside as Jimmy, Micah, and Bitty came over to help me push and pull the little spinet over wet grass, the wheels sinking into soft earth. All four of us were panting by the time we were finally back in Micah's driveway.

"I'll go get Willowdale," I said. "She can pull it home."

"What are you going to do with another piano?" Jimmy asked.

"Play it, of course. I'll give it to Nana for an early birthday present. It was the piano Vienna learned on—she'll love it."

"Or you could have the Blue Mistress pull it home," Gaysie said.

How peacefully she sat, rocking back and forth, looking

out across the field. "Didn't he just love plowing, seeding, and haying those fields. And I loved working alongside him." She sighed. "I miss him every day."

"Me too," Micah said, hugging his knees to his chest.

I finally asked the question that'd been burning in me since the beginning.

"Did you do it?"

With a quick flick of my eyes, Bitty came to my side. If we had to, we would run, and we would run fast. My hands and feet twitched in anticipation. *Instincts.* Sherlock said it was one of the first rules in detective work.

Gaysie eyed me, stopped rocking her chair. "There is a very fine line between good and evil. One small misalignment and you are all at once very far off the path."

"Is that what happened?"

Gaysie studied me. "You would like for me to have done it, wouldn't you? You would like to know you'd been right all this time. Yes, I know what you are thinking. That's what's going to make you one heck of a lawyer someday, Guinevere. You're the hound dog. But as wonderful as your imagination is, there is also the true story."

"Tell her," Jimmy said. "Then Gwyn can talk about something else for once."

"So you've known all along!" I demanded.

"Nah, not exactly, but I know Gaysie."

"Tell me, Guinevere, what is your theory?"

"Your behavior indicates guilt."

"Such as?"

"You stabbed Micah's floatie to bits."

She raised an eyebrow.

"A regrettable moment. Move along."

"You wouldn't let anyone search your property. You threw away the coffeepot and all of Wilbur's coffee. You had his boots! The fingerprints on the Blue Mistress were yours!" I was lying, taking a gamble. I didn't mention my father. I had one more card to play—the most incriminating of them all. "And," I said, delivering my closing argument, "we found his hat in your coffin, in *your* backyard!"

Micah bit his lip, squeezed his eyes tightly together, and crossed all of his fingers, as if he were willing a not-guilty verdict. Even Jimmy looked rattled.

Gaysie considered the evidence.

"My, my, aren't you observant. Fingerprints," Gaysie said.

"We had them tested," Micah said slowly. "On Halloween night, when we got caught outside."

She stared at us.

"We are also pleading the Fifth," I stated.

"She's practicing to be a lawyer," Bitty said solemnly.

"You've told us like a million times," Jimmy said.

"My goodness." Gaysie folded her hands together. "Well, since I'm on the witness stand, I'll tell you right now. I didn't kill Wilbur, may God rest his soul."

"You didn't?"

"Thank goodness," Micah said, exhaling.

"But I did take care of his body. Hence the hat. And the boots."

Micah came back to attention.

"Wilbur was an old man. He died of old age, doing what

he loved, up there on that tractor. One day I saw him out there, his hat pulled down like he was taking a nap. That's how I found him. The good Lord had taken him home. I like to think Myron was waiting. Fitting, don't you think, to go like that?"

"Didn't you—call someone?" I burst out.

"I most certainly did."

I had a sudden and horrible revelation. I knew exactly who she would have called.

"My father?" I asked weakly.

"Yes, but he didn't pick up."

"Phew," Bitty exhaled.

"There was blood," I said.

Gaysie looked at me.

"On your clothes that day."

"Yes," she said. Slowly, she held up her hand with the missing finger. "I felt very strongly that I would take care of it myself, but it was a bit tricky getting him off the tractor. He fell and was trapped underneath the wheel. I lifted the Mistress myself!" She sat up and shook like a ruffled rooster. "But my finger got caught on the undercarriage— cut it right off!"

Gaysie's eyebrows sharply came together. "I was crazy, like a madwoman! What a scene that was, me bleeding all over creation, near death from the shock of it all, holdin' on to Wilbur. Ms. Myrtle saw me, of course. Didn't lift a hand to help, but she had every right to think I'd done the unthinkable."

"What unthinkable?" Micah asked.

"Murder."

"Why didn't you just *tell* what happened?" I asked. "Why not tell Officer Jake?"

"Why would I do that?"

"Because that's what you do!"

"Well, it's not what I do."

"You were hiding evidence."

"No. I never imagined what a scuffle Wilbur's disappearance would make. He wanted to be buried close to me so I could keep talking to him, not in one those overpriced fancy-shmancy formal cemeteries no one visits."

I scowled.

"But you're correct, I miscalculated. I never thought it would matter. And when it did, it was too late. I am sorry, Guinevere. Judge me if you must. I have so many faults. I have a terrible temper. I'm not everyone's cup of tea, but in this case I did exactly what Wilbur would have wanted me to do. I dug a hole, took off his boots, and put him in my very own coffin! If that's not love I don't know what love is. I buried him in the field he loved best, in the earth he had plowed his whole life. We had an agreement worked out a long time ago, he and I, but the town would never have allowed it. The parked tractor was in lieu of a headstone. I believe he'd have been mighty pleased with that."

"Then how did he get in the water?" I shuddered at the memory of being under the cold, frigid creek, seeing his hands and arms.

"Obviously, his burial was a tad too close to the river," Gaysie said. "Again, a miscalculation on my part. Wouldn't you know it? We had more rain than we've seen in twenty years—just my luck! When it began to rain, the whole river rose and the banks washed in." She raised her shoulders. "And so did Wilbur. Right into the river. I knew that coffin should have had a sturdier top."

"Where will he be buried now?"

"The town cemetery." Gaysie rocked back and forth. "Not quite as nice as my backyard."

I remained standing, feeling both a sharp relief and a disappointment. My father was not involved in a murder—that was the relief part. But I had been wrong—that was the disappointment. And somehow it felt all mixed up with Vienna, though I couldn't tell you exactly how. I wanted there to be a reason for everything that had happened, but maybe, like so many things, there wasn't any.

"Guinevere," Gaysie said.

I looked at her.

"I sometimes wondered if your obsession with Wilbur's disappearance wasn't about Wilbur at all. You're a child who needs to have answers, so let me tell you. I knew your mother. Vienna couldn't possibly have known what was going to happen to her, but I do know this: She loved Jed St. Clair from the moment she met him. You are part of the greatest love story I have ever witnessed—then and now. That story is not over. And you take after her; you're both fighters."

I considered this.

Gaysie nodded, the matter settled. "But now it's time to rest awhile. Rest, rest. Soon it'll be time to get up and fight some more."

Jimmy punched the air like he was already thinking of more ways to annoy me.

Was this, I wondered, what it felt like to close a case?

Bitty and I started for home.

"I wonder if an insanity plea would get her off for improper burial," I mused.

Bitty kicked a rock down the road with the toe of her mud boot. We watched it hit a bigger rock and stop dead in the road. Bitty reached up and took my hand.

"Maybe just this once I can let it go. Lawyers have to make deals all the time, you know."

"It's a good deal," Bitty said.

"I guess I won't tell on her, even though she tried to bury me that one time."

We turned around, the clementine house almost completely lost from sight. My eyes found Micah and Jimmy on the porch. They waved wildly, like they'd been watching for us to turn the whole time. Jimmy gave a rooster call. Micah jumped up and down, his newest accessory—an old cowboy hat—lifting off his head, while the orange sun set large and bright behind them both.

"Which one should I marry?"

"Mmmm . . . I can't decide," Bitty said. "I like them both. Race ya there."

Bitty and I turned toward home again and began to skip large, jumping skips. My little sister's face, so much like our mother's, broke into laughter.

We skipped until cows came to the fence to see what we were doing.

"Moooo," said Bitty, sounding like a real nice Holstein. "Run, Gwyn! Run with the cows!"

We began a full-out run down Lanark Lane, the wind carrying us both as it blew our hair and buoyed us off the ground. There was Nana, up ahead, hands on her hips, waiting for us on the porch. Boy, I couldn't wait to see her face when Willowdale pulled her new piano home.

Vienna was visiting, her profile a shadow in the window, as if she was waiting, anticipating our arrival. Our father stood, smoothed her hair, and pulled back the living room curtain. Watching him I realized we hadn't moved to Crow just for Vienna. We had come back for me and Bitty and Nana. Maybe even for Gaysie, Micah, and Jimmy. We had come for my father, too, so that every time he passed the school or a field or sat at the kitchen table, he could remember the girl he would always love.

Vienna sat up straight in her wheelchair and clapped her hands, seeing us.

Lolly was right.

Not everyone comes home.

But sometimes, they do.

ACKNOWLEDGMENTS

My most heartfelt thanks:

To my parents: Mary Cope Nelson, our family storyteller, who showed me that lying in bed with a good book (and chocolate) is a daily essential. Steven Nelson, who taught me all things cows and who loved the real Willowdale Princess Deon Dawn as a boy in Idaho. Thank you both for raising the fab five to love words, God, and family, and for teaching us to believe we are capable of choosing our own destiny.

To my other parents: Heather Makechnie, another storytelling tour de force, a woman who championed us her whole life, and who, along with Arthur, gave me that all-too-real burial scene. To the entire Makechnie family, who has very little patience for sub-par word choices and grammatical errors; you're tough but I love you.

To my first and last readers: Andrea McDonald, Mary Nelson, Allison Nelson, Jill Makechnie, Kate Johnston, Sarah Will, and Shauna Turnbull. All excellent writers, strong women, and nurturing mothers. Thank you for reading my messy drafts and helping me find the narrative arc every time. I'm so appreciative.

To my brothers: Patrick Nelson, for reading and always checking in. Eric Nelson, for sharing insight on the law, and to Peter Nelson, for all things dentistry. Jed St. Clair came as the result of knowing amazing fathers who shoulder heavy loads.

To Jessica Lawson, for answering all of my questions ALL OF THE TIME, and to Tina Wexler of ICM. You both led me to Zoe. I'm indebted forever.

To Julia Tomiak, the #wordnerd, for her encouraging Monday check-in. Every writer needs an accountability buddy!

To Kit and Chris, for the Blue Mistress.

To Norman Doidge and "The Brain That Changes Itself."

To James Anderson especially, for your honest and powerful love story, medical knowledge, and for guiding me to further research—both scientifically and spiritually. And also to Laura. Thank you.

To my wonderful literary agent, the kind and insightful Zoe Sandler. Thank you for taking a chance on me! I am so so grateful.

To my editor Alexa Pastor, for knowing just the right balance of push and praise—you are SO good. To jacket illustrator Abigail Dela Cruz and cover designer Michael McCartney—it's beautiful. To Justin Chanda and the entire team at Simon & Schuster. Thank you for bringing good books for children into the world.

And finally, to Gregor, and our greatest creations: Cope, Nelson, Brynne, and Paige. Thanks for always coming home.